THE HOUSE BESIDE THE CHERRY TREE

BY

L TAYLOR

SCARAMOUCHE PRESS

Stories that challenge
Stories that intrigue
Stories that linger

Facebook: Scaramouche Press
Twitter: ScaramoucheP

For all press and enquiries contact us at:
scaramouchepressinfo@gmail.com

DEDICATION

Dedicated to Michael, June and Stephen.

ACKNOWLEDGEMENTS

There are so many people I need to thank for their support, advice and encouragement with this project without whom this wouldn't have been possible. Most particularly, a heartfelt thanks to Claire Steele, who started my whole writing journey off; her support, encouragement and editing have been invaluable. Huge thanks to Mary Craig and Mark Hodgson and the team at Scaramouche Press; to Tyne and Esk Writers Group, Yvonne Dalziel, Elaine Robertson, Dorothy Robertson, Elena Neira Sinclair, Fran Stone & Kath Burlinson for showing me that I could delve deeper; to Mary Turner Thomson and Susan Cohen - for the sausage sarnies, coffees and all the joy and nonsense you bring with The Book Whisperers and ultimately, to my family and my parents

Diane: Spring 1980

The cherry tree was blighted. Its leaves curled and black. Strange resin oozed from its trunk; a cut that never healed. Small grubs and creatures crawled around its gnarled bark. That area of the garden was dark and unpleasant to visit. The tree had never borne wholesome fruit or attractive flowers.

I hated the tree right from the outset. I complained to my husband, Richard, but he continued digging and planted it anyway, whistling a Nat King Cole tune as he did so. I hated whistling and didn't care much for Nat King Cole either. I spent that afternoon sulking. I spent a lot of afternoons sulking. After planting the tree, Richard left. He jumped in the car, started up the engine and drove off - I didn't know what time to expect him back, I never did.

Twenty-six years on and the tree was still there. Standing solid, its bold outline scratching at the sky, blighted leaves lying on the ground infecting everything they touched. Then, in the springtime, it burst into blossom, spreading pink petal showers around the garden, leaving a trail of small confetti drifts in odd corners. It seemed a poetic act given I had buried Richard in the January.

I felt a tinge of pleasure as I stood at the kitchen window and watched the tree surgeon start up the chainsaw. With an air of nonchalance, he carved and cut. Shavings flew on the air as the cutting chain whined and bit. Branch after branch fell to the ground. As each one fell, I felt lighter, giddy almost.

When they hauled all the logs and debris away, I went down to the bottom of the garden to inspect the work. The stump looked stark. I bent down to look closer at the rings and suddenly, spontaneously, spat on its heart.

Diane: Beginnings - Early July 1959

I squatted by the toilet bowl, spittle dribbling from my mouth, my body no longer responding in the way I want. This was the fourth morning in a row I'd thrown up.

I heard my mother calling from the foot of the stair 'Diane, hurry up. Diane? What are you up to? Your father's waiting.'

I stood up slowly and straightened my skirt, wiped my mouth and splashed my face with water. The face looking back from the mirror looked wan. I pinched my cheeks in an attempt to brighten my complexion then, heart pounding, descended the stairs one step at a time. My knuckles white where I gripped the bannister in case I passed out.

Mother appraised me as I came down. 'You look pale dear, are you sure you're not coming down with something?'

'No, Mum, I'll be alright,' I responded. 'It's just a bit of a headache.'

'You are a little hot,' she put her hand on my forehead. 'Shall I fetch you an aspirin?'

'No, Daddy's waiting, don't fuss. We need to go. I'll be fine. Please.' But I knew I wasn't fine. I was far from fine.

There was no mistake, as surely as any woman ever could know! If only I had more time to think about this. How long could I keep this a secret?

My parent's anger would be dreadful but the thing I couldn't bear to contemplate would be the weight of their disappointment and shame. They'd poured everything they had into giving me an education and all the opportunities they never had. God, how I wished this had never happened, how I wished this had just turned out to be a false alarm. But I knew, I knew.... Those subtle changes in my body, the ripening and tenderness of my breasts, the overwhelming tiredness, oh Christ, the smell of Daddy's pipe. It made me want to vomit on the spot.

Mum and I were going away to Jersey that very morning. There was nothing I could do short of breaking the news. I wondered whether I should risk ruining the holiday and confess there and then, or sit tight? My seventeen-year-old head just couldn't decide. I kept thinking that something would turn up while we were away holidaying for two weeks - 'Kill or Cure!' So, I kept quiet, waiting for the moment of inspiration to appear.

I thought about confiding in Val, my best friend, but every time I thought about it my stomach tightened. All those conversations we had about silly girls who got themselves in the family way. How we had laughed at their stupidity. We, on the other hand, had it all figured out; we had planned how we would marry well and live next door to each other in the salubrious Battledown area, trading recipes and childcare stories. I dreaded confessing. The idea of Val's reaction, particularly to all the lies I'd told. The thought of her inevitable disgust and disdain made me quail. I'd find it difficult to explain how it happened, really.

I shook my head and wrung my hands in the vain attempt to assert myself and stop this non-stop worrying. All that useless, doubting clamour going round and round. In the end I decided against telling Val, for the time being at least - although I would have given anything to confide in someone and get advice.

I looked at the suitcases, everything neatly packed and ready for the off. Months ago, I was really looking forward to this, but now I'm filled with doubt. One more hour before we leave. Daddy said we had to get away promptly for the drive down to Weymouth. We were catching a boat. It was a miserable morning. Out of the window I could see big heavy-looking clouds throwing themselves across the horizon. It was as if the wind had got up and dragged away all the colour leaving behind a dull, slate grey.

We got down there in good time. The boat was due to leave the harbour at 12.30. We said goodbye to Daddy and boarded at

4

12.10. We found a spot in one of the large third-class rooms and left our luggage and coats there. Mum decided we needed lunch, so we made our way to the dining room. It was crowded and noisy and smelled of boiled cabbage and cheap perfume. I couldn't understand why all the tables had lips around the edges until Mum explained.

'It's to prevent you from wearing your food on your lap.'

I wasn't the best of travellers in any mode of transport.

The meal was pleasant enough, meat and two veg with a splash of gravy but I chased the vegetables round the plate with my fork. I could see through one of the portholes that the boat was being tossed back and forth and felt myself lurching with it. I began to feel queasy. My stomach didn't seem to appreciate the good food it had been blessed with. Mum spotted me turning green around the gills and ordered a brandy. I knocked it back in the vain hope that it would put my stomach to rights but felt quite ridiculous, particularly since the boat hadn't even left the harbour.

The brandy made no impact. I excused myself, telling Mum I was going back to where we left our coats and luggage. But with the boat lurching from side to side I quickly changed tack and focused my attention on getting to a toilet. Somehow, I managed to climb a flight of stairs, march unsteadily across part of the deck; then descend another flight of stairs to find where I needed to go. I ended up emptying the contents of my stomach and much regretted having bothered with lunch. Such a waste of good food.

The only consolation that cheered me was to think that it was better to be ill on a full stomach than an empty one.

I stayed in the toilet quite a while, losing all track of time. When I opened the door, I found it impossible to plough my way through the crowd of women that had gathered. All in the same state as me: pale as death and not looking forward to the rest of the journey.

By this time the boat had left the quay. I had no idea how long we had been moving or how much further we had to go. My legs refused to carry me, so I stayed crouched in the corner, handbag clutched in one hand and in the other, a cardboard container specifically supplied for rough passages. These were fast littering the floor in every direction. Desperately, I attempted to work my way round to the door to escape but it was no use. No one was willing to give an inch to let anyone get past. It was a case of 'every woman for herself,' and I was thoroughly stuck.

After a while the toilet door opened again. I couldn't bear to look. 'It'll be another woman looking like I feel - and she's got the worst part to come,' I thought, simultaneously worrying it would start me off again.

I heard 'Yes, thank you very much, that's her over there in the corner.'

I knew that voice and have never felt so relieved to see Mum than at that moment. She was busy instructing the steward and pointing in my direction. He clambered through the door and pushed his way past the women who were blocking the exit to rescue me from my corner. With a deftness that demonstrated this was not the first time he had done this sort of thing he steered me clear of the heap of moaning women. I remember having to pause momentarily to grab another cardboard container, then I staggered out into the passageway.

I thanked him profusely as I steadied myself against the swaying ship. 'Part of the service,' he replied and disappeared up a flight of nearby stairs. Mum had been frantic for nearly an hour. It was well past two o'clock and virtually all the available stewards had been searching for me - she was convinced I'd gone overboard.

Together we made our way up a flight of stairs and out into the fresh air. We both appreciated the rush of wind on our faces. My head began to clear but my legs were still unsteady. My stomach was another thing altogether.

We spotted a clear space at the side of the rails and, running up against the rolling deck, grasping at the rail as if holding on to the banisters of steep stairs. We stood for a moment with our faces looking away from the wind and our hair being whipped up and about beyond all recognition. Then, some unfortunate creature staggered out on deck and, with neither time nor thought for anyone standing in the way, emptied the contents of his stomach. It was soon apparent why that part of the rail had been unoccupied. Mum and I moved inside.

Bodies were stretched all over the deck. Little cardboard containers were lying in corners. Stewards rushed back and forth with extra buckets. It was a chaos of smell, green faces and harsh, animal-like noises.

We made our way back to the luggage and sat. I tried to sleep while Mum read. As I sat there, eyes closed against the world, I thought for a long time about the future and the options available to me. If I was right about my condition, then the only thing I could do was obvious. I couldn't disgrace my parents. I turned it over and over in my mind, like a hot coal burning through my fingers, something I couldn't hold on to, couldn't stop. Exhausted, I eventually slept. The sea was very rough - later we learned that it was one of the worst of the season.

I woke to a terrible crashing sound and was convinced that we had either struck a rock or another vessel. I conjured up images of a sinking ship, rather like the Titanic, of it fast slipping beneath the waves while I was left to flounder in the freezing water. I'd never learned to swim and the thought of being submerged petrified me. Earlier I had contemplated suicide at some point during the holiday, or on the way back, but now I wanted to live, in spite of the future and what was sure to happen.

I thought of my parents and what it would do to them if I took my own life. Surely it would be worse for them if I did - worse than the disgrace I would be involving them in ultimately? I made my mind up to ensure that Mum enjoyed the holiday and put my trust in fate, whatever it was to be. I owed her that much at least. I couldn't let my parents think that, over and above anything else, I was also a coward. I had never learned to stand on my own two feet before, but I knew that this time I had to step up and it wasn't going to be easy.

I recognised in myself the weak, self-centered creature who had left home that morning, uncertain of what to do. Now my life was about to change. I was ill-equipped to know how to deal with what lay ahead. I had only been working in the real world for a short eight months.

I barely knew how to cook. The kitchen - with its myriad array of pots and pans, bowls and utensils - seemed like another world to me. Sometimes I watched Mum at work; sleeves rolled up, fingers rubbing the butter into flour, or standing over the kitchen stove, stirring the pots, with a profusion of mouth-watering smells wafting out of the kitchen. Her eyes seemed to be everywhere, checking the oven, hovering by a spitting grill, appearing through clouds of steam from a bubbling pot. She never needed to refer to a recipe book, it was all 'in there,' inside her busy, domestic head and she never wasted a thing. The pantry was a testament to that - a world of herbs and spices, pickles, jams and chutneys all lined up in carefully labelled jars. It was a world into which I was never allowed to enter. When I tried, I was always rebuffed. It was the same reply every time:

'No, Diane, I can't afford to allow you to play with the ingredients, there's still rationing going on.' She said it so often that I anticipated it before even bothering to ask. I retreated into my books instead. What did I care for domestic chores anyway? I was never going to need them.

My friends talked of similar experiences. The kitchen was off limits and none of us knew much about the rudiments of cleaning either - heaven forbid that we would have to stoop so low. Gals from private schools should only learn how to direct other people to clean, not do it themselves. So, under parental guidance, our attention was turned to the arts. Piano, dance or attending theatre shows and the after-show teas. There were so many social skills and graces to be garnered from such endeavours. I took up piano and horse riding, but what I really excelled in was drama. There I lost myself to the worlds that the plays provided, acted out the frustrations I couldn't give vent to at home. My tutor said I was destined for great things and I always got the juiciest parts, much to the other girls' displeasure. Not that I cared, I had a strong sense of who I was and what I could achieve. With my friendships I usually got what I wanted, complete respect and loyalty. It wasn't always a two-way process. Val, I'd known her since nursery. We gravitated to each other, held each other's hands in our play, always sat together, dressed alike even down to our plaits and ribbons. Val was like my shadow, always doing as I directed, even letting me win when we held guinea-pig races. She hated to see me sulk. I had it down to a fine art, skills I had picked up from Mum. She could cut anyone down with just a look, so much power with every nuance.

When the school holidays came round my parents allowed me to choose a friend to accompany us on our excursions. It was usually Val. My father, Joe, would send a man with a car from his garage to collect us and we would drive down to the coast to take in the sea air or walk along the cliffs.

I never wanted for anything. Even my extended family members, whom I saw little of, claimed I was 'spoiled rotten.' They were so proud, and rather overawed by what Mum and Dad had achieved, rising out of the Birmingham slums. Yet, I've no doubt there was also jealousy too. It must have stuck in their craw to see my parents swanning around with their well-dressed, perfectly spoken, self-assured daughter, the antithesis of who they were. I'm sure they envied our valeted motor car and big swanky house while they still lived on top of one another in their broken-down homes and lives.

My parents did everything for me, giving me the best that their hard-earned money could buy. They worked particularly hard to ensure that there was nothing for the neighbours prying eyes to gossip about. Mum, the force behind the family, always ensured that what happened in and around our family went smoothly and fitted with social convention. She was a stickler for that. Lunch was at one o'clock prompt, with a napkin, not a serviette, and all the cutlery, set out in the appropriate manner. Sherry had to be at the correct temperature - pale cream at nine degrees or dry sherry at thirteen and could only be imbibed from the appropriate glass before dinner and must, at all costs, be sipped not slurped.

'Hello! Cheltenham 26218, who's calling please?'

'Hello, Sophie, it's Diane here. Could I speak to your brother please?'

'Yes, just a minute, I'll call him. He's in the basement cleaning his bike.' She put the telephone down heavily and I listened to her footsteps echo along the corridor and clatter down the stairs. After a while I heard Sophie's soft voice call, 'Riiiiichaaaaaaaard, it's the telephone.'

A door slammed and a pair of boots thundered up the two flights of stairs. I imagined Richard taking them two at a time, all legs and gangly body, a hand gripping the banister to give further purchase as he climbed at speed. Breathless, he picked up the telephone.

'Hello?'

'It's Diane,' I'd pitched my voice to be low and measured. 'We need to talk.'

'Oh, do you want to meet?'

'Yes.' There followed an awkward pause. 'How soon can you get away?'

'I have a couple of errands to run for my Dad but how about later this morning? Will I come and collect you?'

'No. No, I don't think that would work. Can you meet me at the end of my road at eleven?'

'Oh, yes, ok if that's what you want.'

'I think it's best.'

'Diane, is everything alright? You sound a bit off.'

'We'll talk about that when I see you. Don't be late.'

At ten to eleven I told Mum that I needed some fresh air. Daddy was engrossed in the paper and she was working in the kitchen. I'd virtually been sent to Coventry since returning from holiday.

I put on my coat and shoes and took the dog lead down from its hook. Our dog, Bunch, responded with delighted yelps, dancing around my feet as I clipped on his lead.

As I walked, I noted a faltering in my steps as if I couldn't quite decide how to proceed. My head was so full of the things I wanted to say - but would I have the courage to say them?

Richard was sitting on his bike, his back to me watching the traffic. He looked sloppy and immature. Hands deep in pockets, probably dreaming about cars. How would he respond? How did I want him to respond? I wasn't sure what to expect but suspected that whatever he offered it wouldn't come up to par.

He looked like a boy on the edge of manhood, lacking confidence and blinking when nervous. His body was awkward and angular as though he didn't know what to do with it or where to put his outsized hands and feet. An untied shoelace dangled from the bicycle peddle where he rested his foot.

Bunch barked. Richard bent down and ruffled the dog's shaggy head. A tangle of blond hair flopped over Richard's face. He scooped it back to reveal a smudge of oil across his cheek.

He then indulged Bunch's exuberant attention by producing a dog biscuit from his pocket. It piqued me that the dog had been given attention before me. Bunch was my dog and yet, evidently, he adored Richard, possibly more than me. I stiffened at the thought.

'You okay? he made to kiss me on the cheek, I deliberately turned my face away. Richard frowned and I felt slightly triumphant.

'What's up?'

'Not here. Let's walk a little. Head down the park.'

We walked together in a strained silence, a perplexed Richard scanned my face. Battling to keep my composure I avoided his gaze. We found a suitable bench with a view of the lake and the park beyond.

'So, what's with all the cloak and daggers?' the smirk on his face really rattled me.

'This isn't a joke.' A swell of emotions overtook me and I struggled to keep it all together. 'It's ...' I turned my face to hide my tears, stifling a sob with my hand.

'Diane?' he reached out to touch me but I shrugged him off.

'Diane?'

'We've made such a mess of things.'

'Mess?'

'Bloody hell, how can you be so stupid?'

'Diane, you're not making sense. What on earth is going on?'

'What's going on? I'll tell you what's going on Richard, I'm pregnant.'

'What? Are you sure?' He blinked wildly, which I always found irritating.

'Yes, very sure.' My words came hard and bitter. He fixed his gaze on the lake, and said: 'Well, what do you want to do about it?'

'What do you mean, what do I want to do about it?'

He half shrugged. 'Well, do you want to have an abortion?'

'Richard, we're talking about a child. Our child. Not a bloody car that you can sell or get rid of at a scrapyard.'

'Hmmmn.'

'Anyway, there's nothing I can do about it. Not now - I'm too far gone.'

'Oh Lord! How long have you known?'

'I had it confirmed last week.'

Richard leaned forward and put his head in his hands. 'Do your parents know?'

'Yes, I told my mother when we were on holiday. She guessed. I was sick all the time.'

He lifted his head and looked at me. 'How did she react?'

'How do you think she reacted? Very bloody badly.' A silence elapsed between us and then we both giggled. I laughed until my face broke with tears. Richard fished in his trouser pocket and pulled out his hankie. After a quick examination he offered it to me. 'It's clean.' I took it and blew hard. Awkwardly, he tried to comfort me but I batted his hand away.

'It's not funny though. What are we going to do?'

'I suppose we'll have to get married.' I sensed a tinge of excitement in this voice.

'That's just what my Dad said. He said he's going to call your Dad today. He said if he saw you, he would knock your bloody block off.'

'Oh, hell. How did this happen?'

'How do you think it happened?'

'But it was only the once.'

I couldn't help myself and rounded on him, slapping him hard across the cheek.

'What are you implying? You know it was my first time. It only takes the once, idiot.'

Still rubbing his reddening cheek Richard muttered 'Sorry, I didn't mean it like that.' A silence passed between us before he looked at his watch and sighed. 'I need to go, it's nearly lunchtime.' He rose and mounted his bike. 'Will I call you at work?' He tossed another biscuit to Bunch. 'See you Bunny-boy.'

'No, I'll call you,' I shouted after him as he disappeared down the hill, shoelace trailing. He lifted a hand in acknowledgement, but didn't look back and soon he was gone, lost behind the trees.

So, that's it I thought. Should I consider that to be a marriage proposal? It wasn't what I had imagined for myself. Val and I pictured it would be a down on bended knee, with a big sparkly ring and an armful of flowers affair. The stuff of moonlight, dancing in the arms of someone you are hopelessly, madly, in love with. This felt like one great, big, enormous let down.

Bunch jumped on to my lap and covered my face with insistent licks. His hairy paws placed on either side of my neck, tail wagging. 'Oh Bunch,' I sighed. 'At least you love me.' I buried my face in his fur. He smelled faintly of wet dog and fresh air.

I stood up. 'Come on, time we got going Bunny.'

Richard: Late July 1959

The family were at the table waiting for me to get home. The table was unlaid. A twist at the corner of Dad's mouth suggested he was unhappy about something; it was a facial tic I was familiar with. It usually meant he was displeased with me, like the time I broke his watch by overwinding it. A man who hated conflict, he took a long drag on his cigarette, exhaled, a plume of smoke hid his expression. I stood in the doorway, one foot in and the other still in the hall, my knees were trembling. Mum stood up, she was rubbing her hands together, her cheeks tinged with red, her eyes looked damp as if she were about to cry. She pulled a chair from the edge of the table gestured me to sit.

'There's a letter here for you.' It covered the ring stain where I once set my hot cup down without a placemat.

'It's from the M.O.D.' my sister Sophie piped up. 'Go on, open it. Let's see.' I looked over at Dad who inclined his head as if to say *go on.*

My hands were trembling so much I picked up the envelope and turned from them to hide my nervousness. The letter was written on crisp thick paper, signed with an official swirl. Even though I expected this, it still came as a shock.

'Two weeks. I'm getting posted to Aden in two weeks.'

With tears in her eyes, Mum was the first to hug me. 'Congratulations, Son.' Sophie, then Maggie my oldest sister, both hugged me enthusiastically. 'Make sure you bring your friends home in their uniforms,' Maggie winked.

'I bagsy the best looking one,' Sophie chimed. The girls giggled nervously. It all felt a little surreal. Then Dad stood up. 'Well done, son.' His voice was solemn. 'I think we need to go into the sitting room to have a chat don't we.'

My heart skipped a beat. 'Yes, I suppose we do.' I followed him and watched as he carefully poured two glasses of brandy. Handing one on to me, he raised his glass.

'Your good health!'

I went to raise the glass to my lips, but Dad stayed my hand, 'And that of my first grand-child.' I flinched as he drained his glass and it landed with a bang on the table.

'What the bloody hell did you think you were playing at? You've broken your Mother's heart she's been sobbing all afternoon. You ...'

Mum charged into the room, all flustered. 'Freddie, that's enough! And keep your voice down, we don't want everyone to know our business. What's done is done. We'll have no more recriminations, not in this household.'

She gave him a hard *I mean it* stare before retreating, closing the door quietly as if to impress her point. Dad responded by pouring himself another stiff drink and downed it.

'You heard your Mother ...'

I looked askance at my Dad, I bit my lip as I made an effort to stand up straight, shoulders back, like a man should.

'Now, I'm meeting with Joe tomorrow to talk about your future ...' he paused as though trying to find the missing word, 'marriage'. You realise, your conscription complicates things. I have to say, I'm disappointed with you son. It's not the start we had hoped for you. Do you have anything to say for yourself?'

I searched the floor as though looking for the answer.

'I'm sorry, Dad.'

'So am I, son. Let's just hope you don't live to regret it.'

Diane: August 1959

The wedding was hastily organised, both sets of parents took control, making all the decisions for us - we weren't even consulted. Our fathers shook on the final details over a pint at the Vauxhall. It was agreed, it would be a quiet affair with little fuss and no guests. The registry office was booked for a week's time. Nothing more was said. All Richard and I had to do was turn up.

I barely showed beneath my cream suit. Richard and I made our vows in front of the Registrar and our four witnesses; parents of each side. The registry office was cold and perfunctory, smelled of lavender waxed floors and moth balls. There was no white dress, no lace wedding veil or long march down the aisle on my father's arm. No flowers to scent the occasion or throw at random to waiting hopefuls. No showers of confetti or wedding car dressed with cans and ribbons. Everyone cried for all the wrong reasons. What the ceremony lacked in love and vibrancy it made up for in abruptness. It was all over in ten minutes.

'A life sentence made so quickly and with such finality,' Mum later said.

Us newlyweds blinked before the flashing bulb - forever stunned in our wedding photo. At our sides stood both sets of parents, looking pained and awkward. Mum in particular, appeared decidedly peeved. She gripped her handbag with her cotton white gloves and pursed her lips so that they spread thinly across her teeth in an effort to force a smile.

I spent my honeymoon in the damp basement of my in-law's house, a two-storey pile on the edge of town. From the outside it looked the epitome of home comfort and respectability. Everything a girl like me would want. Richard's parents ran a renowned and well-respected dental practice. The surgery was situated on the ground floor and catered to the great and good from Cheltenham's populace. In our bed, curled up on a lumpy old mattress, I cried bitter tears until my pillowcase was sodden and my face red and swollen. Tears of remorse and regret. Married to a boy I didn't love, soon to have his child and all he could do was worry about polishing his shoes ready for the morning. Was this it? Was this all that I had to look forward to? Richard was not a conversationalist, he didn't read, wasn't interested in the arts - we had virtually nothing in common. He had no understanding of my needs and when I told him he laughed, said I was getting above myself or being too sensitive. I wanted to scream with frustration, and he knew it, smiling at me in that patronising 'Oh, Diane,' way.

He tried to placate me with tea and a cheese sandwich, left over from the meagre wedding reception; a buffet at The Mission Hall, with curled egg and cress or cheese sandwiches placed on doilies and an iced sponge cake. Tea was served from a dented urn with cups and saucers that had seen better days. Mine had a chip in it. There were no speeches, not even a telegram.

My face had puffed up I cried so hard. In the end he gave me the handkerchief from his top pocket and took the back stairs up to his parents' sitting room where all the family were assembled, listening to the wireless. He stayed there long after I'd cried myself to sleep. It was dark when he silently slipped between the sheets taking care not to wake me. He remained on his side of the bed all night. I woke every now and then, disoriented, hearing his soft snores. In the morning Richard made me breakfast, then kissed me on the cheek before leaving to start his conscription.

Neither of us spoke about things that really mattered - how we felt, what we wanted or even the impending birth. I suppose we were both overwhelmed with the roles now prescribed to us. They were taken as a given, a fait accompli.

I was left to face the changes alone. My fears of childbirth, being alone and managing all these new responsibilities, weren't factored in. They didn't count.

'You've made your bed, now lie in it!' my Mother chided.

As my body swelled, I felt I could no longer hold my head up high as I walked down the street. I imagined the neighbourhood's eyes upon me, judging, nudging, whispering, 'Oh, did you hear about Miss Bloody La-de-daa. She got herself in the family way, had to get married. Serves her right, Miss Bloody La-de-daa.'

Shame covered me like a smog, seeping into my thoughts, my body, my friends, my family. I was adrift, I had lost my anchor point. I, who used to be the golden girl, was now tarnished, dirty and worthless. It choked me to the core. Right down to my words, they betrayed me, they lost their power. Each sentence started and finished with an apology. Until the I'm sorry's became me. I wanted to remain in the shadows, hugging the walls so as not to be seen, not reminding anyone of the disgusting thing I had done. Tears couldn't wash me clean or flush away my sense of gloom. I rose each day feeling dull and numb and nothing, not even the life within my belly could change it.

I doubt I'll ever get over Daddy's face when Mum broke the news to him. He didn't say a word, just stood up from the table and withdrew to his shed at the bottom of the garden. Since then, he had barely exchanged a word with me, the way his face grimaced when he saw me, or how he would reach for the paper holding it like a barrier between us, begrudging his one-word answers. I could tell by the way he carried himself that he was nursing a deep disappointment. His shoulders drooped, and worse he no longer sang or whistled when working in his shed. The silence was unbearable.

Mum was the polar opposite and certainly made her feelings known. I picked the moment while on holiday, I just couldn't help myself. She had noticed me being queasy and said, 'The way you are carrying on anyone would think you are pregnant.'

I didn't want to lie anymore so I told her over breakfast, keeping my voice low and steady, trying not to raise it above the clatter of the cutlery and the quiet conversations of the hotel patrons dotted about the room. Mum left the room speechless her eyes blazing and face white. I just sat there and tried to sip my tea, but my hands shook so much I kept spilling it. This is it I thought, this is the cutting of my umbilical cord. When I finally went back to our room it was evident that Mum had been crying. She rounded on me and slapped me hard on the cheek.

'Trollop, Guttersnipe. Whore! We've done so much for you and this is how you repay us?'

I just wanted to curl up and die. In a way I was glad Mum had slapped me, I deserved it. My cheek felt hot and was still smarting some ten minutes later. All Mum could scream was 'Who is the father? Do you know?'

The words stuck in the back of my mouth. Despite all my efforts I just couldn't summon them.

'Your Daddy will have a fit. This will break him. You have no idea what you have done …' She continued to rail through snot ridden tears and then snatched up my neatly folded clothes and ripped several items to shreds. The shock had stripped her of all her veneer, revealing her working class roots she worked so hard to hide. 'Youse 'ave ruined things. Clarting about in your cack-handed manner,' she threw the items across the room. 'I could lamp youse, I swear to god.' Then she lifted up my suitcase and hurled it at me. 'Go on, get out of my sight you guttersnipe whore.'

I left the room having never witnessed such terrifying ferocity from her. What if the news had driven her mad? What if she never returned back to normal?

I was horribly unsettled for days after the event, jumping at every little noise as though I'd been ambushed. My sleep was broken with disturbing dreams and my hands trembled all the time. I couldn't decide whether the fluttering in my belly was the baby or the shame remaining trapped within me. My world had tilted on its axis, making me anxious and dislocated as if I were no longer part of it, as if I had been shaken out and had fallen onto another place where I didn't belong. Dreams were ragged and fraught, unable to reach back into a world that was known and safe.

After my shocking revelation my parents quelled their lavish attentions retreating into what they considered 'the right thing to do.' No one spoke of what was to come next, each withdrawing onto their own island of disappointment.

There were so many hurdles to be surmounted. Breaking the news to my neighbours - Mrs Teague, my favourite, muttered under her breath and shut the door on me. My cousins, they revelled in it, their smiles that said, 'see you're no better than any of us.' As for Val, she was shocked but didn't reproach me. At least I can thank her for that.

Telling my colleagues of my rushed wedding date left me feeling humiliated. I wanted to curl up in a dark corner and never come out. These were the people I looked up to, respected and wanted to impress. They said the mandatory 'congratulations' but I could sense a look of confusion. I suppose it was a natural reaction, given that I had never even mentioned Richard until the day I announced the wedding at the office. I overheard the secretaries gossiping in the kitchen the day before I got married:

'Office juniors don't normally get married that quickly do they?'

'Did she ever mention this Richard to you?'

'No. Not at all. But then again, she has never mentioned any of her boyfriends.'

'Do you think she's in the family way?'

'No, not Diane. She's just a very private person.'

'I wouldn't be so sure. It's always the quiet ones...'

When I walked into the office everyone hushed and feigned being engrossed in something. My outrage overcame my fear. I pulled myself up tall and faced them.

'Actually, you guessed correctly. I am in the family way and that's why I have to get married so quickly. I'm not proud of it but that's how it is. Do what you will with the information.'

I then flounced out of the room and went and sat behind my typewriter, trying to keep myself occupied and not burst into tears.

That afternoon, at five o'clock, Bill my boss, presented me with a huge bouquet of flowers and a card signed by all the office members, some of them looked rather sheepish. Their good luck wishes seemed to be genuine, which puzzled me. Based on my parents' reaction I'd expected adverse responses from all of them. Bill did look disappointed but didn't reproach me. At the end of the day, he took me aside and said:

'Diane, you know there will always be a job here for you after the baby has arrived, don't you? And if you need anything you just have to say.'

I managed to mumble a 'thank you' and fled to the toilet.

I didn't realise that Mrs Webb, the charwoman was in the next cubicle. Had I known I would have made an effort to cry quietly. When I eventually came out she handed me a cup of sweet tea and patted my hand. 'Don't take on, pet, I'm sure it will pass.'

I crumpled into her arms and sobbed. 'Oh Mrs Webb! It's all such a mess. I should be happy about getting married - but I'm not. I don't want to get married. If truth be told, I don't want this baby either.'

She looked at me with her kind old eyes, 'Why, my dear, it's natural to be afraid of change. It will all turn out well in the end, you'll see.'

'No,' I wailed. 'You don't understand.'

She reached deep into her tabard pocket and produced a packet of cigarettes. I watched as she carefully lit two and handed one to me. 'Go on ...'

I took a puff of the cigarette to steady myself. 'It's like this. I'm not in love. I didn't plan on having a baby. I didn't know what I was doing. It's all happening too quickly,' I paused to draw breath.

'I haven't even had a life yet. It was only four months ago that my parents started to allow me out until 10.30. Now look at me. And my parents hate me.'

She shook her head slowly, 'Shhh, I'm sure they don't.'

'No, really. My father has hardly spoken to me and my mother ...'

'It's probably been a bit of a shock for them that's all. They'll come round, I promise, and they'll love your baby when it comes.'

'Are you sure?' I looked up into Mrs Webb's lined old face. She smiled. 'Yes, I'm more than sure - you see my daughter had a similar thing happen to her.'

'Really?'

'Yes. Only the father scarpered and left us to pick up the pieces.'

'How did your daughter cope? It must have been so hard.'

'Yes, it was. It was too much for her. She left her baby with me to bring up.'

I reeled backwards, my hand flew up to my mouth. 'My goodness, Mrs Webb. I didn't know.' In my head I was reconfiguring all my preconceptions about her. 'You really are an amazing woman. Does the child still stay with you?' She half smiled in a manner that hinted at all the hardships she had had to endure.

'Yes, Gilly is twelve now and doing really well.'

'I bet you and Mr. Webb are very proud of her.' She glanced down at her wedding band.

'Unfortunately, my husband died in the war.'

'I'm so sorry, I didn't know.'

'You weren't to know pet. Now, dry your tears and put on a brave face. That's a girl, hold you head up because no one is going to hold it up for you.'

She put her rubber gloves on and disappeared through the door into the office humming a little tune as she went.

Mrs Webb had worked at the office for a great many years. She never took a day off sick and always arrived at 6pm prompt. Sometimes she had Gilly with her. A solitary child with hair in two plaits who sat quietly in the corner as she watched her grandma work. When I think about Mrs Webb my mind conjures up a picture of seeing her on her old hands and knees polishing the floor with lavender wax, grunting a little when she got up - the old lumbago! Her face, although kind, had her life etched on it, like cracks in dried mud but the creases at her eyes spoke of a life rich in laughter and tears .

She had been there so long that people didn't seem to notice her. She had become invisible, haunting the other world outside office time, cleaning up the debris of the day, quietly putting everything back in its place, clean and tidy. It left me feeling profoundly sad. That little family unit cleaved together, living on a cleaner's wage. Were they happy? I hoped they were. Mrs Webb was always grateful for any hand-me-downs passed to her for Gilly.

Then I realised, I didn't recall seeing Mrs Webb in anything other than her tabard worn over a straight tweed skirt and white shirt, her hair in pins covered by a hairnet and sometimes a red scarf. Occasionally I saw her in the street, limping along in her long black coat and sensible fur-lined booties. I thought it odd that no one in the office, aside from Bill, acknowledged that Mrs Webb was bringing up her granddaughter single-handedly. I, along with the others, had assumed that the mother was still around, and Mrs Webb was just helping out. When I grasped this, I suddenly felt incredibly ashamed of being so self-indulgent and self-centered.

Diane: September–November 1959

As the months ticked by, I was pressed with many fears as my body swelled with the new life I carried. The move to the flat beneath my new in-laws seemed too sudden, too soon. I felt as though I was rattling around there on my own, playing at being housewife. My mother rarely visited, and I was just too ashamed to encourage friends to drop-in. Besides, the place didn't lend itself to that. The only continuity was my work just a five-minute walk away. Sometimes I would wake from a jangly sleep thinking that this was all a nightmare, only to find that my nightmare was a reality that couldn't be undone. In those twilight hours, lying in the dark, my heart fluttering like a trapped bird beneath my breast. After a while the sensation would pass but come morning, I often found myself feeling foggy and worn out.

The in-laws kept a careful eye on me, too careful, for my liking. I found their questions intrusive, judgmental, abrasive. They were always there in the shadows on the landing, watching as I entered or left, the twitch of the curtains in their front room up the stairs, even the click on the phone. 'It must have been the party line.' was the standard response, but I wasn't buying it.

Maggie and Sophie seemed to know my every move. They made it their business to look after their brother's wife. They didn't match up to my idea of what a sister-in-law should be. Sophie was once my best friend at school, we did everything together but now... now all I got was laconic responses and tight-lipped smiles. I began to wonder if they kept a notebook on me, I wouldn't have put it past them.

I gave up fighting the silent barriers and decided that they weren't worthy of my time or concern. But all that soon changed. I found myself cursing them under my breath, particularly when the door slammed for the umpteenth time and Sophie and Maggie's raucous chatter receded as their high heels tapped up the road. They maddened me, especially when it seemed everyone spoke so highly of Richard's bloody sisters. They were out every night dressed to the nines with a different boy on their arms. I hated their lipstick, the smell of their perfume trailing through the house long after they had left and all those pretty dresses they flaunted about in while I could no longer fit into any of mine. Sometimes I'd hear their muffled laughter coming from up the stairs - all the young folk in the front room, sitting round the piano, singing and having fun while I ballooned and seethed with envy.

I noted all my grudges against 'that bloody family', nursed them in ritual fashion, going over and over them like rosary beads, refining and polishing my reasons until truth was no longer party to the stories I told myself.

At seven months something within me snapped. The spying, the intrusions into my flat when I was out, the sound of them clumping about in the front room upstairs - it had all become too much and left me wondering what it would be like when my child was born. I had visions of them trailing in and out of the flat as it suited them - their grubby fingers pointing and poking at my child, claiming it as theirs. It was my baby, I did all the hard work, I had taken all the flak. Where was Richard in this? He had scarpered, left me to pick up the pieces and I'll be damned if they thought they could just swan in and take all the joy of my new-born from me. There was nothing for it but to leave.

Within a short space of time I had moved out into a cramped dingy flat, situated up several flights of stairs, on the other side of town. For what it was, the rent was exorbitant but, to me, it was worth it. I could claim and carve my own space. Of course, my Mother questioned my reasoning, my colleagues raised their eyebrows and gave me sidelong glances. But what did I care? I was going to show them all exactly how capable I could be. Now, I would jettison that family from my life and never, if I had my way, provide them with an option to come back in.

The day I moved into my new place, I found myself looking out through rain drizzled windows onto the grimy street below. A steady stream of traffic thrummed past making the windows rattle.

The flat wasn't in great shape. The pipes clanged and banged through the night; the neighbour's radio warbled from the floor below and I found mice droppings in the kitchen cabinets - I hate mice, odious little vermin. As I looked around me, the reality of my situation loomed large. Was this really a good place to bring up a child? How would I manage? My shape had changed, I lumbered rather than walked, I could now feel the baby moving inside me yet I still didn't experience that frisson of excitement and anticipation that one of the girl's in the office said I would experience. I told myself I didn't care, I pretended not to feel lonely and frightened, I was away from 'them' and that was all that mattered. The fluttering behind my breast made regular visits, waking me in the early hours of the morning. I put it down to hormones, to the impending birth, anything that made some sort of sense.

I'd arranged to meet Val at the Cadena Cafe that Saturday afternoon. I couldn't really afford it but needed cheering up and hadn't seen her for months. Since the wedding she seemed to have distanced herself, been less available, but her reasons sounded valid enough. She was learning to drive, started a new job, got a new beau. I was the first to arrive. The cafe was busy, so much so that the windows had steamed up, spoiling the view of the Promenade.

Heads turned when Val arrived. She was perfectly coiffed, not a hair out of place. Her red lipstick accentuated her bright smile, and her dress emphasised her slim figure, particularly her legs; she looked stunning.

I smoothed my dress and lifting my handbag to my lap, covered my belly. It was a self-conscious act. Shortly after she arrived, I noticed a definite shift in our friendship, it was subtle, but it was definitely there. I had always been the one that exuded the poise and charm, I was the one that took the lead, had the confidence and the looks. But now…

The chatter was light and casual at first. We talked of friends and work. Val became animated when she mentioned her new beau, John. He was on a board of directors for a company based in Malvern. He owned a red sports car, *'an Aston Martin.'* She positively savoured the words as she spoke them aloud noting the effect it had on those eavesdropping from the near-by tables. Her voice grew louder, shrill almost, when she added that 'he was the most divine and handsome man you could ever meet.'

I forced a smile and stabbed at my cake. It was hard to swallow. She was beginning to grate.

'So, Diane, tell me, how is married life?'

I know I should have kept my reserve, not said anything. I shouldn't have put my woes into her hands or expected her to be sympathetic. She had been lording it over me and relishing every moment. My words came gushing out like a river in spate I couldn't have stopped myself even if I had tried. Tears welled up as I spoke.

'I never thought things would turn out like this, Val. Never in a million years. Paying for my own *wedding ring was bad enough.* That really stuck in my craw. If Daddy had found out he would have had a fit. I can see Richard now fiddling with the change in his pockets like he does when he doesn't want to deal with something, and that simpering voice 'but Diane, I just don't have the funds.' And yet he had enough funds to go out with his bloody friends right before the wedding. I wasn't supposed to find out about that but Carol, the office junior, let slip at work. Said the boys had been over to Gloucester living it up, whatever that means!'

Val put her hand to her mouth in horror. 'Oh Lord, Diane. Whatever are you going to do?'

'I wish to God I'd never gone along with the marriage. It felt all wrong. It was all wrong. I was ambushed into it because I was made to feel guilty and Mum wanted me to be respectable.

'What was I thinking? How did it all turn out like this? If I'm honest, brutally honest Val, yes, I was attracted to Richard at first in a comfortable sort of way. At least I thought it was attraction.

He was safe and steady, I knew that he adored me - but he didn't challenge me, I never thought of him as my 'forever' guy. We were imbalanced right from the start. There was nothing exciting about him, the sex ...'

Val recoiled, stunned that I was even using the word in a public place and tried to temper me with a hissed 'Diane, keep your voice down.' But I continued undeterred.

'I think that came about because I was curious. I know I wanted to see what it was like, I assumed he would be careful, I thought he knew what to do.'

'Diane.' Val reached out and laid her hand heavily over mine. I looked at her obliquely and continued, my voice a little softer.

'When it happened ... I don't really know what happened. I was drunk, he'd been feeding me alcohol that night. It was a party. I felt a bit sick so he took me outside to get some fresh air. Next thing I knew we were in the car and he was heaving away on top of me.

Afterwards, I couldn't even stand the smell of him, all Brylcreem, body odour and his precious cigarettes. It repulsed me and then I repulsed myself, I couldn't understand why I had allowed him, us, to go that far. I found it hard to fathom what all the fuss was about. It just felt dirty and sordid. And here we are now, in this rotten pickle, expecting a baby and married.'

Val looked down at my bump and grimaced, like she was trying to wipe the words, the very ideas from her head.

'Married, what does that word really mean? I think his idea of what it entails is a far cry from mine. I don't even think he's really thought it through. I'm just a captured trophy - something for him to brag about. He got me up the duff - he doesn't fire blanks. To him it's like a badge of honour among his friends. I saw Simon, his best friend, clapping him on the back congratulating him. They were both smirking. It made me feel sick. He would have been better off marrying Simon than me, wherever Simon is, Richard is never far behind, tagging along, picking up for him, being his lackey. The two have always been thick as thieves - only Simon always seemed to have the upper hand. The RAF did us all a favour there. Maybe it will make him grow up.

Richard: January 1960

I was posted to Aden in Yemen just before Frankie was born. I had hoped Diane would join me out there, but she outright refused. *'Why would I want to go all the way out there to be isolated from family, friends and leave a job I love?'* She looked at me with disdain.

I knew it was no place for a wife, let alone a child, besides, the political climate was precarious, to say the least. But oh, how I missed her. How I wished I could share the things I witnessed there - the sunrise in the mornings. A big red sphere that filled half the horizon and rolled slowly as it climbed its way up. I could swear I could see huge flames leaping from it visibly heating up the earth as it rose higher and higher. Then there was the call to prayer, a haunting wail at various times of the day from the tall minarets standing out on the skyline. The call entered my dreams, snaking its way into my secret places soothing like a lullaby and yet woke me from my slumbers in a strange and comforting way. These were but a few of the things I wanted to share with her, see the wonder on her face as it lit up with her dazzling smile.

But something had changed. If I'm honest it began when she found out she was pregnant, as though a part of her had retreated. She had battened down the hatches and stopped talking, giving only short, clipped responses, to get her to share anything was like pulling teeth. My mum said it was probably due to the pregnancy, so I didn't push it. There was also an edginess, it was there at our wedding reception, the way her eyes darted round the room as if she was checking for reactions and making a mental note - who was in and who was out. The face she wore looked more like she was facing the death sentence, a half-smile that wasn't reflected in her eyes.

There was a fear there, I wasn't fooled by the *just get on with it* front. Her shoulders, all rounded and the way she placed her feet, turned inwards, all said that same thing. But she wouldn't let me reassure her, kept pushing me off saying 'stop pawing me.'

It didn't help that her father wouldn't look her in the eye, I'd seen her looking over to him, but he would just look away and shake his head. Every time it happened her bottom lip trembled, my poor love, what with his rigid stance and her mother tightly gripping her handbag as if its contents might try and climb out. I'm sure it affected Diane. They left quietly after the toast and then Diane disengaged completely. When we got home, she curled up on our bed and cried, shuddering and sobbing. I didn't know what to do.

'Leave her,' mum said, 'she'll come round eventually.'

So, I did.

Diane: Late January 1960

I was ironing, almost a month shy of full term, when my waters broke. Calmly I descended three flights of stairs, made my way to the nearest telephone box and called an ambulance and then my parents.

By the time the ambulance arrived twenty minutes later, it had started to snow. It drifted down in swirls and flourishes, barely settling. I remember feeling the playful tickle of the odd snowflake as I was being loaded into the back of the ambulance. Snowflakes landed on my hair, face and eyelashes and on the blanket that had been wrapped around me. It made me think of a snow globe I once had when I was a child. A scene with pine trees and swathes of whirling snow when I shook it. I was both anxious and excited at the prospect of seeing my new baby but even more than that I couldn't wait to get back to being a normal size. My ankles had swollen, physical activity over-taxed me and I felt emotional all the time or so it seemed.

En route the ambulance crew were advised that the local hospital's baby unit was full and were diverted to the nearest hospital in Cirencester some sixteen miles away.

'There's plenty time,' the crew assured me, 'nothing to worry about.'

The weather conditions deteriorated, Cirencester had it worst. The ambulance wheels lost traction several times and the vehicle fish-tailed dangerously across the road twice. Still, it ploughed on through the snow-covered roads until treacherous blizzard conditions prevented any further movement. The wind howled and whipped around us; huge dollops of snow fell eventually trapping the ambulance in a deep snow drift. Inside the vehicle, I screamed, bore down and pushed my breach-birth baby out into the world to the encouragement of both the male ambulance staff. I witnessed with awe and fear as my baby took its first lungful of air and lifted a tiny but defiant fist.

Gently, I cradled my baby, a precious girl, while outside the ambulance crew shovelled snow. I felt as vulnerable as my baby, my child, wet with life and crying. Never had I needed my parents or my husband more. But I was alone. My husband, thousands of miles away in the Middle East doing his bit for Queen and country and my parents, unable to come on account of the weather.

During the days when I was confined to my hospital bed, I changed from being a frightened young girl to a woman of grit. Knowing that Richard probably wouldn't get the news of the birth for a week or so I resolved to move things on myself and give my child a name. *'It's the one thing I can do and be proud of doing and nobody can take that away from me,'* I thought.

Prior to the birth I'd thought of delicate, feminine names for a girl, like Felicity, or Penelope but looking at this child in my arms I thought better of it. No, this child will need a strong name, and just like that, the name Frankie came to mind.

'Ah, Frances, what a pretty name,' said the nurse when I first tried saying the name out loud. Even I was surprised at how I responded, rounding on her sharply, 'No, it's Frankie, not Frances.'

We stayed in hospital for a week while a steady stream of visitors came to wish us well. I kept the name a secret until after I had my daughter officially registered. I didn't want anyone to steal my thunder, not even my parents, I knew they would resist. I could just imagine my mother's reaction, 'but that's not a real name for a child.' But Frankie wasn't theirs to name, she was mine. She had come from my body and so I'll call her what I bloody-well pleased, that was my prerogative.

Frankie cried a lot. She was premature and weighed only 5lbs. They placed her in a cot at the side of my bed, it was the same for all the other mothers on the ward, but I found it beyond trying. When I looked down at my child all I saw was a little screwed-up face like an old man, gums dribbling, tiny fists balled - the crying was incessant. I tried to reassure her, swaddled her gently in her hospital blanket, rocked her back and forth, tried feeding her. But all attempts failed, she refused to suckle and wasn't easily calmed.

There was something about Frankie's frailty that petrified me: her small body, its tiny limbs, the pulsing fontanelle, the way her hands gripped hold of my fingers with a fierce determination. I thought all this would provoke an instant feeling of love, of wanting to protect this minute creature, my child. But all I felt was dread, fear and revulsion. Despite the nurses' entreaties, I let her cry for longer and longer periods before picking her up; I was sickened by the smell of regurgitated milk, and found her squalls irritating. I handled her roughly. I waited for the flush of maternal love that everyone one talked about, but it never came. I felt cheated and confused.

Silently, I wrangled with my sense of estrangement. How could I broach this subject with anyone? Who would be willing to listen to what I had to say? I didn't feel confident enough to mention it to Mum, I had expectations to live up to and none of my friends had any experience of childbirth. The nurses were far too busy and efficient to deal with this and they probably wouldn't understand anyway.

I began to think that what I was experiencing was unnatural. It was easy to jump from that to the conclusion that I wasn't normal, a monster even. The thought of it turned round and round in my mind until I was convinced it was true. Just looking around me there was evidence enough to prove that. Every mother I looked at in the ward appeared to take to motherhood easily. I watched them, brimming with love, fussing, cosseting, with wide smiles of pride. They didn't seem to be all fingers and thumbs when changing nappies or bathing their babies. If anyone mentioned terylene nappies again, or what a wonderful sight it was to see them hanging on the line, I thought I would scream. I didn't relish the idea of scraping shit off a used item or leaving dirty nappies to soak in an enamel bucket - a present given to me from the girls in the office.

'How thoughtful!' I just didn't know how or where to begin.

The nappy pin frightened me; I didn't trust myself not to stick it in Frankie. The pin seemed to be the same size as her foot, bigger even. I hated having to be reminded by the nursing staff - 'Feed your baby, bathe your baby, pick it up, don't pick it up'. It was all so confusing.

Mum's first comment to me when she saw her was 'you're holding that child all wrong Diane.'

I wondered whether this would be a good time to give Frankie up for adoption before I got too deeply embroiled. I tried to broach the subject with one of the nurses who found me crying in the bathroom. 'I don't think I can do this. I think it would be better to give the baby up, have her adopted.'

But the nurse just patted me on the arm and said 'Don't be a silly girl. What would your husband think?' She then ushered me back into the ward and busied herself tucking me into bed, speaking over my protestations in soothing tones.

'There now, a nice cup of tea and you'll soon be as right as rain.'

I was perplexed. Why was it that everyone considered my husband's feelings, or what my family would think? How come no one took me seriously or really listened to what I had to say or how I felt?

The other new-borns around me in the ward didn't scream and bawl but lay in their mothers' arms peaceful and contented. These mothers all appeared to have a natural bond whereas I felt disconnected. I was playing a part, imitating everyone else, trying to live up to what was expected of me and not facing what I really felt.

I could see that Frankie was a small helpless baby whose tight little fists showed her spirit, even when so young, but I couldn't help my wanting to reject her. I had no love for her, I had nothing left.

The birth had ripped me open and laid me bare. The ambulance men had been kind and professional but all the same, they were men bearing witness to parts of my body that even I had never really seen. The twenty stitches administered in the hospital to put things right had been both frightening and disorienting. Suddenly it seemed that everyone had access to me. Everything hurt, my private parts were constantly sore and jabbed me with a sharp pain every time I moved.

I couldn't help but think, 'all that fuss and for what? A twenty-minute fumble in the back of an old Austin Healey car.'

I felt as though I was the one being punished again and again for that one stupid mistake - and now I would be paying for it for the rest of my life.

Richard: Early 1960's

Visits home were infrequent and short, left me with the sense that the gulf between myself and Diane was growing increasingly wider. She had moved out from the flat my parents had provided before the baby was born. Maggie kept prying, was it the decoration, did she not appreciate the new cooker? It was humiliating, I'd leave the room if the conversation started going that way or change the subject. It hadn't crossed anyone's mind that she found them suffocating and boring.

How was I to explain that to my parents? What would they make of it? I'd painted, laid carpets and fixed it up to make it look nice. And it was rent free. If she could have accepted it, I imagined we would have money saved to buy our own place within a couple of years. We would have had babysitting on hand and Diane would have had a five-minute walk to work. But she didn't like the smell of the dental surgery above her, could sometimes hear the sound of the drill. The toilet was noisy, and the drain gurgled too loudly. She objected to my sisters wanting access to the backyard to hang out their washing! Did it matter? They were family, they had always used the backyard to hang out the washing.

'Why does she have to be so cussed?' my mother asked in her last letter.

I was at a loss to know what to do, particularly from Aden. In my mind's eye I could see her, hands on hips, her swollen belly beginning to show beneath her colourful skirt, staring defiantly at one of my sisters, probably Sophie, refusing her access to the backyard. She was spirited, like a wild horse that refused to be tamed.

Correspondence from her was infrequent to say the least. If I did get a letter its contents were perfunctory and brief and mostly pointed out what a poor husband I was and how much she detested my family. I understood that things were difficult for her. Juggling work and impending motherhood on her own wasn't an easy road to take. But if she would just come down off her high horse and accept the help and support that was available to her - my sisters and parents were there in the wings willing and able to help as were her parents, I had no doubt about that. Yet I still couldn't fully understand what her gripes about my family were or where they stemmed from. There was a time when she and my middle sister Sophie had been the closest of friends at school, Sophie even went on holiday with her family to Bournemouth.

I wanted so much to learn about Frankie, what stage she was at with her development, how she was doing generally. My parents, especially Mum, was always asking. She was desperate to get to know her first grand-daughter. But I had nothing to tell her.

What was her first word? I didn't know. Was she potty trained now? Did Frankie have a favourite toy?

The sad fact was I really couldn't say. There were no funny comments about what she had been up to, no recent photographs. Each time I returned home I had to learn to get reacquainted with Frankie all over again. It was a slow painstaking process and required time. Time that Diane guarded jealously, she worked hard to find excuses to make Frankie unavailable. She needed a bath, needed to be changed, had an appointment with the district nurse, she was tired. I felt my child getting further and further beyond my reach and felt powerless to do anything about it.

I felt acutely embarrassed that I didn't have any boasting pictures of my daughter to show anyone. My colleagues often asked but I made weak excuses or changed the subject. When their questions got too personal, I just shut down, put up a wall of silence. The only picture I had in my locker was one that was taken the day I got married. A small black and white photograph of the two of us standing not quite close together on the steps of the registry office. Diane wore a neat cream suit and pill box hat drawing attention away from the almost imperceptible swell of her belly. On my lips, a wistful smile, I was the happiest I had ever been as I looked down on her - she, on the other hand was looking away off to the right.

I spent every spare moment I had in the workshop learning my craft, working on the airplane engines. If no aircraft engine was available, I turned my attention to cars - anything and anyone's. It was my way of thoroughly getting to grips with engines. I found it hard to get the grease and oil out of my hands. It had become ingrained, right down to the fine fingerprint lines. My fingers bore nicks and callouses from wielding wrenches and spanners. I liked nothing better than the sound of metal against metal, dismantling, unscrewing, refitting. I loved the sounds of the workshop, the smell of the oil, the thrum of a smooth well-oiled engine.

My work ethic and meticulous attitude paid dividends. Soon people sought me out to help solve a problem or to ensure that a job was finished and done well. I loved to work, it provided a means of keeping me occupied, stopped me over-thinking about things that would only drive me crazy. Not that anyone had any inkling of that. I never let on what was on my mind, kept my cards close to my chest. I was friendly enough but didn't open up; I didn't seek out company or go drinking with the rest of the crew. I know I was considered to be a bit of an odd-ball, useful for getting things done but not one for mixing or socialising. I think the adjutant kept a close eye on me, curious to know what it was that made this man tick. Whenever he questioned me about home, I always responded with one-word answers.

'So, Richard, how's the wife?'

'Okay, Sir.'

'Does she mind you being out here?'

'No, Sir.'

'And you have a child, a daughter isn't it?'

'Yes, Sir.'

'A toddler.'

'Yes, Sir.'

I wasn't prepared to venture any further information, even when pushed. I just kept my mouth shut.

Diane: Early 1960's

I went back to work a fortnight after Frankie was born. I never thought I'd ever have to work, let alone when I had a child. Imagine the indignity of it all. I even had to go and express my milk in the office toilet. Everyone considered me odd for wanting to breast-feed, I didn't understand why. It was a perfect way of bonding with my child. Nonetheless, there was so much I constantly leaked. Milk marks appeared on my blouse leaving an oily residue that spread into the material and smelt sour. The only positive to be had from it was that I suddenly had womanly curves in all the right places. But the milk was no good. It didn't matter how much I produced, Frankie refused it, turned her head away and clamped her mouth tightly shut. She just wouldn't latch on, no matter how many times I tried. The health visitor cajoled me to switch to formula, 'It's what everyone else is doing Diane. But I was determined to try and feed her myself even though it just made me feel hopeless and angry. I took it personally, even though a part of me knew it to be irrational. I felt as though my unhappiness had curdled the milk and somehow Frankie sensed that. Of course, she knew, she had grown inside me, heard my tears, felt my desperation - knew that I hadn't wanted her then and this was her way of punishing me. Her refusal felt personal, spiteful.

This wasn't how I expected motherhood to turn out. When I was younger, I imagined spending my days baking cakes and taking strolls in the sunshine with the pram when the au pair had the day off. I'd joked with Val about having five children, a big house and two nannies. Now look at me, barely scraping by. No husband around on a regular basis, working all the hours and hardly a bean to show for all my effort. Richard didn't send money home regularly, God knows what he did with his wages, I've given up asking ...

I hated handing Frankie over to the child-minder, that sour-faced old trout with her judgemental opinions and pointed questions. Her disapproval followed me down the garden path and along the road, I could feel it clinging to me every time I left her house. *She* got to see Frankie's first steps, hear her first words. *She* got to see and do all the things that I should have done with my child and she revelled in it. Dripped every little detail into my ear until the poison consumed me.

Work was a relief, my refuge. Bill didn't judge me on my private life only on my merits as a secretary and I knew I was a good one - my shorthand was second to none and I never got any of my typing returned. Bill, said I was his right hand, told all his clients that he couldn't do without me. High praise indeed from an accountant of his calibre. My life pivoted round work and childcare for the next three years and pretty much nothing else. Just one never ending dull monotonous routine, I felt old at 21.

And then came Tom Morton. Initially I didn't notice him when he came for his first appointment. He was already seated and waiting his turn when I got to the office. An early bird, evidently. Bill liked to summon his clients in by sending through a call on the switchboard, said it was more efficient that way.

'Mr Morton, would you like to go through to Mr Wilson's office now' was all I said in my usual manner.

Then he stood and I had to catch myself, stop myself from gasping aloud. It was the way he stood and carried himself, emitting a quiet self-assurance through the whole length of his long body. Such a perfect frame, broad shoulders and a sharp dresser. I found myself briefly imagining what he looked like beneath his suit. He smiled, made a point of thanking me as he walked past my desk and I blushed. I don't think he saw, but I'm sure Bill, who at that point had come to the doorway to give him a warm handshake, noticed because he raised his eyebrows in an amused fashion and said, 'Can you bring through some tea, Diane?'

I replayed that moment over and over again in my head. He specifically thanked me, it was pointed, and communicated very subtly that he was interested, that I had his attention, he wanted me. I knew it and it thrilled me.

Tom had cause to come to the office twice that week. The second time he arrived early, and we struck up a conversation about nothing in particular. The dance had begun, as though the Tarantella music had struck up and we were both players leading up to the inevitable. I drank in everything about him. The cut of his brown tweed jacket, the colour of his fine curly hair, his dark eyes with their long lashes. His broad hands with a peppering of black hair from his wrists. But most of all it was the timbre of his voice. Self-assured and smooth as chocolate. I wanted that voice to whisper into my hair, murmur at my neck, speak directly to me. But decency dictated. I was a married woman, and he, he was out of my reach. Or was he?

Six months later it was Race Week, the highlight of the office calendar. Race Week was a time when Cheltenham threw out all sensibilities and the good and the great descended upon it, pockets filled to the gunnels. Bill had hired a box at the Race Course; we spent the time with clients, entertaining. Tom turned up and perhaps it was the liberal amounts of alcohol or the conditions were right, but we were both unguarded. He touched me lightly when we talked, even fed me an olive, his finger lingering in my mouth. When it came time to leave, he offered me a lift home. It seemed a natural thing to do. He escorted me to the car, his hand lightly touching the small of my back. It wasn't so much as guiding me but taking the opportunity to touch me again. Don't ask me how I knew, I just did. He opened my door and held my hand as I seated myself. It was that hold, so gentle and reassuring that sealed it for me. I knew then I was in love with Tom. Stupid I know, I hardly knew the man, but at some level we knew there was something between us.

We were heading to the child minders' when it started to rain. It was so heavy we could hardly see through the windscreen; the wipers couldn't cope. The rain pummelled on the roof and bounced off the windows like an endless round of applause. Inside the car it felt warm and safe. That's when he pulled the car over to the side of the road, our breath misting up the windows, then he kissed me passionately. It was intoxicating, never had I felt anything like that: his hand in my hair, I could feel him breathing me in, kissing my face, my neck, tender and reverent. He held my face in his hands and looked me in the eye, I mean, really looked at me, as though there was something there that he recognised. I felt both naked and exposed but incredibly beautiful and powerful. I know I should have stopped him but after the first kiss there was no turning back.

We met every day after work for the following month. He'd pick me up after work, we'd collect Frankie from the childminder and from there, go on to my flat. It was perfect. I lived for those meetings, the tenderness and laughter. The intensity of the love making. The fact that he was interested in me, laughed at my jokes, listened to my every utterance all meant that something deep and powerful was blooming between us. I felt so alive. We were completely compatible, like a pair of gloves reunited. My world seemed whole and complete. I never wanted it to end. We both declared our feelings and I meant it with every fibre of my being. Tom asked me to consider going away with him. Let's make a new life together, that's what he said.

I used the babysitter a lot over that time. After our love-making Tom and I would go out for meals or dancing or for walks out near Winchcombe or Crickley Hill. I did worry that someone might have seen us, but we were discreet, taking our trysts to out of the way places, He was good in that way, always thinking about me. He said he didn't care about what people said, 'let the gossips say what they like,' he'd say waving his hand dismissively and we'd both laugh. 'Soon you'll be mine, my love,' and he would wrap my hands in his and kiss them tenderly.

I felt as if I'd known him a lifetime. He was gregarious, commanding, passionate, intelligent and incredibly attentive. When his eyes were on me I felt like I was the centre of his world. He bought me an expensive gold locket in the shape of a heart. I implored him to let me have a bit of his hair to put in it, so I could carry a piece of him close to me, just like they did in the old novels. He ribbed me for reading too much Jane Austen. I loved the fact that he was a reader, such a contrast to Richard.

I thought my life was changing for the better and although it had only been a short while, it just felt right. Here was a man who really knew how to make a woman feel like a woman, knew how to touch her body in such a way that it came alive.

It was a giddy time. We talked of going away together, of our new life. We fantasised about what it would be like to live abroad. It was always something that he had dreamed of. He thought the States would be the best place for a new start, 'The land of milk and honey where dreams come true.' His eyes would come alive when he spoke of it. He liked the idea of the south because of the heat, the sound of the cicadas, the Spanish moss dancing in the trees. He filled my head with his dreams, made me part of them so I dreamed them too. He was even prepared to take on Frankie and, as he said with a mischievous grin, provide her with a sibling or two.

This made all my other worries pale into insignificance. I felt claimed and nothing, nothing else mattered. I was in love and he loved me.

One evening we had gone out of town to Broadway for a drink. We stopped in one of the little pubs on the way. He said it was an interesting watering hole which made me laugh. A full, smoky bar with a lot of the patrons drinking the local cider. Tom loved to observe people. He casually pointed out the man in the corner and the size of his big red nose, he called it 'the tell-tale cider nose' and to watch out as that would happen to me if I drank too much of the local brew. I threw my head back and laughed out loud and then someone familiar caught my eye. It was one of the girls from the office. It had totally slipped my mind that she lived out that way. She jutted her chin out acknowledging me and then turned her back. I didn't really think much of it. I was having such a good time with Tom.

The next day at the office she took me aside in the kitchen and tactfully asked: 'Diane, do you know what you are doing?' I acted as if I was affronted. 'There is absolutely no impropriety going on, it was just a harmless drink.' She apologised. 'I just thought you needed to know. Tom is not all he seems.'

Her comments rattled me, but I was so in love I dismissed them. Not my Tom, he would never hurt me or let me down. I thought that perhaps she was jealous - it was understandable, he was a good-looking man with everything going for him. Besides, we had even discussed starting divorce proceedings, he said he would make me an appointment with his solicitor, so I knew it was serious.

Richard: April 1964

We didn't get the best of starts, either of us. We were too young, too naive, too busy trying to figure out what was going on. Christ, we didn't even know who we were then. I know I should have tried to explain, tell her what I was thinking, but before I knew it, I had signed up for a further three years. I thought she'd be pleased, that somehow, she would understand that I was trying to think ahead, think about us, our family.

I knew I didn't want to follow my father's trade. I hated dentistry and everything to do with it. God, the thought of having to speak to people - make small talk with relative strangers. It left me cold. I'm just not a people person. I'd probably fare better making or fixing the dentures if push came to shove, but that would still mean I would be left to take over the business. Then I'd be tied, have to live in the same place I work in. That rattly old house with its sloping floors and draughty windows and I'm sure my parents would expect to live with us. I can't see Diane accepting that one. No, we'd both feel trapped and tied. I decided that I needed physical things, not in an office, but doing my own thing. Something that didn't entail having to empathise or reassure like Dad is obliged to do.

I decided I'd be better off staying on with the RAF, get trained up. It's a guarantee that I'd have a trade by the time I'm out the other end. It's only three years. That would give me more options, more choices, a better income and a sure-fire way of providing for my family with something that I like doing. It would give us stability.

I was never happier than when I was trying to find a solution to a mechanical problem. I revelled in engines, all those small intricate interconnecting pieces. How they all fit together, what makes them tick, and then there's the sound when all the parts are moving. There's nothing better than the smell of the oil in a smooth-running engine – it's like winning the Gold Cup of car mechanics. If only people were that simple and easy to read. If only Diane ...

But Diane - she wasn't interested, she didn't want to know why I made the decisions I did. According to her all my actions are based on selfishness, 'doing as I please.' Even planting the cherry tree in the garden to symbolise our family growing together was wrong.

It was the letter from my sister Maggie that gee'd me into action. I read it, like I read all my letters, lying on my bunk in the cool of the day just after mess. It was a routine I'd developed and grown accustomed to - saving my little treats until last. I hated trying to work with my mind all cluttered up - I needed to be able to focus. But Maggie's letter worked like a cattle prod.

That night I hardly slept a wink, my mind conjuring up all kinds of scenarios, none of which were favourable. Come the morning I was sick with worry and went to see the adjutant to plead for special home leave.

Taking my private business to someone else made me feel cornered, it was like admitting I was inept as a husband and father, but I couldn't think of any other way to handle it. The officer was very understanding, far more than I had anticipated. I think he knew it was a hard thing for me to discuss. Got me to talk about what had been happening at home. I explained the circumstances, how awkward things were. How Diane was. My guilt at not being there for her when Frankie was born, how we were struggling to hold things together as a family. Then I told him about Maggie's letter and as I began to talk about it, I could feel this tightness in my chest till I could hardly breathe. He asked me to read the letter to him.

My dear little brother ... it pains me to tell you that something may be amiss with Diane. She has been spending a lot of time in the company of that Tom Morton. Remember that odious character from school? Two years above you, in Sophie's class. Lived up the Leckhampton Road, his father owned the jewellers', down the lower end of the High Street ...

I remembered him alright, particularly that time in school ... the day I was playing football in the playground with my mates. We weren't bothering anyone, just having a good kick about and then Tom turned up. He muscled in on the game, belted the ball so hard at us that some of us fell, writhing in agony and he, the big bully, stood over us and laughed. 'Aww who's a little cissy then? Do you want to run home and tell your Mummies?' Then he picked up our ball and took it to his friends to play their own game. We all had to wait about until the end of break to try and get our ball back knowing there was nothing we could do. Tom and his gang were bigger, older and their fists hurt when thrown.

It made my headache just thinking about him. an aggressive know-it-all with delusions of grandeur but smarmy with it. He could hoodwink the teachers into thinking that butter wouldn't melt. I knew he was the ringleader responsible for damaging my bike. They'd punctured my tyres and ripped the chain off and stood there blatantly laughing as they watched me discover their handiwork. I had poured hours into that bike, painting it, fixing it up, it had carried me on many rides around the Cotswolds, my prize possession.

Oh God, to think that he has been around my Diane - taking her in with his smarmy smooth talk. She was so naive and vulnerable. Hell's teeth - I couldn't even be there to protect her from him.

The adjutant agreed to sign me off with special leave and within twenty-four hours I was packed, off the base and on a plane heading back home. I didn't have time to let anyone know I was coming, and I was relieved. It gave me that element of surprise.

When I arrived home, weary from travel, Simon was the first person I turned to. We'd been friends since nursery. Mum always said 'when you found one the other wasn't far behind.' We were like chalk and cheese, I was the quiet and practical one whereas Simon was gregarious, unpredictable and tremendous fun. He had a great capacity for wit and could create a party in an empty room. He kept everyone entertained with his quips, could talk his way out of trouble and across any threshold if the urge took him and he nearly always spoke on my behalf. Simon's biggest failing was that he didn't possess an ounce of common sense. 'Couldn't boil an egg, let alone the water to put it in!' his father was wont to say. I, on the other hand, was calm, rarely got over excited and great with practical problem solving. I always came up trumps when faced with a crisis. Simon's father would testify to this, harking back to a camping holiday us boys took in our early teens.

'Had it not been for Richard, they'd have got lost and either died of hypothermia or hunger or possibly both. He had the sense to bring a serviceable map, fix the boat's outboard motor and catch, prepare and cook the fish.'

So, it was Simon who came with me to Tom's house. Just for a change he was the one doing the supporting. He tried to talk me out of it, could see that I was angry and was very concerned that I was going to do something I might regret later. He couldn't just leave me to get on with it alone. He later told me that he came with me with a view to talking some sense into me on the way. I'd told him I was going to rip Tom's head off and castrate him on the spot. He knew I meant business that was for sure. Simon had no intention of getting physically involved. He couldn't handle himself in that way besides as a newly qualified solicitor he couldn't afford to get implicated in anything sordid. He was there to ensure that I didn't kill the bastard and to keep me legally safe.

I remember him starting up the car engine, hands gripping the steering wheel, looking at me sidelong, 'are you sure this is what you want to do?'

'Yes,' my answer was like a forceful punch. 'Just drive for God's sake. Let's get this bloody mess over and done with.'

Then Simon put the car into gear, indicated and swerved out into the road as if he sensed he was on an important mission.

At Tom's door I had steadied myself, locked down my anger and focused. Simon had never witnessed me act this way and I think it proved to be quite a revelation. Military life had made a man of me. Catching an image of myself in the car window, I could see the physical changes myself. The evening light exaggerated my chiselled features; my physique had bulked out during my time away, lending gravitas to my stance and frame. There was an ice-cold malice in my eyes, Simon said later that it had unnerved him. I had always been so placid and malleable when we were kids. he added that he was relieved that he was not the one on the receiving end of my wrath.

After ringing the bell, we waited on the doorstep for what seemed like an age. A light came on. I pulled myself up to full height. There was movement from behind the door. A voice shouted, 'just a minute.'

Tom took his time answering. He stood there, bare chested, a towel slung around his neck. He smelt of shaving foam and Old Spice after shave. His chin shiny smooth from his clean shave, his hair all slicked back. He opened the door with a swagger that lost its effect when he saw me standing there. His smile flickered momentarily then set, crocodile fashion, his eyes, cold and calculating. 'Hi Richard, what brings you here?' He merely nodded to Simon.

My frame filled the doorway. I stood there and deliberately sized him up. Now I had three inches height on Tom and was in much better shape. My first thought was cutting this man down to size would be easy pickings. Then I looked at Tom's hands and thought of where they had been how they had trailed over my wife's body, held her, touched her in the most intimate places. I thought of Tom's lips, pressed against Diane's and suddenly rage was pumping through my body like some kind of super-charged electricity. I could vaguely hear Tom's voice. There was a tremor in it. I registered the fear and took full advantage. My left hand went for Tom's throat and I lifted him from the floor. Then, putting my face up close to Tom's, I growled 'now, let me make things clear ...'

By the time we walked away from his house I had achieved what I'd set out to achieve — a promise from Tom to leave town and to leave my wife alone.

Simon remained unusually silent for the duration of the journey home. He dropped me off at the flat and just as I was opening the door he looked up and ventured: 'You were formidable. For a moment there I thought you were going to kill him.' I looked him full in the face, hesitated for a moment and said, 'so did I.'

I hoisted my kitbag onto my shoulder and put my key in the lock and wondered what kind of reception awaited me.

She was putting Frankie to bed when I appeared through the front door. In the kitchen sat Caroline, the babysitter. I recognised her as the young girl who lived with her family on the ground floor beneath us. I motioned to her, putting my fingers to my lips, sshhhh. Diane called through,' I won't be a minute,' I could hear her trying to persuade Frankie to settle down and go to sleep.

She came into the living room, a smile on her face. It was casual and open. Her face was relaxed and bright as though full of optimism. She was all dressed up, her hair done in an elaborate beehive, I could smell the hairspray as soon as she came near, and her make-up was perfectly applied. Her smile froze the moment she set eyes on me. 'What are you doing here?'

'Aren't you pleased to see me?' I said, in a mock jovial way expecting her to bite.

'No, I. I just wasn't expecting you, that's all.' She looked down awkwardly.

'You look like you are planning to go out.'

'Yes, I am...' She looked flustered and paused to look at her watch.

'Do you have you a hug for your husband? I've been travelling nearly twenty-four hours.' I made to step towards her but she held up the flat of her palm and narrowed her eyes.

'You look and smell like you need a bath. I'd rather not if you don't mind.'

'Point taken, but that can easily be remedied.' I dropped my kitbag. 'Can I have a look in on Frankie?'

'Do you have to? I've only just put her down.'

I didn't stop to listen and marched past her to Frankie's room. By the time Diane got to me I was holding my sleepy daughter who was mewling in my arms.

'Now you've gone and woken her up,' Diane's voice was raised and strained.

'She'll be fine,' I said softly, not taking my eyes off my daughter. 'How's Daddy's little girl then?'

Frankie responded by lifting her hands up to my mouth and tried forcing open my lips with her fingers. I giggled and Frankie followed suit.

'Put her down, Richard, if she doesn't sleep now, she'll be cranky in the morning and I've …' Diane held her arms out to take Frankie from me, but I turned away. I was still drinking my daughter in, how she had grown. She looked the spit of my youngest sister when she was her age. Irritated, Diane snapped at me, her voice swelling, 'Put her down.'

'Diane. Do you still want me to babysit?' Caroline called from the kitchen.

I was quick to respond. 'No, she'll not be needing a babysitter anymore thanks, not now her husband is home...'

'Oh, goodbye then, Mrs Miller.' Caroline left swiftly. The front door closed. Her footsteps thundered down the stairs landing heavily on each landing as she went.

Diane rounded on me, 'How bloody dare you? I have plans!' There it was, that spark in her eyes, she was up for a fight. I turned my face back to my daughter, kissed her once more. 'You can go out if you want, I'm not stopping you. I'll stay and look after Frankie.'

Flustered, she searched her handbag for her cigarettes as though stalling for time, a moment to think. She wanted me gone, anticipating Tom's imminent arrival.

She was probably thinking: 'Who the bloody hell does he think he is just turning up unannounced and upsetting things? This is my flat'. Her actions indicated her thoughts.

She struck a match, lit her cigarette and blew out the match with force. She threw the dead match into the ash tray and pulled hard on her cigarette.

'If Frankie wakes later on you'll need to ...'

'I can sort that.'

'Yes, but I don't have time to tell you all the details. I'm due to go out shortly. Will you be going to your parents when I come back?'

'No, I hadn't planned on that, why would I?' I fixed my gaze on her as she looked away and moved to the window likely searching the dark street for Tom. Wondering where he was. She checked her watch.

'I just don't think it'll work. Besides, you didn't give me any notice you were coming.'

'Since when does a husband have to give his wife notice that he's coming home? She remained unresponsive, her back to me as she stared out of the window. I could feel the anger bloom up from my chest and into my neck but hid it from my voice. 'You haven't even tried to make this work. It doesn't matter to you that I'm doing my damnedest and you can't even give me the courtesy of an answer.'

She tapped her fingernails against the window frame.

'And I'm not going to my parents, this is my flat just as much as it is yours, I send you money to pay the rent. Besides, my parents'll wonder what the bloody hell we're playing at.'

Frankie began to squall and wriggled in my arms.

'Now look what you've done.' Diane held her arms out. 'Give her to me.'

I kissed Frankie on her forehead, rocking her gently as I did so. 'No, I'll take her through to her cot and make sure she goes down.'

Diane: April 1964

'You need to leave Richard. Now, I don't want you here.'

He didn't flinch, remaining rooted to the spot. There was something about his demeanour that I found unsettling. He seemed different in a way that I couldn't quite fathom. I was both drawn and repelled by it. Tom was late. The doorbell remained silent. What was keeping him? Outside it started to rain, I watched the raindrops slant against the fluorescent streetlights and come-and-go shadows expand and contract as the occasional pedestrian walked past.

Richard put Frankie back down to sleep and ran himself a bath. He whistled tunelessly, I wanted to cram something into his face to shut him up, stop that mindless noise.

'Richard! Shut up, you'll disturb Frankie.' But he would have none of it.

'Nonsense, Frankie's happy to see her Daddy home.'

He knew it annoyed me and did it all the more with an exasperating pleased-with-himself look on his face. I stood at the window, eyes fixed on the street below, smoking cigarette after cigarette as I waited. I busied myself around the flat, little thankless tasks, I drank tea, endless cups of it. I did the washing up and tidied it away. By nine pm I knew Tom wasn't coming. Then I didn't want him to come. What would he think if he saw Richard here? What would Richard think? Not that I really cared about what he thought.

I tried to imagine a scenario with Tom here, the two of us sitting on the settee together opposite Richard. Tom breaking the news that we were in love and leaving together, us holding hands as he delivered the news. But he didn't come, he was nowhere to be seen. I took my shoes and earrings off and sat on the sofa with a magazine. I must have read the same sentence over and over.

After his bath Richard took his kit bag into the bedroom and began putting things away in drawers. Like he was staying here for a long while. I hadn't asked him what he was doing home. I was too preoccupied, too irritated.

The steam from his bath mingled with the cigarette smoke making strange patterns around the light in the hall. It made me think of a crystal ball. Which way was my fortune heading I wondered? What would it see?

I'd forgotten to tell him to leave the bathwater in the tub on account of the pipes clanging and gurgling. The noise woke Frankie up and she started wailing. He went through to her with just a towel wrapped around his waist and I couldn't help but notice the alteration to his physique. He'd gained more muscle, his neck looked thicker, his back broader. I only looked when I was sure he couldn't see me looking.

He was good with Frankie, managed to calm her down and had her back to sleep within ten minutes. She looked so content nestling in his arms I felt a pang of guilt thinking that soon I would be taking her away from him.

He put on his dressing gown. It had been hanging up on the back of the bedroom door and came into the living room. Tom had worn it only the other day and I held my breath for a moment in case Richard smelled a hint of Tom. He sat quietly and just looked - like he was studying me, flipping his zippo lighter lid open and shut. I braced myself. Any minute now I thought. But the moment never happened. After a while he ventured 'So how have you been?'

My response was perfunctory. 'Alright I spose.'

'And Frankie, how's she getting on. You don't say much in your letters.'

'As if you really want to know. You're never bloody well here.'

'That doesn't mean I don't care, and I do want to know Diane.'

'What, so you can keep tabs on me? Report to your parents what a rubbish mother I am?'

'Not at all, who said anything about reporting to my parents. I've never done such a thing.'

'Why are you home now? Have you gone AWOL? Why didn't you let me know you were coming?'

'I wanted it to be a surprise. Can a husband not surprise his wife and daughter, is there a law against that?'

'Surprise, a tornado would be more of a surprise than this. I'm so sick of this charade. Let's face it Richard, it's a part time marriage at best - with me shouldering all the responsibilities. Don't kid yourself that this hollow gesture is going to change things. It doesn't pay the bills, kiss Frankie goodnight, mend a broken toy or fix the kitchen cabinet door when it comes off its hinges for the umpteenth time. You have no idea of how it has been for me. This isn't love and you're kidding yourself if you think it is. Love doesn't leave a family to do its own thing. We were just a fumble in the back of a car that went wrong and now look at us. It's all a lie. A sham of a marriage, just going through the motions and for what? The sake of our child? Surely there's a better option for us than this.'

I wanted to challenge him, annoy him, push him away but he managed to head me off each time. He was always so reasonable in the face of my unreasonableness, sometimes I wondered if he enjoyed it. That game of cat and mouse that went on between us. By eleven o'clock we were both exhausted. So, we went to bed, me on my side, curled up tight and resentful thinking about how I'd washed and pressed those cotton sheets, sprinkled them with rose cologne, the smell of romance, but the wrong man was in my bed.

The flat was quiet, barring the gusts of wind whistling round the building and rattling the old window-panes as it went. Occasionally the coils on the electric bar clicked. The kitchen tap dripped relentlessly drip drip and Richard's snores drifted in and out. Everything seemed amplified. His snoring irritated me, reminded me that he was there and would still be there in the morning.

The night hours stretched long. Every time I looked at the clock the minute hand had barely moved. I was tired, I was always tired, but tonight I couldn't sleep for wondering why Tom hadn't turned up. Had something happened to him? Did he know about Richard's return? Surely that wouldn't stop him. Had he changed his mind and had second thoughts about all the plans we had made? Was there someone else?

I hoped he would call by the following day with some feasible excuse and all would be forgiven and maybe, maybe we would tell Richard of our plans. But Richard suddenly appearing unannounced... I hadn't fully thought through the implications of what that would mean for the custody of Frankie. Could I leave Frankie behind? It would certainly make things easier, give Tom and I a better chance of starting afresh. It's hard asking the man you love to bring up another man's child. What would I tell my parents? How would they react? It had been hard enough for them that I had had to get married, but the disgrace of their daughter having an affair and running off with another man - surely it would kill Mum? And what was I going to do about Richard? He turned over in his sleep and threw his arm around me, I flung it off and pushed him away. It should have been Tom doing this not *him*. I punched my pillow and turned over. Richard barely noticed.

In the morning I woke to sounds of movement in the kitchen. I could smell bacon cooking, hear eggs sizzling in the pan. Radio One playing in the background. I could hear Richard's voice he was talking to Frankie. They were having a conversation with Sal Floppit her favourite doll.

'Want some more Sal? Open wide, here it comes. Mmmmn she really likes it doesn't she. What's that? Oh, Sal Floppit you should say pardon me when you burp!' Frankie was all giggles, probably watching Richard pretending to feed her dolly and obliging by eating the same, putty in his hands. It made me seethe, he had been here less than twenty-four hours and there he was playing happy families as if everything was easy. And Frankie usually screamed around strangers, it wasn't as if she knew him that well. I lay there with gritted teeth, listening, but couldn't just lie in bed and enjoy a much-needed sleep.

I got up, washed and dressed anticipating having breakfast in the kitchen, but that pleasure was denied me. It looked like a bomb had hit it. All the pans used, mess all over the surfaces and the floor and Frankie had food in her hair.

Fuming I bellowed: 'Look at this mess. Did you have to use every bloody pan available. And who is going to clean it all up? Certainly not me.' I opened the fridge to find all the milk gone. There was nothing left for me, not even for a cup of tea. 'You're nothing but a selfish bastard.' I swept it all off the counter, plates, cutlery, pans went crashing to the floor. Frankie started screaming which made me raise my voice even higher and louder. Richard just stood there in his dressing gown with a stupid smirk on his face, looking at me not saying a word. It made me even madder.

'Damned it, you've already created chaos and you haven't even been back twenty-four hours.' He lifted Frankie out of her high chair keeping his eyes on her as her stroked her cheek.

'Calm down, it's upsetting Frankie and you're getting yourself all worked up over nothing. Frankie was hungry. She had all the milk, that's what children need, milk. Did you think I would just go out and get some more and leave Frankie to her own devices? I'll go and get some for you now shall I? Do you need anything else while I'm there?' He tickled Frankie under the chin and put her back in her highchair. 'And leave the mess, I'm happy to clear it up.'

I was so angry it could have curdled the bile in my stomach - angry that I was angry, angry that he was there and not Tom, angry and tired and so the thoughts spiralled on and on until my head hurt.

Diane: June-November 1964

Richard's unannounced arrival changed everything. I knew it, and Tom knew it, as sure as the sun rises each day. Richard swanned back in as if he had never been away thinking he could pick up where he left off including all the marital duties. How could I refuse?

I remember hearing it in Tom's voice over the phone. It sounded broken, strained, 'Bill tells me your husband is home.'

I wanted so much to explain but the office junior was in the room, ears like an elephant and a penchant for tittle-tattle. I acted casual, like this was an ordinary work call. I opened my mouth trying to find the words, struggling to order my thoughts but he beat me to it.

'I'll leave you to get reacquainted,' and then the phone line went dead.

He never called again.

Two months after that I found out I was pregnant with Danny. I knew it was Tom's but by the time I'd had it confirmed, he'd left town. Sophie told me the news. She called into the office to drop something off for her 'dear brother.' It put me on the spot, I couldn't ignore her, especially given that her new boyfriend was friendly with Bill. She gave me a blow-by-blow account, told me they'd all gone out for a big send off the night before he left for America, some big job in Connecticut. I cried so hard that night my eyes were still swollen in the morning. I looked so bad that Bill let me go home early. I told him I was having a bad allergic reaction. After putting Frankie to bed, I went to bed myself and lay there. I didn't want to move, I didn't want to do anything except dream, relive all those moments I had spent with Tom. All the things he said, all the things we had promised each other. I went about things like an automaton. For weeks I hardly slept, hardly ate. In truth I wanted to die, everything else seemed pointless. I couldn't accept it was over, that he would drop me without saying a word. I believed he loved me too much to do that to me. I waited for Tom to call, write, something. But nothing came. No word at all. All I had left of him was the child I carried inside me.

It was the only thing that anchored me, kept me going. But only just. Nothing else came close. There followed a long period where I forgot how to smile. Frankie was forever saying 'Why don't you smile Mummy, why are you sad?' I was more than sad, I was heart-broken, trapped. I wanted the life that I was meant to have. The one where I loved everything and everyone in it. But this life was joyless. Everything a drudge. It took an enormous amount of effort to just get out of bed and face the day. Little things like dealing with the post got out of proportion, the letters in the hall piled up unopened.

My secret weighed heavily. I wanted to tell the world I was carrying Tom's child but, how could I? He was gone. Richard came home just before the birth. Everyone was congratulating him, slapping him on the back, making crude innuendos. He beamed with pride. It would wipe the smile off his face if he knew. Old ladies stopped me in the street and told me it was a boy. 'You can tell by the way it's lying.' some even presumed to put their hand on my bump as if it would bring them good luck. That's all Tom ever wanted, a son. He even had a name: Daniel Jeremy.

When Danny was born, the first thing I noticed was Tom's chin. He had such a strong jawline and now his son had it too. Nobody else could see it, why would they? It was my little secret. I don't think Richard suspected a thing. Of course, he was delighted when Danny arrived, he went out and celebrated having a son. An heir to carry on his family name. What a joke!

I thought of Tom every hour of the day, relived the precious moments we had had together. Our time together didn't feel cheap or sordid, just natural and as it should have been. I couldn't understand why he backed off so quickly, especially after all the things he said. 'Come away with me Diane and we will live the life we were born to live together.' I lived with that line running over and over in my head until the day, five years later when Bill told me Tom had got married.

My world stopped. I was rabid with jealousy. I couldn't concentrate and made a bunch of typing errors. It was at that point the shaking started. It felt as if it came from deep within as though my heart was out of rhythm. Bill was standing there in the doorway to his office, sunlight glaring through the windows illuminating him in a vaguely saintly fashion. He had a huge grin on his face, 'marvellous news about Tom isn't it?'

'Marvellous?' I wanted to scream. 'What about me? What about our son? Can you not see the likeness?'

I went to the bathroom and threw up. I cried like I'd never cried before, sitting there in the tiny cubical, it was like a copy of my life, bare bland walls, closing in. My mood sank so low and I couldn't pull myself out of it. I couldn't sleep and then was so tired I couldn't function. Everything became such an effort and all the while I had this repetitive thought, Tom. Tom. Tom.

I couldn't decide whether I was angry or hurt and I still couldn't fathom why he had left. Was he jealous that Richard had come back? He knew we didn't get on. Had someone said something to the contrary? These thoughts circled round and round like vultures picking at the bones of my insecurities.

Diane: October 1967

I couldn't exactly say what it was that made me decide to go to the Doctor. I was aware that something in me had changed. It was getting to the stage where everything had become such an effort and yet I just couldn't talk about it to anyone. Not to my parents - they would tell me I was being ungrateful. Not to Val, my best friend. She wouldn't have understood. Our friendship had radically changed since she got married, happily married. I don't think she had ever experienced sadness, longing or disappointment. I didn't know where to begin to start to try and explain all of that to her - and then I felt ashamed for not being able to manage when it seemed that everyone else around me appeared to be coping admirably.

My hair looked a mess, my clothes barely pressed and shoddy. I longed to wear the clothes that all the other people my age wore but that was out of the question. I had bills to pay, even more now with the new house. I couldn't even afford to have my shoes resoled, not until the end of the month but then Frankie needed a new coat and Danny was growing so fast. Richard sent money but it was never enough. I was at the height of my youth so why didn't I feel this?

Just deciding what to wear in the mornings brought me to tears. Frankie would cry and I'd get cross. Poor child, she tried her best to be a good girl, to help. But as her Mum I was constantly letting her down. She didn't get the toys, the outings, the play time and love she deserved. Danny swallowed up a lot of my time. All she got was a grumpy, tired not-good-enough

Mum. Guilt held me back, and widened the gulf between us. Exhaustion and sadness settled in my bones, the ache spread throughout my body and grew into a pain, in my stomach, my head, my hands. It manifested in trembling but grew out of exhaustion and fear.

My parents, they cared, but left me to get on with it, after all this was the life I'd chosen wasn't it? On occasions Mum came round to clean the house - but left me with a list of 'shoulds' and 'musts' that I knew I would never be able to follow through. I just didn't have the energy, the inclination or the know-how. This made me feel even more inadequate, like I'd never quite managed to prove I was capable of being a fully functioning adult.

The doctor's surgery was on the floor below my office, so it was easy to get a quick appointment. My doctor, Dr Atkins, was an elderly gentleman. He had been our family doctor ever since I was little.

He was very attentive, listened without interruption, took the odd note. I didn't tell him everything, just that I was having trouble sleeping and that my heart kept racing, so he prescribed sleeping tablets. They certainly knocked me out to start with. I slept well for the first couple of days and began to feel a little better in myself. Then Danny got the croup. His coughing wracked his little body and caused the air to bubble at the back of his throat. At one point his lips turned blue. I panicked, gathered up the children, put them in the car and drove to the hospital. We spent a long night waiting to be seen and get his breathing sorted. After that I knew I needed to have some semblance of alertness for the sake of the children and so I took only half a tablet.

But I still struggled, instead of feeling better I felt anxious and jangled *all* the time. I worried about what people thought of me as a mother, as a secretary, as a daughter, as a friend - not that I had many. The children and the exhaustion put paid to that. I had bags under my eyes, my skin rough and papery; sideways on I looked like a whip, I'd lost so much weight. The trembling rumbled on, starting from my heart and spread outwards. I had nothing in my life but an endless round of getting up, working, coming home sorting out the kids, cleaning, cooking and doing it all over again.

The girls in the office, all my age or a little younger, seemed to be having the time of their lives. They were off to dances, being courted, flowers arriving at the office, flirty gossip at tea break. Not a care in the world unless were talking about the colour of their nails or new hairdos. What did I have? Nothing.

Simple tasks began to overwhelm me. I started to cry at everything, even cried because I was crying. Mum kept telling me to pull myself together, that I had responsibilities that this was my life now and to just get on with it. But I couldn't, I just couldn't.

Doctor Atkins suggested Valium. That took the edge off things a little. It made everything so easy at first - there was no mention of it or the Mogadon being addictive. It didn't occur to me how dependent I would become on the pills. I never dreamed that it could apply to the likes of mothers. To the likes of me.

It wasn't until I almost got arrested in one of Cheltenham's elite stores, Cavendish House, that I began to question things. It was a simple mistake that just spiralled out of control. I was shopping with the children. Frankie kept going on and on about visiting the toy department. I'd told her 'no' several times, but she kept at me until finally I just snapped. I slapped the back of her legs. She started wailing like a banshee and in response I shouted and found I couldn't stop shouting. The next thing I knew, I was shouting and crying, Frankie was crying, Danny was crying. Store assistants and customers were looking and whispering under their breaths. A small crowd began to gather before several store assistants appeared and pulled us apart. I was taken to the manager's room and the kids? I didn't know, at that point I didn't want to know. Fortunately, they called Bill, the manager was one of his clients and knew us all well enough. Bill came and got us. He opened up the office and took us back there. He poured me a brandy to stop the shaking. Then he kept the kids occupied by giving them pieces of office paper to draw on in the board room while he talked quietly to me in the office. He was so kind, it made me cry harder.

Ashamed and embarrassed, I could hardly speak for tears, I stammered my way through excuses, and he listened patiently without interrupting. Finally, he said, 'Diane, you're exhausted, that's the problem. I'm going to give you the week off.' I tried to remonstrate but there was nothing left of me to do it with. Inwardly I was panicking, I couldn't afford the time off. I had bills and debts that needed paying. That would just make the situation worse. He obviously understood my reasons for being distressed. 'Listen, I'm giving you the week off with full pay. I just want to see you well. Besides, the office needs you well too. You're my right hand, where would I be without you?' He was being kind I know, but to me it was just another burden to carry. Then he loaded us all into his car and drove us home.

That night I went to bed early. I must have slept a good ten hours. When I awoke, I felt a little refreshed but still drowsy. It was then it began to dawn on me that I was stuck in a cycle, unable to wake up properly after the sleeping tablets, I had upped the dose by then, and not able to get through the day without a Valium or two. But being aware and being bothered or having the energy to try and do anything about it was another thing entirely.

The week off work helped to restore my sanity. I had time to sleep, to breathe, take a walk, clean the house, have an uninterrupted bath. But then I had to fend off my mother's prying questions and disdain.

'Why aren't you at work Diane? You shouldn't be lying in your bed until this time in the morning. What on earth are you doing taking a bath at this time in the day? Why did you want to take a walk when you have a pile of housework to attend to? Tired? Well, whose fault is that? You should have thought about that before you went and got yourself in the family way with him.' She still hadn't forgiven me my fall from grace. I felt powerless to put that right.

I worried about her disapproval. I'd call her each night after the kids were in bed. 'What do you think Mum, should I do it this way? How would I go about doing that?' In a lot of ways, I suppose I hadn't fully left home. I relied on her. She told me what to do when I couldn't decide and let's face it, I couldn't decide a lot of the time. Sometimes I wondered what the point of that expensive private education was when I could barely tie my own shoelaces.

I worried more that she would find out who Danny's true father was - that one day she'd look at him, see that he didn't take after Richard and realise my infidelity - that her daughter really was nothing but a whore.

I was drowning in guilt and shame, so much so it numbed me, everything I did seemed mechanical, without feeling and pointless.

My body began to balloon, that grey skirt, the one I wore to work, began to pinch at the waist. I couldn't get the zip all the way up, it gaped at the top. It wasn't because I was eating too much, just the odd biscuit now and then at the office, no more than usual. Granted I had developed a liking for a packet of crisps or two in the evening, but why not, I had nothing else to do! My confidence, what little was left of it, disappeared and everything just crowded in. I was slowly collapsing in on myself - like a plastic doll thrown on a fire, its hair and limbs melting into the flames.

Frankie: October 1967

I was sitting on the back of the sofa playing lookout through the Venetian blinds. I wasn't allowed to sit on the sofa like that really. I was watching the rain streak down the windowpane, trying to guess which ones would win.

Outside, the road was quiet, sometimes a car passed making great splashes of water. Whoosh! Mr Kent from up the road went past. He was taking his old dog out for a walk. They were wet through, they looked away from the rain, so they didn't see me wave. I was watching Mr Kent stop his dog falling off the kerb with his big curly walking stick. The old dog limped like Mrs King next door and kept stopping, even in the rain. I thought the dog was blind because it had white eyes. I wondered what it would be like to be blind. All darkness, like the cupboard under the stairs where the hoover is kept.

Danny was lying on his tummy playing with his Meccano. He'd made a gun cos he wanted to be a cowboy. Every now and then he shouted, 'reach for the sky' and drew his gun from his pyjama bottoms and aimed it at me. I had to play dead or he got cross. He loved cowboy films and every time he got dressed or undressed for bed, he sang the tune to The Ponderosa really loud. He coughed a lot. I had to tell him to put his hand to his mouth coz he was always forgetting, and I was the oldest. The cough made his breathing funny sometimes.

Oh no! Quick! I leapt off the sofa. Tipped the blinds shut and picked Danny up. He didn't like it. I had to drag him to sit beside me under the windowsill. 'Quiet, Danny' I whispered, 'keep still. The milkman's here.'

The two of us huddled against the wall and held our breaths as a sharp knock came. We listened to the milkman standing on the doorstep rummaging about in his leather pouch, jangling the change. He rapped the door again and waited. Then he moved from the step and stood at the front room window, his hand shielded over his eyes trying to see inside. We could see his long shadow and were frightened. We heard his big shouty voice from the other side of the window.

'I know you're in there. If you don't pay me next week, I'm stopping the milk.'

Danny started to whimper, so I put my hand over his mouth. 'Sshhhhhh.'

The milkman and his shadow left after posting a note through the letterbox. We sat, still flattened against the wall for a bit as we listened to the sound of the milk float disappearing up the road. Its motor sounded a bit like the lift in the ladybird shop, making a noise that got higher as it moved further away; all the bottles rattled too, ringing away along the road. Then Danny started coughing a lot, more than usual, and his breath was whispering in.

He wriggled out of my grip, cross at being held so tightly and thumped me hard on the arm.

'I'm telling Mum on you.'

'Go on then, see if I care.'

'You're going to get in trouble,' Danny teased, his voice all breathy. I pulled a face and shrugged my shoulders. Danny went up to the bedroom where Mum was lying down. I followed him from a distance. I watched as he crawled onto the bed and leaned over her, his breath all squeaky as it came and went. Mum struggled to open her eyes, she lifted a weak hand and touched his shoulder. He snuggled in beside her.

I stood near to Danny, his eyes were open. I put my finger to my lips and whispered 'shhhh, don't wake Mum, she's not very well.' He nodded and stuck his thumb in his mouth. Something wasn't right. Mum didn't smell like Mum. The usual lemony perfume I smelled on her clothes was gone. I could follow that smell with my eyes shut and be sure to find her. But she smelled nasty, like smelly arms and poo. Her red hair was sticking to her head and she had dark circles round her eyes. Mum said you get circles and bags under your eyes if you don't get enough sleep. Mum had been asleep all day and hadn't spoken since yesterday, or was it the day before? I couldn't quite remember.

I went back downstairs. I wanted to help her, so I did something nice for her. I dragged a chair to the sink and got a cup from the big pile of dirty cups and plates lying in there. I washed and dried it. Then I fetched the kettle and filled it with water. I dragged the chair to the stove and put the kettle on. It whistles when its ready. Then I put some tea leaves in the teapot, one for Mum and one for the pot. Just as the kettle began to sing someone started banging on the door. I kept very still. The letterbox lid lifted, and a pair of lips ordered. 'Open the door!' I knew that voice. It was Grandma.

Grandma came and brought in the fresh air. She had a lot of bags and her Mary Poppins handbag too. It was always full of exciting things, a key with a bell, a mirror, a penknife that I was not allowed to play with, yet. Plasters with holes in them for her onions, funny things for her 'stays' and best of all, Barley sugar sweeties.

By then the kettle was really singing on the stove.

Danny came running down the stairs shouting 'Grandma, Grandma!' while I clung to Grandma's hips with all my might. Grandma set her bags down, took off her coat and bent down to scoop us children into a hug.

'My goodness look at you. You look like you haven't washed for days,' she paused to look around and caught sight of the kitchen. Jam jars with their lids off sat on the side, along with butter-smeared knives, an open packet of cereal, spilt milk and a trail of breadcrumbs. 'Or eaten for that matter. Frankie, where's your mother?'

'She's upstairs Grandma. She's not very well. But it's alright, I've been looking after her. I was just about to make her some tea.'

Grandma eyed me crossly. 'That's all very well and good Frankie, but how many times have you been told not to go near the stove? It's dangerous. Now, what's wrong with your mother?'

'She's got the grizzles.'

'Oh, has she now? Will you stay here and look after Danny while I pop upstairs for a bit?'

I nodded. Grandma disappeared upstairs. I could hear her voice from where we were below.

'Right young lady. What is all this nonsense? Lying here feeling sorry for yourself when your children have been fending for themselves downstairs. Have you seen the state of the kitchen and Frankie? Thank goodness I came when I did. She was just about to attempt to take the boiling hot kettle off the stove. What has come over you Diane? Get up, go and wash yourself for goodness sake and when you're done, come down and eat.'

I stood looking out of the kitchen window at the bottom of the garden.

'Can we play football now?' asked Danny following my gaze.

'No, coz look, the ball is still stuck up the tree.' I pointed at the ball high in the cherry tree branches, lodged there from an over zealous kick by Danny.

'Still?' he sighed and threw himself to the floor verging on a tantrum.

'I'll try and climb it again later, but remember the tree scraped my leg and I got sticky stuff on my dress.' I showed him the welt on my leg as if to prove a point.

'I hate that tree,' he said putting on a petted lip.

Grandma came downstairs and busied herself in the kitchen. Soon soup was bubbling on the stove, the dishes washed and put away and the kitchen looked spick and span. Spit spot! Grandma was always clean and tidy, she said it was important. She washed her step every Monday morning just to please the neighbours because otherwise 'they would talk.'

Diane: October 1967

I was so weak when I sat at the table. Mum had made soup, but I could only manage a few mouthfuls as the children scraped the bottom of their bowls. I didn't have the heart or the urge to eat. Seeing Mum tackle the mess, make soup, sort the children effortlessly, added to my sense of helplessness. Mum had always been that way, capable, efficient and understated. Whereas I was the direct opposite. I couldn't keep up with myself let alone the children. Merely doing a household wash for the week took up the whole of Saturday. I hated that twin-tub with a passion, it robbed me of my time and energy. Added to which, I had to shop, cook, clean the house, keep on top of the children and hold down a full-time job during the week.

Mum didn't have time for any of 'that nonsense,' couldn't understand what it would feel like to be broken and so profoundly sad.

'You're too self-absorbed, that's your problem, just pull yourself together,' is what she'd say.

I tried to explain how I was feeling but Mum refused to understand. She cited the trials and tribulations that she and her family had undergone during the war years.

'They didn't break us and Lord knows we had it a damned sight tougher than you my girl.'

Her restless fingers always fussing, smoothing, folding, tied me into emotional knots, left me feeling inadequate, ashamed and bound me with their constant activity.

'But Mum, you had a community around you, people to go to who would help lighten the load, provide support.' I bit my lip and held back … I wanted to tell her about the emotional support I craved and needed but words failed me. Fear filled my mouth, stopped me from speaking or being able to form the words. It was like trying to speak a foreign language you've never heard before. I knew, deep down that I wasn't good enough - would never be good enough. I knew that all my misdeeds and shortcomings would be gathered up and turned on me.

A loud crash came from the front room. The children were fighting, Danny was squealing, his voice raised in anguish. 'Mummeeeeeeeee.'

I couldn't move. All I wanted to do was put my hands over my ears to blot it out. Mum intervened, her voice firm but soothing. Danny's sobs died away and I was relieved. When she came back to the kitchen, she gave me a hard stare.

'You have to step up Diane, this idleness won't do. Your children will end up running wild if you don't watch out, and I can't always do it for you.'

In my recent dreams I found myself running from a baying mob hell bent on taking me down. I run with all my might but my legs don't work, they move of their own accord, disconnected, as if treading deep viscous water and all the while the mob are gaining. Laughing at me with cruel upturned mouths and broken teeth.

Mum reinforced my sense of ineptitude by continually reminding me of the shameful deed, of how I had undone myself. Everything seemed to refer back to that big ugly stain on the family landscape, like spilt tea on a starched white tablecloth slowly spreading, getting larger by the minute. Sometimes I wanted to take a whole teapot and empty the lot, just put that big stain all over the prissy white tablecloth and be damned - but I always held back.

Mum had some backbone, stronger than mine at any rate. I was at a loss to know how to navigate getting through to her.

'Nonsense Diane, you're just being lazy. It won't take you more than two hours to get the washing done.'

'But Mum, I can't keep the children occupied at the same time. Danny can climb out of his playpen now and I'm worried he'll fall into the fire.'

'Well then, don't build a fire until after the washing.'

'It's too cold for that Mum.'

'Then take them out to the park and give them a run around before you do the washing. That should warm them up.'

'I don't think I'll have the energy to do that.'

'Find the energy Diane, I did it in my day. You're young and fit enough. Stop making excuses and get on with it. I shan't be coming round to do for you. You'll have to learn, Diane, and that's all there is to it. You need to be firmer with your children, they have to know who is in charge.'

I found her emotional landscape could change with the wind from kind and sunny to cold and distant. Mum was well versed at pulling down the shutters to put on a front. She could sulk for days with Daddy at the merest slight.

'Pull yourself together Diane and get on with it,'

Like a boot pushing me further down into a deep black hole.

Unaware of, or perhaps inured to my delicate state Mum continued, 'Do you realise what we have done for you? What we have gone through to give you a good upbringing? All the shame you brought upon us. Some of our friends don't even speak to us now because of your careless actions. And now you behave like this, like a mad woman, are you deliberately trying to humiliate us Diane? If you can't think of us, at least think of your children.'

There were times when I wondered whether I had taken things too far. Had cutting myself off from Richard's family been an altogether wise decision? In those moments where I questioned my actions, felt vulnerable, I glimpsed a portal that could potentially lead to other possibilities. But what could I do now? How could I find my way back? I'd said and done some things that couldn't be undone.

I thought of the letters I'd exchanged between myself and my father-in-law just after I moved out of the flat he had provided. His reference to my immaturity had hurt, like a sharp slap in the face, but then I'd retaliated and gave as good as I got, if not better. Perhaps it was a little childish. No, that door of opportunity slammed shut a while ago. Pride had much to answer for where I was now.

Then there was my big secret. Danny. I felt guilty, conflicted. And I felt hurt, deeply hurt that I'd been so rudely abandoned. Thoughts of Tom still swam round in my head. I would never get over why he had simply disappeared off the face of the earth, no goodbye, no explanation. Nothing.

I questioned myself constantly, turning the consequences round and round in my head, trying to figure out better solutions and compromises until I could no longer remember the difference between fact, consequence or compromise. It had worn me down.

Richard: April 1968

The kitchen windows were steamed from the pots of bubbling potatoes, peas and gravy. The radio chattered softly in the corner sending out its Sunday glow to its listeners. I'd almost finished mashing the potatoes and was busy plating up: the Yorkshire puds were proving difficult - they'd stuck fast to the tin. In the dining room the rest of the family were sitting at the table. Anyone looking in from the outside would have seen a normal family ritual. Outside the rain came down in torrents, streaking the windows and leaving a great belching pool at the blocked culvert by the front door. Diane started screeching:

'For God's sake, I thought I told you to fix it!' She jerked a finger in the direction of the growing puddle.

I let out a pained gasp. My mouth moved as if I was ready to say something, but then I thought what's the point? I felt my body deflate. I was tired of feeling stoppered. It was always an uphill battle. I didn't have the vocabulary where it counted. She was always one step ahead, goading, criticising. It was like being around a crazed terrier that constantly nipped at you. I mashed the potatoes with renewed vigour, my mind split between thought and task, and took the food through.

All the things I had hoped to achieve. The simple things, and Diane was at the heart of all that. But if I really thought about it, I couldn't see a way forward. My fears surfaced like unwanted bits of flotsam and jetsam. Failure loomed large. I feared losing her, wearing the mantle of defeat, being a divorced and single part-time parent. Why stay? It certainly wasn't because I was stubborn or a martyr to the cause. She drove me to the edge of reason at times. The tantrums and accusations, telling me to leave and then accusing me of not staying around. Embarrassing me in front of my friends with comments, 'He's never here. He doesn't care about his family.' or being rude to my parents after all they did for us when we were first married. There was no tenderness, no care, just tears and complaints.

I stayed for the hint, the promise of love. Yes, in spite of the vitriol she doled out in copious heaps, I believed there was something there between us. Hell, I couldn't figure it out. Half the time I didn't understand myself, let alone understand her. She was wild and unpredictable, dangerous sometimes, but she was mine, in spite of it all 'for better or worse'.

'You can never do anything right can you?' She pushed her plate away, her voice on the edge of shrill. 'I can't eat this mess. You're giving me a headache, you, all of you, and this mess.' Her chair grated as she rose from the table and pushed past me in the kitchen. From the table the children heard her filling a glass of water at the tap. Through the doorway I saw Frankie watching her mother throw a couple of pills into her mouth and swill them down.

'I'm going to lie down. And turn that crap off,' Diane motioned towards the radio warbling in the corner.

No one at the table moved, all eyes were down avoiding her gaze. We never knew what was to come next, especially when she was in a mood. Then she lunged across the kitchen picked up the radio and hurled it across the room. It shattered against the wall scattering bits of radio parts across the floor. The Clithero Kid was silenced mid-sentence.

'Get that bloody drain sorted and all this cleared away by the time I come back down. Bloody useless good-for-nothings all of you. I'm fed up of cleaning up after all your messes.'

She slammed the door and we listened to her stamp up the stairs and bang the bedroom door shut.

The children ate their food moving their cutlery with care across the plates, pretending nothing had happened. Not a word was spoken. I ate joylessly, sinews stretched across my lean jowls, temples working mechanically as though with each mouthful I was swallowing the words I should have spoken. Angry words, that made my eyes blaze and my grip chalk white. I held onto my cutlery like I was holding on to myself.

The children left the table without speaking, they knew the drill. They lifted the plates and carried them into the kitchen. Rhythmically they washed, dried, stacked and cleaned. There was a resignation about the way they worked, withdrawn into their own little worlds, closed, buttoned up tight. When they were done, they dispersed, Danny to his bricks, and Frankie put on her boots and anorak and stepped out into the rain. She didn't say where she was going, I called after her, but she didn't answer.

At five o'clock I checked my watch, slugged back the last of my tea and stood up. I looked out of the kitchen window, past the full ashtrays, nail varnish bottles and chipped cups scattered on the sill and watched four magpies hopping about the cherry tree. 'One for sorrow, two for joy, three for a girl, four for a....' Sighing, I placed my half empty cup down on the bunker and reached for my car keys.

The central heating attempted to fire itself into life, sending the pipes belching and banging. I knew it wouldn't be long until it broke down again but didn't want to consider trying to fix it; I didn't have the time and to be honest, I wasn't entirely sure what I was dealing with. Car's okay, but central heating was a whole new ball game. I knew she would give me bloody hell over it, no change there, but I had so much to do and as usual, so little time.

My mother sensed I wasn't happy when I last saw her.

'You always looked happy, as though you had a purpose when you were with the RAF, but now ...'

'It's taken me a while to adjust to civvy life Mum, that's all.'

'I thought as much. And Diane, how is she adapting to the new change? Does she like the new house?'

'Yes, she's getting there.' Getting there indeed! I'd hoped coming home for good would change things, that Diane would be pleased. I'd hoped that we could try to make a go of things. Had I not already provided us with a house and garden and our own front door. I even planted a cherry tree all those years back to signify a renewal, a new beginning. The fresh start I promised just before Danny was born. Instead, she made it impossible, let me know in no uncertain terms, that I was not wanted, and she had no intention of letting her children near my family. She wouldn't wash, wouldn't cook, wouldn't do anything for me and yet still expected me to fix the car, do the gardening, tidy up the house, pay the mortgage.

The work in Somerset was a godsend, an answer to my prayers. Going to work with an old school chum Geoff, saved me in many ways. It was hard graft but honest money and made use of my mechanical expertise. Travelling back and forth was a pain and I hated being away during the week, but it was the best solution at the time.

Diane was upstairs resting with her headache - she always had a headache or so it seemed. I fetched my things. A small, battered suitcase and a threadbare washbag which, when packed, left little evidence of me in the house.

I needed to leave before it got dark, the roads were dangerous at night. The drive would take me two hours at least. I also figured that if I headed off then I might have been in time to catch a quick pint at the pub.

I picked up Danny and placed him in his playpen with his bricks then looked around for Frankie, but she was nowhere to be seen. Diane wouldn't have appreciated me disturbing her to say I was off, so I slipped quietly out of the back door.

Some days I felt guilty for leaving. There were times when I looked at my children and I wasn't sure if they were happy. But kids can't happy all the time can they? Danny seemed to have an easier time of it - he was the apple of his mother's eye. But Frankie, looked wary, on edge, constantly nibbling at her fingernails as though she was consuming her fears. I was always asking her if anything was wrong, but she remained tight lipped and just shrugged. It was worrying but what could I do if she wouldn't say anything? It made me wince when I thought of how often Diane's moods drove tears into Frankie's play.

Not that she was the perfect child, far from it. She could be a handful at times, wilful and defiant. She had that look about her where her chin jutted out, and she'd tilt her head to one side and look you full in the eye. It was a look that penetrated your soul, drilled right into you. It was that look that would send Diane apoplectic with rage. It didn't matter how hard or often Diane hit her, Frankie would not back down. I admired that in Frankie, she had more bottle about her than I had. I wondered who it came from? Had she inherited it from her mother? Frankie had it in spades - enough to be her undoing. But Diane hadn't broken her ... not yet.

I got into my car, lit a cigarette and saw Diane's outline descending the stairs. 'Just in time,' I muttered under my breath as I put the gears into reverse and backed out of the driveway.

The tension ebbed the further I drove away from the house, my grip on the steering wheel relaxed, my jaw slackened. It had been like this for the last three years - travelling back and forth up and down the motorway, home late on Friday nights and leaving on Sunday afternoon. My life during the week was centred on work. I had room and board in a small guest house, its facilities were meagre but preferable to living in a war zone.

I'd tried my best, taken counsel from my parents and sisters, ignored my friends' advice to leave but still I found it hard to decide what to do about my marriage.

I knew this wasn't a normal marriage, not the conventional kind I'd envisioned. I wanted something like my parents' marriage, a doting wife, happy children, a lovely home. My parents had been happily married for over thirty years and even during misunderstandings there was still a deep love between them. They still danced cheek-to-cheek to their favourite songs; I'd often found them sitting at the kitchen table, heads bent close together, giggling. That was the kind of marriage I wanted. One brimming with love.

My parents' love for me never wavered, even when they found out Diane was pregnant and all the scandal it created. I recalled the time when I crashed my Dad's car, his beloved Austin Healey. I was convinced he would kill me when he found out. I remembered it like it was only yesterday. The shaky cold sweat. Coming home through the front door and taking the stairs two at a time up to the sitting room. Everything stood out. It was uncanny, all the little details like the loose stair treads I'd never noticed before, the loud tick-tock of the grandfather clock, sunlight pooling through the tall sitting room windows and the dancing dust motes. Dad was sitting in his favourite wing-backed chair beside the fireplace, he looked like he was part of a film set - Hitchcock in repose. He was studying his chess board, didn't even look up when I came in.

'Yes?' he said in his distracted voice.

'Dad I ...' I searched for the words, but nothing came. I shoved my hands deep into my pockets so that I could feel the seams strain against my fingers.

'Dad I ...'

'Come on son. Spit it out.' He was always a bit impatient.

'Dad. I crashed the car.'

He raised an eyebrow, took in a deep breath, picked up the rook and made his move. He didn't even look up. 'You hurt?'

'No, but the car's a write off.'

'It's only the car. We can replace that.' He moved his knight to replace a pawn, his calmness was unnerving.

Dad had a particular view on how a man should be and react. Once, when I was young, I'd argued with one of my sisters. I can't remember now what started it, but I know that it was pretty fierce, and blows were exchanged. Being the youngest I came off the worst and ran crying to Mum for solace. She hugged me and produced a starched handkerchief to mop up my tears. I remember, it happened to be lunchtime and Dad had come for his lunch. I heard his footsteps coming up the stairs from the surgery on the ground floor. He stomped into the kitchen annoyed that I was making such a racket and 'crying like a girl.' He slapped my legs despite Mum's remonstrations and spoke sharply. 'Pull yourself together Richard. I'll have no son of mine behaving in this manner. It's disgraceful, you should be ashamed of yourself.'

'Freddie, Stop! You're being too hard on him.'

'Lilly,' he gave her a sharp look then raised his voice and slammed his fist down on the kitchen table. 'I'll not be countermanded in my own house. He will learn his place.' Then he turned and stooping over me said, 'Never forget son, a real man keeps his emotions in check and He never, ever, cries. Now, dry your eyes and don't disappoint me again.'

I took my hankie from my short trouser pocket, dabbed my eyes and straightened my stance. From that day on I was mindful of following my Father's credo until it became second nature.

I made an effort to be a good husband. Tried my best to replicate what my parents did. I complimented Diane on the way she looked, made jokes, bad ones. I bought her gifts. She never appreciated the gesture - said I'd wasted my money and often threw them in the bin. I worked, kept the money coming, what little there was. I tried not to respond to her outbursts - fearing how it would affect her, she was delicate and highly-strung, but it seemed that whatever I tried somehow it made her worse. Words failed me they came out wrong.

'Language cannot do everything son' Dad would say, as if offering me a get-out from my failings.

When I was a child my Mother sent me to Miss Power the elocution teacher, she said it was to bring me out of myself. My sisters thrived under her care, but they didn't really need much bringing on really. They were already out-going, gregarious and full of excitable chatter. They'd taken my share of conversation genes according to Mum. When it came to my turn to stand up and recite my piece I pleaded, 'Miss Power, do I have to?'

She would sigh and indulgently say, 'What am I going to do with you Richard?'

Perhaps I should have persevered and heeded her instructions, maybe it would have helped me with Diane. She had me spellbound, I guess I loved her too much to argue with her.

I couldn't help thinking about how Diane had reacted the other day - how we are with each other, how she is. She's resourceful, I'll give her that. I was hardly through the door, home after a long drive. All I wanted was to sit down, have a cigarette and rest. I'd begun reading the newspaper in the front room when in she came screaming the odds about what? I don't recall now. Her face was all contorted as she ranted and wailed. I raised the paper a bit higher to blot her out, hoping that she'd just stop her noise and go away. On reflection it was a stupid move, but I was tired, just needed a breather. This small act really escalated things.

'Don't ignore me. Put that bloody paper down.'

I kept the paper at half-mast and said nothing.

'You bastard, you do this all the time'.

A yellow flame licked up the newspaper extending upwards and outwards. I leapt from my chair throwing the paper to the floor and stamped on it. Diane stood before me defiant, lighter in hand. Now she really had my attention.

'You drove me to this. You're never bloody here, you don't listen, you don't communicate - you just leave it all to me.' Her eye's blazed spilling with tears. I felt ashamed, I'd pushed her too far, this game of cat and mouse we played. We both knew we were doing it but neither of us would admit to it. This time I tried to put up the white flag. It was time to stop this nonsense before something got broken or hurt. But every time I tried to remonstrate, make a point, she shot me down, finishing her diatribe with her brittle fists and anything to hand she could lob at me. Throughout it all Frankie and Danny looked on from their place on the stairs. What could I do? I couldn't argue with her, there was no point. I was rendered mute, emasculated before my own children. Yet still I hadn't dealt with it, whatever 'it' was.

Simon called her 'the ogre' and made jokes about her antics - like the time when she threw my new tape-to-tape reel out the bedroom window. It exploded into smithereens as it landed on the front lawn. She followed it with a volley of insults. Simon had come by at the time to show me his new car. When the insults were hurled, he opened the passenger door, started up the engine and I jumped in. We sped off at high-speed laughing all the way to the pub. I don't think he'll ever let me live that one down.

'She's not been well,' I protested, but it was a weak defence against the relentless jibes. By this time several of Simon's friends had joined us and had been regaled with the whole story. Diane's antics bested everyone else's girlfriends and wives.

'Unwell? Is that your excuse Richard?'

'You need to give her a slap, that'd sort her out.'

I slugged down my pint, trying to think of something to counter that. Something that would make an acceptable valid response. 'Violence isn't the answer,' I countered.

'No, but euthanasia is.' The whole table erupted in laughter.

'She's a bloody mental case!'

Simon was pointing a finger to his head and twisting it, which caused more hilarity.

I shifted uncomfortably, it seemed they all had an opinion about mental cases and all of them negative. I tried to remonstrate, 'yes, but....' They shot me down, talking over me.

One of them piped up, 'She's never been right that one,' to which the rest of the group laughed uproariously.

'How did you get anywhere close to that?'

I got up and left.

The comment sent me momentarily reeling. I processed it on a different level, not the jibe alluding to the state of her mental ill-health, but her elusiveness. At heart I'd always known I was punching above my weight she was gorgeous to look at. People often commented saying she looked like Jackie Onassis, I was proud of that. It made me want to claim her like a prize possession, but you don't claim prize possessions when they are broken do you?

I'll admit, I struggled with my feelings for her against the opinions of my friends and family, particularly when Dad said, 'She's damaged son, best you give it up as a bad job'.

But I wasn't for walking away. I didn't know what to do, but I knew that walking away was not the answer. Maybe she was ill. I didn't know what being 'mental' really meant, hadn't really thought about it much. People didn't talk about those things. All her behaviours were just part and parcel of Diane being Diane. My Diane. It was a rare occasion she willingly allowed me close, but I took every second I could with gratitude. The last time - she fell pregnant again but then lost it. Makes me shudder even thinking about it.

She'd fished the baby out of the toilet and put it in a bucket to show me when I got home, like some gruesome medical exhibit. She had kept it beneath the kitchen sink for almost a week and with it stored up all her anger to unleash on me when I arrived. It was her tangible proof that it was *all my fault*. It lay there, all shrivelled and curled in on itself at the bottom of the bucket, like some alien with a big head and not quite formed body parts. It shook me having it thrust in my face. My child! She hadn't even mentioned she was pregnant. How could it be my fault? It was another of her swords of reason with which to cut me with. It was hard to fathom what was just *'a woman's way'* and what was normal.

Diane's behaviour started to become more erratic. She sulked, she screamed, pitching from one extreme emotion to the other. She nursed unrealistic grudges, blamed everyone and everything for things going wrong, she was constantly tired but didn't appear to sleep much, hardly ate; the house often looked like a pigsty with piles of clothes and toys scattered over the floor. Dishes in the kitchen sink piled up for days and the cooker was filthy with burnt food and detritus. I'd come home and spend the day sorting it out only to find it exactly the same the following week.

She accused me of not caring, of staying away and not being part of the family. Then in the next breath she'd be screaming about how much she hated me, my bloody family and wanted me out. Gone! There was no middle ground. I felt lost, the spaces in between what was and wasn't said were like dark voids, barricades piled too high to find a way through for either of us.

Initially I thought Diane was managing. I'd assumed everything was well in so far as everything that needed to be in place was. She juggled organising the children, her work, she even said herself that her boss couldn't do without her. It was just the domestic things that were wanting. Admittedly the house was a mess but then again Diane had been brought up to think she was a princess. She had no understanding of the nuances of domesticity.

I was working late one evening when the phone went. I picked up the call, 'Is that Richard, Richard Miller?' The voice sounded vaguely familiar.

'Yes, how can I help?

'It's Margaret here, from across the road at number 12. I hope you don't mind me phoning but I didn't know what else to do. It's Diane, I'm wondering if everything is alright?'

Alright? How do you mean?' My mind was racing. How the hell did they know where I was and how did she get this number? What the hell was going on?

'Well, its Diane. She was at the shop round the corner earlier. I don't really know what set it off but she broke down in floods of tears, dumped all her shopping on the counter and ran out the door with the little one leaving Frankie behind.'

'Where's Frankie now?'

'Oh, she's alright. I brought her home with me. I dropped in on Diane, said I'd give Frankie some tea and let her play with our George and pop her back across later.'

I didn't quite know what to say. I thanked the caller and made up some excuse. Later that night, I called home.

She was raving, so much so, I could still hear her shouting even when I held the phone at arms-length and she still hadn't told me why she was so upset. I remember hearing Frankie sobbing in the background. I had this image of her little body folded in on itself, all bone and sinew, and wondered if this time Diane had really crushed her. I felt helpless, I was too far away to drop everything and sort it out, douse the fire. Chances are that it would have been all sorted by the time I got there anyway. And if I called anyone for help, got them to pop by, that would just make things worse. Poor Frankie. I felt bad and wished things weren't the way they were but was at a loss to know what to do. It was like a living nightmare for all of us. As I put the phone down, I caught a snatch of Frankie whimpering, 'Sal Floppit' and Diane hissing 'if you'd have behaved, she wouldn't have been confiscated.'

Shame, I thought, she loves that doll.

Diane: May 1968

I was wakened early that morning by Danny crawling onto my bed. 'Mum,' he wheezed into my ear, 'Maaa ma me.'

'Lie still son,' I murmured half asleep.

'Mummeee,' Danny coughed. I felt his little chest heave as it searched for air. I opened my eyes, suddenly alert. Danny's breath was laboured, rasping. I turned to look at him. His face was pale. His skin clammy, his lips - his lips were tinged blue. Fear catapulted me out of bed. 'Danny? Danny, look at Mum. Can you hear me?' He was struggling, now slipping in and out of consciousness.

I touched his face and leaned in close. Listless, Danny's eyes fluttered open - all his effort was going into taking a laboured, wheezy breath.

'Danny! Danny?'

I stalled for a moment, not quite sure what to do: *Call an ambulance? No, the phone box was too far away to run to. I needed to be close to him. Could I trust Frankie to do it?* I looked at Danny, I didn't have time to wait. I'd have to take him to hospital myself. I called to Frankie in the other room, 'Frankie, wake up. Quickly, I need you to help me.'

Frankie appeared, still rubbing her eyes, half awake, tousled hair. 'What is it Mum?'

'Danny's not well. We need to get him to the hospital.'

'What's wrong?' Frankie whimpered her little brow furrowed with concern.

'What's wrong with him Mum?'

I struggled into my dressing gown and forced my feet into the nearest pair of shoes.

'Go and find my keys and get a blanket for Danny.'

But Frankie remained rooted to the spot staring at Danny, biting at a fingernail.

'NOW Frankie.' There was an edge to my voice, like a teacher drawing a day-dreaming child's attention back into the classroom.

I then scooped Danny into my arms and carried him down the stairs. Frankie shivered in her coat and pyjamas as she waited at the bottom with the keys.

'Open the door for me Frankie. Quickly!'

Frankie: May 1968

I couldn't reach the door. I tried but even on tiptoes the latch was way too high.

Danny's body was limp in Mummy's arms. Her voice was rising in pitch, increasing in volume and my head was spinning. She hoisted Danny up on a shoulder and snatched the keys from my hands. I watched through the open door as she banged frantically at the neighbour's door across the road.

Mr West appeared looking grumpy, but he quickly grabbed a coat and started his car. Mummy settled Danny into the backseat of the car. Somehow, I ended up there too, with Danny's head on my lap. Mum cried and cried. Mr West drove us fast through the early morning streets to the hospital. We passed the petrol station. Went through a set of red lights and headed on up to Montpellier and the Gordon Lamps, over the roundabout and on to the hospital. I tried to think about the tall trees lining the side of the road, like they were great angels looking down on us. If I squeezed my eyes almost closed, they looked like big people with outstretched arms. With open eyes they were just coming into bud, lumpy and strange against the grey early morning sky.

The hospital car park was quiet. Mr West dropped us at the door. The Accident and Emergency sign blinking above the entrance. Mum crashed through the doors, Danny in her arms, me at her side. Shouting and shouting, 'Help me. Somebody help me please!'

A man dressed in a white coat stepped forward and took Danny; Mum followed, her shoes click-clacking as she half ran.

Suddenly doors opened, more people in white coats appeared. They rushed into Danny's 'cubical, number three' and swished closed the curtain. The doctors and nurses were talking quickly, talking loudly. Mum was still crying. I was standing just behind her, watching, crying too. Someone pulled me aside and lead me away. She said she was a receptionist.

Above the receptionist's small questions all I could hear was the clatter and rush of hospital staff behind the cubical curtain, a trolley being wheeled in. Then the sound of Mum's sobs. In my head I saw a picture of a small bird flying so high that I couldn't see it against the shine of the midday sun and no matter how hard I tried to look, all I got was white.

'Shall we go and get you a hot chocolate and a biscuit?' The receptionist lady stooped over me, standing right in front of my view of Danny's curtain. I bit my nail and looked at the floor. The lady got down low so she was the same size as me. She looked me in the eyes and holding out her hand. smiled.

'Come on. We'll make sure Mum knows where you are if that's what you're worried about. You look hungry. Are you?'

I nodded and took the lady's hand, I kept looking at her fingernails. They were flame red and reminded me of Mum's fingers flying across the typewriter - long red claws. Those nails that she used for pinching. For a second I squeezed my eyes shut and held my breath. I wondered whether the lady used her nails in the same way.

As we walked along the corridor I looked up and asked, 'Will Mum and Danny be alright?'

The lady stopped short and, bending down close to my face said, 'The doctors are doing their level best to help, of that you can be sure.' She patted my hand and gave one of those pretend smiles that grown-ups do. She took me back to the place where the chairs were. I was told to be good and wait quietly.

I went to sleep outside Danny's curtain. Later I was awoken.

'Wake up sleepy-head, time to go home.'

I was lying on two hospital chairs pushed together. My school coat had been placed over me to keep me warm with a hospital blanket on top. Someone had taken off my shoes.

'Mum?' I looked around bleary-eyed.

'No, my dear, it's Grandma. Come on, up you get.'

I sat up slowly, screwing up my eyes. I yawned and shivered in my pyjamas.

'Let's get your coat on, shall we? Then you can come home with Grandma.'

'But what about Mum and Danny?'

'Don't worry about them love, Grandad will fetch them home later. Come on now.'

Grandma hauled me up into her arms and, still full of sleep. I clasped my hands behind Grandma's neck and snuggled in, reassured by her lavender smell.

At breakfast, Grandma made porridge, but her usual hawk eyes didn't notice me ladling spoonful's of sugar over mine. We ate in silence, just the sound of the spoons chasing porridge round the plates. I had learned it was best to wait to be told something than ask and get a clout for *not minding my own business*.

The phone rang in the hall. With a sigh, Grandma rose to answer it, her footsteps quickened on the Lino flooring.

'Joe? Any news?' I listened between mouthfuls of sweet porridge.

'Oh, dear Lord, no! And Diane …?'

I craned my neck to hear, imagining what Grandad was saying.

'Best you fetch her home. Will you let Richard …? Yes, I'll get Frankie to school, it'll be easier that way.' I heard the receiver being placed back in its cradle, then nothing. Grandma stayed in the hall for what seemed an age before she returned.

When Grandma came through the kitchen door, I searched her for signs, of what I wasn't sure. I noticed that her body looked all hunched and deflated as though age had caught up with her since walking from the kitchen to the hall and back. She almost vanished against a watery beam of sunshine which shone through the kitchen window, highlighting the dishes piled up by the sink. Outside the wind lifted the leaves and tossed them up in the air. I watched them dance. They looked like how I felt, a jumble of tumbling thoughts.

Grandma told me to get down from the table and go and get ready for school. She had pressed my school uniform and made it look like new. I could smell the love pressed into it, and when I did up my blouse, I found she had replaced a couple of buttons too.

We travelled together on the bus to school. It wasn't the usual fun like it had been on previous journeys with Grandma all happy and pointing out things of interest or feeding me barley sugars from her pocket. This time she was quiet, preoccupied with looking out of the window and blowing her nose. After a while I slipped my hand in hers and tried to cheer her up by singing a song that would usually raise a smile.

'If you're happy and you know it, clap your hands...' but as I sang Grandma looked at me and her tired old eyes welled up.

Diane: May 1968

A nurse took me by the arm and spoke to me quietly. All the while we were taking steps away from Danny. I wanted to protest but she kept walking. We stopped and she turned to face me. Her mouth was moving but I couldn't make out what she was saying. Sounds were muffled, like something barely heard under water. I tried to read her facial expressions then I looked at the watch, pinned to her chest like a medal, with its upside down clock face.

Shouting filled my head. *'Who is making all that racket, where is all the shouting coming from?'* Then, as if someone had flicked a switch my senses were on.

It was me! I was the one shouting: a desperate sound, raw and wounded, emptying my lungs; pushing out every ounce of air with a fierce urgency. My body collapsed, folding in and down on itself. I was adrift on inky black waters and wailing like a siren into the dark as if I believed my raised anguished voice could reverse things, keep us away from crashing into the rocks.

'Save him. Bring my Danny back.'

He had been on the brink - teetering between the two worlds, when they made me step away. The medics were pressing in and down on him, doing their best to stop his spirit rising, inserting tubes and cannulas, injecting liquids, attaching things to monitor his heartbeat and brain activity. Danny, my boy, was lying there, surrounded by a sea of masks and gowns, people he didn't even know. He didn't like strangers, they frightened him. If he woke, he'd be afraid. He needed me.

'Help him. Help him, please!'

'This way, Mrs Miller, let the doctors do their work.' The staff nurse rustled towards me, she led me out, her firm hand gripping my arm.

As we headed down the corridor, away from Danny, I heard it. A thin but unmissable sound sitting on the very edge of my perception. That noise, the one you got on those stupid bloody hospital dramas like Emergency Ward 10 where the equipment registers a patient flatlining. That one continuous note like all the air was leaving the body; signifying that all the bodily functions had stopped, that death had taken over.

My knees buckled.

I had to wait for them to finish what they were doing - to tidy him up. I sat waiting, alone in the relatives' room with its green chairs and muted colours, a mere fifty yards away from where my son lay. The nurse had given me a hot sweet tea and asked if she could call anyone for me. I don't remember what I said. I knew daddy was on his way. I was shaking so hard I kept spilling my tea.

After a while, the Doctor came into the room and sat before me, I watched his mouth move, the words colliding, not making sense. He handed me a tissue. I was trying hard to breathe normally.

'Can I see him? Can I see my son?'

He looked as though he was sleeping under the bright lights, all quiet and peaceful. I saw his freckles spread over his nose and cheeks I hadn't noticed he had so many until then. How could that be? And those long, sweeping eyelashes, how I wished he would just flip them open... his lips were too pale for someone who had died only twenty minutes earlier. Two hours previous he was alive. If I'd woken up earlier, acted quicker would things be different?

I stroked his hair.

His body wasn't yet cold.

He didn't have Duffy, his favourite toy. He didn't go anywhere without Duffy! I cried harder.

I was leaning over him apologising, promising to put it right, when I saw Dad enter the room. He folded me into his arms, and I surrendered. Through my tears I tried to explain but he stopped me, cupping my face in his hands. He kissed me on the forehead then put his arm around me.

'Come on, Pet, let's get you home.'

'I can't leave Danny, Daddy, not now. He needs me.'

'Diane, that's enough now. There's nothing more you can do. Now, come on home, you've been here for hours. You need to rest now and besides your Mum and Frankie need to see you.'

'But Daddy, there's so much I need to do.'

'Don't worry about a thing. It's all in hand. Come on, let's go.'

We said our goodbyes and I followed him to the car. It was a cold soulless drive. Mum was waiting for us on the porch, still in her overcoat, back from taking Frankie to school. We stood and buried our faces in each other's necks, sobbing before Daddy gave us both a brandy.

Diane: May 1968

The death certificate recorded 'sudden-onset fatal asthma' as the cause. I read and re-read the certificate as if re-reading it could undo the event. Daddy and Richard had gone to the Registrar's office, he insisted, saying it was something I didn't need to do. Mum, in the background echoed their words which made the decision final.

'Hurry up Joe. Richard, go and get it done before the office closes. Look at her, she's in no fit state.' I know they meant well, were trying to help but in doing that they took something away from me.

I should have seen it through, it should have been my name on the certificate not his. It was all wrong. I brought Danny into this world but feel so guilty for not being there when he left. It should have been left to me to complete the circle.

I felt jarred in so many ways. Angry and cheated. This should never have happened, not to Danny and not to me. He had his whole life before him, such a beautiful child and to have it all snatched away so suddenly. A child made from love and he was loved, so loved, my happy secret. Was that why I lost him, because of my transgression, denying me any semblance of happiness? Is this God's punishment? Is there a God at all?

All I wanted to do was sleep, to free myself from this horrible nightmare. But real sleep was elusive, I dozed in snatches, full of fidgets and falling sensations. I always woke just before the anticipated landing and struggled to get my bearings. Then, as if my mind had hit re-set, I remember all over again that Danny was dead, and the trauma would replay once more. That hollow ache in my chest, the lightness in my arms where his body should be, holding me, hugging me, had now become all too familiar. The place beside me in the bed where he would snuggle was now cold and empty. I'd imagine him laughing, machine-gun-fire giggles, I'd hear him wheezing, replaying over and over in my head, followed by that dreadful rasping at the back of his throat. A sound I couldn't eradicate no matter how hard I tried, leaving me desperate and broken, *Danny, my boy. Come back. Come back.*

I slept with his little stuffed dog pressed to my chest, his smell still clinging to its flattened fur. I lay in my bed for two days refusing to answer the door. My mother came by each day and called through the letter box.

'Diane, answer the door. Let me in. Diane, Diane! Frankie needs you.'

Richard: May 1968

I sat Diane up in bed and fed her soup. I held her as she curled into my arms and cried. It was the first time that we had really come together as a couple, shared something that we could both relate to. All our other experiences had been collisions, experienced from opposite ends, our wedding, the births of our children, our jobs, nothing that either of us wanted to discuss, not like other couples. But this, this was different. A shared pain we both understood.

Diane loved me for this, she told me so. When her mother came and tried to fuss, I gently but firmly sent her away. Her questions were too pointed, too loaded with accusations. Diane was too fragile to handle them. Not right now at any rate. I knew she meant well, that she too was grieving, but Diane had taken it hard.

'I can't believe he's gone Richard. It was all so quick. Why didn't I see it? If I'd have woken and moved quicker, I'm sure he'd still be here. It's all my fault.' I stroked her hair trying to soothe her.

'No Di don't blame yourself, it wasn't your fault. The Doctors said so.'

'But I was in bed. I was asleep. If I'd have been awake, I would have acted ... '

'That's irrelevant, even if you were awake, it took hold quickly.'

'No. Nooo.'

She tortured herself with an endless round of poisonous thoughts. If her mother had come and told us one more time that she couldn't cope with Frankie anymore, I wasn't sure I'd be able to control myself. Surely, she could keep her until the funeral was over. Give us some time and space at least? Not that I didn't want to see Frankie or have her there as part of the family - it was just not a healthy environment for a child. Besides, there wouldn't be much for her to do here and I didn't have the time to deal with both her and Diane. Frankie would be much better off left where she was for the time being.

Dark circles appeared beneath my bloodshot eyes, I'd developed a five o'clock shadow, shaving wasn't high on my priority list. I organised things for the funeral, sorted out the house, tidied things away as though putting things to right in my mind's eye. Doing these things enabled me to function, after a fashion.

I saw to the jobs that needed doing in the garden. A bough had fallen off the cherry tree, ripped off in the high winds during the night. I cleared away the debris, cut the branch up and stacked it near the back door. As I stacked, I was reminded that it was only a few weeks ago I had been shouting at Danny for swinging on that very bough. It felt significant somehow. I fixed the fence, unblocked the drain, turned the compost heap. Then I rolled my sleeves up and lifting the spade higher than necessary, rhythmically thrust it into the earth and stamped it down with force. My mouth twisting with the effort.

After a while, the physical exertion got the better of me and forced me to rest. I bent, hands holding on to the spade handle with my forehead resting there while my lungs drew in deep breaths, my rib cage visibly expanding and contracting. I stayed in that position for what seemed an age, catching my breath and assembling my thoughts. Finally, I stood up straight and, taking my handkerchief from my trouser pocket, mopped my brow.

I didn't see my elderly neighbour shuffle out of his back door and head down the garden path towards me, but I sensed a presence at the boundary fence behind me.

'Alright, son?'

I half turned. 'Yes, Alfie. I'm okay thanks, and you? I said it in a way that didn't genuinely invite or want a response.

Oblivious, Alfie shrugged, 'So-so, you know how it is for us oldies.'

I nodded, raised my spade and stabbed it into the ground.

'You're digging too deep for potatoes,' Alfie ventured.

'I'm just digging Alf, just for the sake of it', I threw a shovelful of dirt aside.

'My days for digging are over, son. But you're making some job of that. Are you sure you're not digging a grave for those potatoes?'

'There are no potatoes. I just thought I'd give the soil a good turning over. Apparently, it does it good.' Vigorously I scooped up another spade full.

'Well, if you say so son. Definitely keeps you fit. You sure you're alright? My Mrs told me about your sad news. We're awfully sorry ... '

I continued working with my back to Alfie. My eyes, now red rimmed and filled with tears. The only way I could express my pain was by driving the spade in deep. Eventually Alfie sensed that I didn't want to talk and went back indoors.

I went back into the house, it was quiet. There was none of the usual clatter and noise of children, the radio was silent, and Diane's presence couldn't be felt. I went into the front room and sat heavily on the sofa. Something hard poked my back, so I shifted position and reached behind the cushion. My hand found the offending object, a small red dinky car, one of Danny's favourites. I sat and stared at it for a few seconds, conjuring up the image of Danny's little fingers closed around it and running it across the floor. His enthusiastic gear change noises always made me chuckle. The moment brought a smile to my face but soon gave way as my face crumpled. I let out one long, agonising cry and threw the toy car across the room.

The next morning, I was up early despite my pounding head. A debris of bottles and spent cigarette stubs lay where they had fallen on the living room floor. Unwilling, or perhaps unable, to stay in the house, I turned my attention to outstanding jobs in the garage. My broad, calloused hands gripped the hammer with fixed determination. Instinctively, I knew my hands could navigate their way through a problem. I hammered away most of the morning, re-attaching a screen to a window like I was trying to re-attach some part of my life. I was never happier than when I was busying myself in my little workshop with its pigeon feathers, its paint brushes standing upside-down in old coffee tins and its rows of jars filled with an assortment of nails. This was my world, one that I could understand and lose my thoughts and fears in, one that I could build or break as I saw fit.

My thoughts settled on the first time I'd laid eyes on Diane. I'd been nine years old and cycling along Beechurst Avenue, eyeing up the horse-chestnut trees for conkers. Hand-like leaves were beginning to fall, quivering from side to side in their descent as though waving goodbye to summer's end. A pale-yellow sunlight picked out great drifts of red, orange and golden-brown leaves that lay in abundance around the tree trunks. I had parked my bike against the whitewashed wall of the old vicarage and was kicking idly at the leaf piles. Occasionally a hard, mahogany-brown conker revealed itself, sometimes still partially encased in its protective spiky jacket.

A hedgehog had uncurled itself from its nest of leaves and started to meander towards the trees. Its beady eyes shone like buttons and its inquisitive nose moved this way and that. I watched it closely, marvelling at its little paws and strange bristly coat before returning my attention back to looking for the conker of all conkers to earn me first prize in the up-coming match. I had crouched down to investigate a particularly large specimen and was just about to pocket it when a voice said. 'That's stealing.' I whirled round to find where the voice had come from.

'No, it isn't,' I ventured, 'this is public land.' Her flame red hair matched the colour of the leaves. She looked like a wild fairy creature that I'd seen in one of my sister's books. Her brown eyes blazed at me through a long fringe and her skinny arms poked out from beneath the sleeves of her blouse.

'Well, you can't lean your bike against our wall without permission. My daddy will tell you off!'

I scoffed, 'Oh really? So now it's an offence to lean your bike against a wall?'

She flushed and was just about to speak when a voice from within the house called 'Diane. Diane! Get down off that wall this instant and come here. Who were you speaking to?'

She swung her legs over the wall, looked back at me standing knee-high in leaves with the prize conker in my hand, and disappeared to the other side. That was the moment I was captivated by her and to this day she still captivated me.

When Diane finally got herself out of bed and went downstairs, she stood in the front room, still holding Duffy, and began wailing.

'Get them out, all of them. Now.'

She was pointing at Danny's toys shoved in a box in the corner and his pictures on the mantlepiece.

'What do you want me to do with them?'

'Just get rid of them. I can't stand it. I can't bear to see his things and not have him here. Take it all away. Out of my sight, now! Please, please,' she sobbed. Her hair fell in strands across her face as she doubled over clutching on to Danny's dog.

All I could see in front of me was a frail, broken creature swallowed up in a sea of emotion. Gently, I took her by the arm and led her back upstairs. I gave her another sedative and tucked her up in bed. When I returned back downstairs, I set about packing away Danny's things in boxes ready for stashing away in the loft.

I removed the pictures from the mantlepiece last of all, lingering over each one. There had been such joy in the boy, his laughter was infectious, and his need to love and be loved was compulsive. I found myself staring at a photo of Danny sitting on the donkey at Weston Super Mare beach.

I recalled that day so well, as if it were yesterday. Danny sitting there, looking as pleased as punch. He kicked up such a fuss to have that donkey ride. And when he got it, he had bounced on the animal's back as it trotted across the sand, hanging on to the reins for dear life with a huge smile spread across his face. He was even more delighted when Billy the donkey stopped for a pooh 'out of his bottom' mid ride. Something he took great delight in informing everyone for the rest of the holiday adding the size, colour and smell into the conversation. Pretty soon the pooh became *that big*, like the proverbial fish that got away. I placed the picture face down in the box and whispered 'Goodnight, Son,' then I sealed up the box and put it in the hall, ready for the loft.

It didn't feel right packing everything of Danny's away. It felt like it was dishonouring his memory, and yet Diane was in such a delicate position. Seeing anything relating to him was, for the moment, potentially going to send her over the edge. Hopefully, given time, some of the items could be reintroduced. I hated the idea of never being able to mention my son within her earshot. It was such an old-fashioned attitude. I remembered an aged aunt whose husband had died in the war years and everyone tip toeing around her making sure no reference to Jimmy was made. I despised the woman, she was mean-spirited, bad tempered and smelled of moth balls. Once, in a fit of pique, I said to Mum that Jimmy was probably glad to get away from the old bag. I was sent to my room for that outburst and later, when I was allowed down, Mum gently explained that for some people loss can just be too much to bear. Aunt Agatha, she said, had found her own way of dealing with her grief and we should respect her for it.

Diane: Mid-May 1968

My parents arrived early. Mum busied herself in the kitchen making cups of tea. She pressed my blouse. I could hear the sound of the steam and the thump of her running the iron over it on the ironing board. Richard was busy polishing his shoes - a rhythmic, rasping sound of brush on leather. The noise grated and seemed to amplify and echo inside my head. I covered my ears with my hands to blot it out, but it was superseded by the sound of blood coursing round my body, pulsing in my ears. I lay there, paralysed by sensation. I felt hollow, my legs strangely heavy; and deep in the core of me I shook, my heart revving and racing. I wanted it to stop. I wanted everything to stop. It all seemed like too much effort, even the simple act of getting myself up off the sofa when the time came. It was as if I had regressed, fallen inside myself and had forgotten how to do things, everything felt layered with a leathery patina of sadness. Richard got me up and into the car, slipped my shoes onto my feet, buttoned up my coat, pushed a stray hair behind my ear and handed me a Valium to swallow. He had been so good, so solicitous - it was like he was a different person, or perhaps a person I hadn't recognised. I gave in to it, let him lead me, leaned on him.

I don't know how I got through the funeral. It all felt so surreal. I held a hankie to my face most of the time, covering my mouth to remind me not to scream. It was one of Danny's with the letter D embroidered in navy in the corner.

I watched the vicar as he smoothed the page before he read from it. His cassock billowed white. It was raining, and I looked down at my muddied shoes at the graveside. There were muffled sobs everywhere and I could hear the raindrops pattering on the coffin as they lowered it into the earth. I wanted to jump down and tear the lid off, cradle my baby in my arms, bawl at the vicar 'Shut up with your bloody *Suffer the little children!*'

Then there was my mother tugging at my sleeve, 'Come on, Diane, hold it together.' bringing me into the moment and Richard's hands holding me up and my shoes, how had they got so dirty?

A lot of people attended - a sea of sad faces in the church and at the graveside where the wreaths and bouquets of flowers lay. Bill had brought a beautiful one from the office, he made a specific point of talking to me at the gathering afterwards, saying everyone in the office was very saddened, especially Mrs Webb. He told me to take my time coming back to work, that I wasn't to worry about anything. Then, just as he was about to turn on his heel to leave, he said, 'did you get the flowers from Tom and Monica?'

'Who?'

'You know, Tom and his wife Monica.'

'Tom!' It was as if I'd been punched in the gut and winded. Just the mention of his name. Tom the father of my son! He didn't have a clue that today we were burying *his* child. How would he react if he knew? If I had known where he was should I have told him his child was dead? I felt a pang of guilt and then remorse. Then I remembered how it all had finished, the last phone call, callous and final. He didn't give me the chance to tell him. I still mourned what could have been - but the depth and nature of that pain had changed over time. I got bogged down with the day-to-day things. Bringing up the children, working, making do. I managed to mumble something but wasn't entirely sure it made any sense.

Richard was hovering just as Bill mentioned Tom, I saw his expression change, had he figured it out? Did he suspect that Danny wasn't his child? For a moment I felt desperate, frightened of being exposed. I knocked back another brandy to steady myself, it burned as it slid down the back of my throat, following the verbal trail of my deceit. I had lied to him all these years, surely, he would have confronted me before now if he suspected. I doubted he would have been as kind as he had been if he knew. I dismissed the thought, too tired to pursue things further, there was just too much going on. All I wanted was to go home and lie in a darkened room and not think of anything.

I took ten days off. Richard left four days after the funeral. He had to go back to work, he had no choice. For once, I was sorry to see him go. He kept his family away from me which suited me fine - I couldn't bear the thought of Sophie's pity.

I was brittle like porcelain, bone dry to the core but knew I was close to shattering. My body showed it, hunched, curling in on itself, getting smaller by the hour. I hardly recognised myself, a thin hollow face with hooded eyes, every crease underlining my sadness. My lipstick-less lips were dry and papery, I must have cried all the moisture out. Every little thing exhausted me, my brain continually ticking over things, even when I slept. I woke exhausted only to do the same thing over again.

Frankie came home the day before Richard left. Her eyes darted here and there as if she expected Danny to suddenly appear. Mum had told her that Danny wouldn't be coming home, that he had gone to Jesus. That night, when I sent her to bed, I told her to say a prayer for her brother up in heaven.

'Is he up in the clouds now, Mum?' was all she asked.

I fell asleep on the sofa that night, after a Scotch to numb the pain and ease my tears.

Going back to work was strange. People gave me awkward smiles but then avoided me. Perhaps they were afraid I might cry in front of them or do something emotionally embarrassing. Mrs Webb was the only person that genuinely asked me how I was. When she turned up twenty minutes early, I was just leaving. She stood before me in her old shabby coat and headscarf, her hair still pinned beneath the hairnet. Her smile was genuine and warm.

'Hello, Diane, I was hoping to catch you.'

'Hello, Mrs Webb.'

'I was so sorry to hear your sad news.' She took my hand in hers. I could feel her papery skin. Her hands were strong but thin and claw-like, rather like a bird's. She had a smattering of age spots on the back of her hand. I wanted to withdraw, snatch my hand away, too much kindness would make me spill over and I worried that I wouldn't be able to stop. I nodded and fumbled in my handbag with my free hand, I didn't really know what I was looking for.

'How are you, Diane? Really, how are you?'

I thought to myself, she is the first person that has bothered to ask me that and really, genuinely want to know. Most people had asked it in a perfunctory way, their body language crying out *'please don't tell me, I can't handle it.*

I let my guard down.

'Honestly? Mrs Webb, I don't know. I feel … I don't know how to explain how I feel really.'

'That's understandable, my dear.' She looked deep into my eyes. Her gaze was kind and gentle. I felt my throat constrict.

'I know I feel terribly guilty. I keep going over and over it in my head. It never stops, even when I'm sleeping it's still going on and I can't stop it. I can't … '

'Shall I make you cup of tea and you can tell me all about it?'

'Yes. Yes, I would like that.' I was still gripping her hand as though my life depended on it when I followed her into the office kitchen.

Richard: Mid-May 1968

Some of the neighbours were very kind just after we lost Danny. A steady stream of casseroles and pies appeared at the door. It got to the point where I couldn't remember who the dishes belonged to and I didn't dare ask Diane. One of the families down the road asked if Frankie would like to go with them on a day out to the local air show. Frankie had never seen an aeroplane up close and was quite ecstatic with the idea. They fetched her the following morning and off they went in the car, Frankie waving frantically from the back window and me mouthing 'be good,' as they went past. I could just see the gap in her teeth where she had lost a tooth the day before, but it didn't take away from her broad smile.

I watched the car disappear up the road and was struck by how little I had really seen or spoken to Frankie since Danny's death. It was as if she had melted into the background, occupying the silences that filled our grief.

In the house I spent a little time tidying up. I went into Frankie's room and started to put away the small scattering of toys she had. One of her crayons had been partially crushed at the side of her bed. I bent down to pick it up and tried and remove the mess it had made of the carpet. Then I came across a pile of paper tucked away in the corner beneath the bed, pictures that Frankie had been drawing. They were an assortment of stickmen pictures. Frankie and Danny in stickman form, red and bigger Frankie, blue and smaller with what looked like a tractor, Danny. The last one made me blanche. It was like a finger poked into a wound, revisiting the initial pain. I put my hand to my mouth to stop the cry. It was a tall stickwoman in a triangle skirt holding a limp stick-child in its arms.

I'd meant to check in with her but had been so caught up with looking after Diane it had been overlooked. My mother-in-law had said that it had all been explained to Frankie and she hadn't really made much of a response either way. She also said that it was best not to talk about Danny in case it stirred things up, 'best to keep her distracted, least said, soonest mended.'

I decided to make a special effort and buy her a new doll to cheer her up. I put the pictures in the bin, she didn't need any more reminders. Perhaps the day out in the fresh air at the air show would help to take her mind off things, it sounded like they had planned to make it fun, ice-cream, hot-dogs and lots of biplanes. I'd have loved to have gone too but had too much to deal with here.

Frankie: Mid-May 1968

At the air show I stood at the barriers watching bi-plane after bi-plane take off, do some stunts and land again. After the first few, the novelty had worn off. I was bored, cold and hungry. The Wilsons, my neighbours had brought with them their sulky grandchild Esme, who didn't like it if I was given any attention. She was mean and showed her dislike in a sneaky way so that the grownups didn't notice. The odd wicked pinch or poking her tongue out when they weren't looking. She even claimed that I had pulled one of her plaits, snivelling as she did so. I wasn't quite sure how to handle it so I tried to make myself invisible so that no one would notice me.

I'd been looking forward to the outing all week, but all the joy had gone out of it. I wasn't told about Esme, she made me feel even more alone. It was strange just having to look out for myself, made me feel like I was off balance and I missed Danny. Without him I didn't know how to be. I felt awkward and uncomfortable and really wanted to go home.

It wasn't long before I needed a wee. All that fizzy pop and burgers. I tried getting the adults' attention, but they were busy talking with another grownup and Esme was being annoying and giving me withering looks. So, I used my initiative, mum's always telling me to do that. I set out to find the public loo on my own. I walked away from the crowd and wandered up the main route: past the ice-cream vans, the big tent with the man sitting at a microphone telling us all what was happening with the light aircraft, past the long line of people at the chip van filling up on chip butties with a generous squish of tomato sauce and the man selling balloons.

Then I saw it, just a little way off, coming out of a hangar, a small biplane. Its movement was quite slow and then it came to a stop. The pilot got out and went back into the hangar. I was so curious I forgot I needed a wee and headed off towards the biplane. Just as I got to it, I noticed a young couple walking my way too. The pilot appeared out of the hangar with a smile and a clipboard. I gave him one of my biggest smiles back, he looked kind and friendly. The pilot ruffled my hair.

'Hello, Curly Tops, how are you?'

'Very well, thank you.'

'And are you looking forward to your ride in the airplane?'

'Yes,' I was somewhat surprised, I hadn't expected a ride but was not about to ruin it.

'Up you get then. You can sit up front next to me if you like.'

He helped me climb up into the cockpit. I was too overwhelmed to know what to say and didn't want to appear impolite. I'd always had it impressed upon me to respect my elders.

The couple, having reached the plane, exchanged a few words with the pilot and climbed aboard. After a few more pleasantries and a brief safety check the plane taxied along the runway and took off. I looked out of the window, mouth agape as we climbed higher and higher into the sky. Far below I could make out an area with rows of little huts all by a big main road, possibly GCHQ (Government Communications Head Quarters) because I could see it from my bedroom window. So, I knew my home was nearby, but the plane moved on and on until all the familiar landmarks had disappeared. I sat tight lipped as the plane ploughed through the clouds. I was disappointed that they were mere wisps of smoke easily dispersed and not at all like the bunches of cotton wool we were given in class to stick on our pictures.

The pilot pointed out the dials on the dashboard, 'the instrumentation panel', the jump seat, the fire extinguishers in the stowage area, the propellers. He told me the length of the wingspan and how long it would take to get to Jersey. Jersey meant nothing to me. I think he could see that I was distracted. I turned my head this way, but I couldn't find what I was looking for. My eyes began to well up with tears.

'I can't see him. I can't see him,' I was getting agitated, clamouring at the window.

I saw no sign of God in his nightie, or the angels sitting on the clouds with their big, feathered, outstretched wings and harps and, more to the point, not a hint of Danny. I had half expected to see him with all his cars set out, engrossed in playing 'heavenly garages.'

'What's wrong? Who can't you see?'

'Danny, where's Danny?'

The pilot turned to the couple seated behind him.

'Your daughter's getting upset. Has she left one of her toys behind, she's looking for Danny?'

'Daughter? She's not our daughter!' They looked rather surprised, looking to each other, the pilot, then me, and back at each other.

'Well, who is she then? isn't she with you?'

I began to wail loudly.

'I thought she was your daughter,' ventured the woman.

'What's your name, little one?' asked the pilot, leaning across to me, I was busy wiping my nose on my sleeve. Between sobs I said my name 'Frankie, Frankie Miller and I'm looking for Danny my brother.'

The pilot adjusted his radio to contact Air Traffic Control. 'ATC this is Nine Three Nine Four November we have an emergency on board and need to return. Can you give clearance? Over?'

Instructions come back over the radio and soon the plane banked to the left and made the descent back to from where it came. I was now not only crying because I couldn't see my brother but also because I thought I would be in hot water.

On the ground, the fact that I had gone missing had certainly caused a stir. My name and description had gone out repeatedly over the tannoy. Groups of people had split up to look for me around the area. The police had been notified and the Wilsons were frantic with worry. It seemed that no one had seen me come or go, except for Esme and she kept quiet. Apparently, I had disappeared without a trace. How were they to break this to my already grieving mother?

The light aircraft touched down in the midst of all the melee. When it came to a halt and the propellers had finally stopped turning the pilot and us passengers disembarked, I held on to the pilot's hand as we made our way to Air Traffic Control. We were stopped part way by one of the air show stewards. He stood fifty yards in front of us repeating the words reported back to him over the walkie-talkie. 'Eight-year-old girl, blonde curly hair, wearing a red duffle coat and black patent shoes - small for her age.' The moment he saw us he held a hand up, signalling stop.

'Is that your daughter, Sir?'

'Err no. I've just brought her back down.'

The steward looked at him quizzically. 'Sir?'

'I'm a pilot. She was on board ...'

The steward hunkered down, 'Are you Frankie?'

I squeezed the pilot's hand and edged a little closer to him. Looking down to the floor, I nodded my head.

'It's okay, you're not in trouble, Frankie, we're all just very relieved to have found you.' The steward smiled and then radioed in on the walkie-talkie advising that I had been found. 'If you would like to follow me.' We walked behind him as he threaded his way through a throng of people. As we approached the tent, several policemen, the Wilsons and a waiting group of people all seemed to collectively exhale as I came into sight, all that is, except for Esme, who was busy rolling her eyes and sighing.

When I was delivered safely back home, I mumbled a thank you and went straight upstairs to my bedroom. Dad lingered at the door a while talking to Mr Wilson, but nothing was ever said to me about the day's events. Dad just asked if I enjoyed my ride in the plane. I said it was okay but didn't tell him about the clouds and Danny. I was glad to be home and away from it all, especially from Esme who glared at me for the duration of the journey home, though it was probably because I'd refused to share any of the sweets I'd been given. In my coat pocket I carried a souvenir aeroplane, a present from the pilot and a reminder of the day I looked for Danny.

Diane: June 1968

A small, but orderly, queue spilled out of the Post Office and onto the baking pavement. I stood impatiently gripping Frankie's hand she was itching to wrestle free. With the queue the size it was I was worried I wasn't going to get to the Post Office in time. Bill had impressed upon me the importance of getting the post away that evening. I prided myself in my ability to get things done - failure frightened me. I might get fired, be considered inept, incapable. Without my livelihood how will I cope? What will happen to the house, to Frankie? I owe the Co-op all that money for the funeral on top of the other debts, Danny's new coat. What will my parents say? I can just hear it now, the scoldings, the reminders of what a disappointment I've been. A bloody failure as a daughter, a wife, parent and secretary.

I waited, Frankie was still twisting on the end of my arm, trying to break free.

'Keep still. Do you hear? Just keep still!'

I took Frankie by the shoulders and gave her a harsh shake. From across the road the church clock struck 5 o'clock. On its last peal the post office pulled its huge wooden doors shut. The queue began to disperse.

I broke from the line and tugged hard at Frankie's hand. Distressed, she squealed, remonstrating loudly, still attempting to pull away. Her little outstretched fingers pointed, 'My dolly. My dolly!' A couple of passers-by slowed their stride to watch, looking back over their shoulders, tutting as they went. I leaned in close to her ear and spoke in a low firm tone.

'Shut up, right now, or I'll give you something to cry about. Do I make myself clear?' But Frankie continued to squirm, her face screwed up as she fought hard not to cry.

'Leave her alone,' a stranger cried. 'Can't you see you're hurting her?'

Another passer-by picked up the doll and handed it to Frankie. She hunkered down and touched her tenderly on the cheek. 'Is this what you were missing, Curly Tops?' Frankie nodded and grabbed the doll. She held it tightly to her chest, as though her life depended on it and crooning into its woollen hair.

I shot the woman a look, how dare she presume to talk to my child when she's been misbehaving. Then I dragged Frankie along the street, I didn't care if my nails were digging into her. Frankie quietened, seemingly distracted by watching our shadows expand and contract as we moved quickly, her dolly dancing in her hand. I had a sense of my high heels rhythmically tapping along the pavement until finally we reached the car.

The white ford Cortina's interior was hot and stuffy, the plastic seats unforgiving, sucking and potentially scorching Frankie's bare legs as I pushed her inside.

'Get in. I'll see to you when I get home. Drama queen.'

Frankie kept quiet, she sat on her hands with her head down and eyes fixed on her dolly.

I slammed my door, started the car and revved the engine longer than was necessary. The engine erupted into life then spluttered off. I tried the ignition again, but it made a half-hearted cough and died. Frustrated, I thumped the steering wheel. 'Shit, shit, shit.'

'Ouch!' I recoiled and looked at my nail. It had completely sheared off at the nub. From my mirror I saw Frankie freeze in the back seat, she watched as I placed my head on the steering wheel and took deep breaths.

Eventually I straightened up, checked myself in the mirror, reapplied my lipstick and searched my handbag for cigarettes. Soon thick smoke unfurled its way around the car. I inhaled deeply, wound down the window a crack and threw out the spent match.

Beyond, the sounds of the evening traffic blended with the soughing wind as it whispered through the trees. Inside, the car was stifling, smoke, heat, hot plastic. Everything felt close and every noise, amplified.

I turned the ignition key. The engine burst into life. I manoeuvred the car into the road and out into the busy, work traffic. By the time we had been round the one-way system and hit the queue waiting at the lights on the Promenade, the needle on the temperature gauge had already edged its way to red. Steam rose from the bonnet, building from small bursts to great funnels. Droplets of boiling water landed on the windscreen. It was sticky with pollen dust and little dead flies. There followed a long-extended gasp and the car died. Water gushed from the radiator leaving a rusty green puddle where it fell.

The traffic lights turned to green, but nothing moved; horns blared, drivers leaned out of their windows gesticulating and shouting.

I ushered my daughter out of the car and across the road. I left her to stand by one of the wide ash trees lining The Promenade, safely out of the way.

As car horns blared. I got back into the car and put the gears into neutral. I tried to push it to the side of the road. As I laboured, one of my shoes collapsed at its heel. I fell to my knees, ripped my tights and scraped my knee as the heavy car continued its momentum. I was still clinging to the steering wheel but was unable to slow its passage.

Two men turned off the street at separate intervals and pitched in to help. Traffic started to move around the car. A woman helped me to my feet. I could no longer hold back my tears. They poured down my cheeks, leaving ugly black mascara streaks and pools beneath my eyes. As I sobbed and gulped for air, I fished in my handbag for a hankie. The catch failed to shut and the bag fell open. Its contents emptied, spilling out all over the pavement. I cried harder, my face twisting in distress, spittle dribbling from my gaping scarlet mouth. I could no longer speak. Words broke and scattered. Each time I tried, the sounds I made felt alien. Hands, my own hands stretched out in front, shaking.

Faces came and went, blurring and morphing into ugly creatures looming large at me. The heat, the noise. A blaring car horn.

'Are you alright?'

Footsteps quick and slow. Fountain water cascading. Engines running, cars moving. More hands.

'Are you alright? Are you alright?'

I squatted on the floor, arms about my head covering my ears, and began to scream. I relieved myself in the process.

The ambulance arrived promptly. No fuss. It parked discreetly up a side street and was accompanied by some local bobbies. One oversaw the traffic, while the other busied himself with the incident, taking notes from witnesses. The ambulance crew steadied me and led me quietly away to the waiting ambulance.

Frankie: June 1968

I was watching from the other side of the road, nervously biting my fingernails. I didn't dare move from the spot because I'd been told not to. I tried to look at the pretty things instead of what was happening with Mum. Neptune's fountain was really lovely. Cascades of water ringing rainbows with fearless Neptune flanked by horses with wild manes. I watched as Mum was helped, into the ambulance. I was frightened and not sure what to do.

'Mum's crying again,' I whispered into dolly's ear.

A policeman knelt down and looked me in the face. He smiled kindly. 'So, what's your name?'

I shrank away a little and forced my hands deep in my dress pockets. My doll's head peeking mischievously out.

'Who is this?' The policeman pointed at the doll. 'Does she have a name?'

'Sal Floppit' I said in barely a whisper, whipping her out and holding her close to my face as though we were having a silent communication. I focused solely on my doll's face.

'Nice to meet you, Sal Floppit. I'm Constable Green.'

For a few moments I ignored the constable as though I was deep in conversation with my doll. Eventually I turned the doll to look at him signifying that we were now ready to give him our full attention.

'Why, Sal Floppit, you have a dress exactly like your Mum's. Very pretty.' Constable Green pointed at the two dresses and smiled.

I smiled back revealing the gap where my two front teeth were missing.

'Have you had a visit from the tooth fairy? I see you've lost some teeth.'

'She's coming on Friday, after she gets paid.'

'Oh, really?! Well, here's the thing. She came to see me this morning and told me all about you and left something with me. Now, what's your name so I know I'm giving it to the right little girl.'

'Frankie Miller, and I'm eight.' I looked at him curiously. He dug deep into his pocket and produced a two-shilling piece and handed it to me.

'Thank you,' I said timidly as Constable Green pressed the silver coin into my delicate little palm. My mouth fell open as my eyes fixed on the solid coin. Slowly I closed my fingers around it.

'Now, keep it safe in your pocket. There's a good girl. Is that your Mum?'

I clutched the doll close again, not quite knowing what to say. My eyes searched the floor as I gave an almost imperceptible nod.

'Your Mum's a bit upset so we're getting her some help. Is she often upset?' Again, I nodded.

'Do you know where your daddy is?' I lifted my shoulders.

The ambulance man waited on the opposite side of the road for a lull in the traffic. He spoke with Constable Green for a moment then came and introduced himself. Stooping low over me he said in a kind voice.

'Hello, my name's Alan. I drive that ambulance over there. Would you like a ride in it? We're going to take your Mum to hospital.'

I looked between Constable Green and Alan and felt my bottom lip quiver.

'Mum, I want my Mum,' I started to cry.

The constable lifted me up into his arms. 'Do you want me to come with you to the hospital?' I sobbed, clutching on to both his shoulder and Sal Floppit.

'It'll be ok. We're going to make your Mum better.'

I continued to sob.

Frankie: the next day

I spent the night at Grandma's and in the morning, I heard her on the telephone.

'No, I can't possibly manage her.'

I didn't get sent to school that day, and before lunch a lady came and took me in a car to a street on the other side of Cheltenham.

From the outside, the house looked small. It sat at the end of a row of houses all huddled together, it had a green front door with a brass knocker and a small, neat front garden. The catch on the gate stuck a little and the gate needed a good shove to open it.

I clutched the lady's hand as she led me up the garden path. I couldn't see into the house because it had white net curtains. The lady that answered the door looked like a granny - the kind sort, like Cinderella's fairy godmother. She smiled. She smiled a lot, especially when she caught my eye. It was a warm, non-threatening smile, wide and happy that creased her cheeks and made her eyes smile too. They were blue, like the colour of a blackbird's egg. I'd found a blackbird's broken eggshell in the park on the way home from school once. I'd been exploring the bushes by the brook when I came across it. It was cracked and so light it surprised me. I placed it carefully in my palm and held it up. The colour on the outside matched the blue of the cloudless sky. Inside it was creamy white. I wondered what had happened to the chick, was it safe? Perhaps, somewhere in the bushes, it was nestled down in a feathery nest. I stood a while and listened in case I could catch a plaintive little peep, peep. But I heard nothing.

We went in. In the hall was an old grandfather clock. It smelled of lavender polish, my Grandma would like that. Its pendulum moved to a steady tick-tock. I thought of a nursery rhyme. Inside my head I was singing, 'The Mouse ran up the clock,' I always did that when I was afraid; it was either that or chewing my nails and at that point there had been hardly anything left to chew.

Does a mouse live within the clock? I liked the way it's sound remained the same, but I couldn't say why. I liked that it was old too. *If it's a grandfather does that mean it has grandchildren?* I wondered where they were?

In the front room was a large mahogany table, *Grandma has a mahogany table too*, a fireplace with tiles the colour and pattern of tortoiseshell, and in the far corner, a box full of toys. On the table was a spread of sandwiches with the crusts cut off and some cup cakes with pink icing. My stomach hurt I was so hungry - I couldn't remember the last time I ate cake.

The lady left after a while. She went without taking me with her but told me that I wasn't to worry, Mrs Jackson was going to look after me now. I watched her disappear through the door and a hot tear rolled down my cheek, I held my breath so as not to make a sound.

Vera Jackson hunkered down onto her old knees and took my tiny hands in hers. They were swallowed up in warm, soft flesh.

'Now then, Frankie. I knows this is 'ard for you an I knows that it will take some getting used to. This'll be your 'ome for the time being. Everyone calls me Nanny an that's what I wants you to call me.'

I so wanted to be folded into her arms but stood woodenly before her.

'A'right my babba, let's get the general stuff out the road first. Any questions, you just 'ave to ask.'

After the tour of the house and being shown the bedroom which I was to share with two other girls, Vera took me outside into the garden. A shed had been transformed into a giant Wendy House complete with dressing-up box, wind-up gramophone, play cooker and an assortment of dolls, games, paper and colouring pens. Vera left me to play while she sorted the lunch.

We ate sitting at the glittery drop-leaf Formica table in the kitchen. I was impressed and convinced that the glitter made the food taste better - but anything was better than Mum's food.

In one corner a large pile of washing towered over its basket. It smelled of soap and windy days. Above the sink was a pulley filled with a variety of clean smelling clothes, some still dripping. Vera stood at the sink, she was busy emptying water from hot pans which were steaming up her glasses. Her talk was chirpy, and she even laughed at her own jokes. Her laughter high pitched and unbounded, somehow fitted with her rounded, womanly figure seemingly all held together by a floral pinny. I observed all this quietly.

After lunch, I ventured to speak. 'Nanny,' I barely whispered.

'Yes, my babba?'

'Nanny, where's Danny?'

I saw the look, like Nanny was caught off guard, recalibrating what to say next. 'Danny?'

'Danny, my brother.' There was a pause.

'I don't know, my dear, but I'll find out. Would you like that?'

I just nodded, sensing that if I opened my mouth the hollowness inside me would have swallowed me whole in that very moment.

Later that afternoon, Nanny took me on the school run to collect more of her charges: Mandy, Marlon and Lindy. They ran out of the school gates into Nanny's welcoming arms and then made a raggle-taggle line walking home, all talking at once, squabbling, laughing, playing tag.

When we got back, I locked myself in the outside toilet and cried, my arm clamped over my mouth to stifle my sobs. I didn't know what was expected of me, what was safe, how to be? Nobody had spoken of my Mum. I didn't know who anyone was or how long I was expected to stay? What if Mum forgot about me, and Danny? What if Mum really wanted to be rid of me and had kept Danny? Nanny wasn't able to say anything when I asked.

Really, I knew by the way Mum responded to Danny, I'd overheard her singing him lullabies when he cried at night. I'd heard her tell him he is her special boy, her favourite. Danny was Mum's perfect child and me? I was just Frankie. It didn't matter what I did, the kisses and hugs never came.

A face appeared at the four-inch crack at the bottom of the door. 'You a'right my babba? I 'ope you've not taken up camp in there because Nanny 'as to do a wee. Can you open the door for me?'

I sat, immobilised, drawing my legs up while sitting on the toilet seat. Then, unexpectedly, I fell backwards, folding in on myself and becoming quite stuck, bottom end through the seat. Outside the door, Nanny called for assistance.

'Marlon, can you come 'ere please. Do Nanny a favour and crawl under the door. I think our Frankie's got stuck down the pot.' Marlon shimmied beneath the door and undid the lock. His look said nothing and everything in that small moment that passed between us

With the door opened, Nanny set about freeing me. 'Bet you didn't see that one coming, did you?' She giggled. 'No 'arm done. At least you didn't yank the chain at the same time.'

My lower lip began to quiver, I couldn't help it. Was I going to get into trouble now? Nanny opened her arms, I flinched waiting for the strike to come but Nanny enveloped me, losing me in her warm softness and holding on like she was never going to let go.

'Nanny's got you. It's okay now.' Then she produced a fruit salad sweetie from her pinny pocket, and with a wink said, 'Ssh, don't tell anyone!'

Diane: One and a half years later

The day I was carried into that ambulance, in June 1968, was the day that everything came to a head. I hadn't been back at work that long, a couple of weeks perhaps. But I was just going through the motions, nothing was really registering. I was hardly functioning. Most of the time, I had a splitting headache and then there was a continuous ringing in my ears. My hands shook and the shaking went deep, like the deep fissures in my heart; love, loss, the tenderness shaken out of me. Sometimes I wondered whether I was about to have a heart attack, it was a strange, unsettling sensation.

I'd lie awake, night after night, watching the hands of the clock slowly move round the dial. It seemed as though I was on a treadmill going over the same things - trying to re-enact that devastating day and somehow radically change the outcome. My thoughts plagued me as if they had lives of their own. They intruded unbidden, kept me awake, held me hostage. I had this constant image of Danny sitting on the edge of my bed, his little hands, those chubby fingers, curled round Duffy. There was always a wheeze in his breath. He's muttering Muuummmeee, but I can't wake up. Why did I not wake up? The prescription drugs were useless, didn't work as I wanted them to. I was a mess and just wasn't able to get myself out of it.

I couldn't even answer properly when questioned directly. I thought I could understand what was being asked of me but just couldn't physically translate it. It was as if my body was taken over and wouldn't function as it should. It was as though my words had fallen through a colander and left only bits of syllables or grunts. Voices came and went. I was left in a room with some magazines but strangely found reading impossible. It looked like a jumble of random words.

I was sectioned under the Mental ill-health Act and was moved to an acute admissions ward. I didn't really know what was happening or care for that matter - the cocktail of drugs rendered me incapable of thought or action.

My days were spent staring into space, dribbling, and responding to things mechanically. I don't really remember much about that time except for the ECT.

I'd get wheeled into the treatment room, strapped to a trolley and have a bunch of wires attached to my head. Then they'd give me something to bite on. It tasted vile, sterilised rubber. I'd try to resist but they'd find a way of forcing it between my teeth - I wondered how many hundreds before me had that put in their mouths to stop them biting their tongues or breaking their teeth. How many others were volted rigid until their eyes bulged and all the air and fluids in their body escaped from whatever orifices they could? I always knew when it was coming because there was a big fuss about going to the toilet beforehand.

'Diane have you been to the toilet? Diane, have you evacuated your bowels this morning?'

It left me feeling no better than an animal; worse even. I'd be so weak it was all I could do to move from the trolley on to my bed.

Lord knows, I needed something to break me out of that depressive cycle. It was my parents who pushed for things, asked questions, cared, prodded, goaded. Mum went on and on about the ECT, how it would do me good, set me straight. They stepped up and took over.

For the next six months I was wheeled in and out of that room, secured to the trolley and shocked. Then it took another six months for me to be deemed fit enough to leave. I'd lost over a year of my life. Frankie visited once; even I registered her distress written all over her face. Mum without make up or her hair done. Mum in a special place where all the doors are locked, and other patients sit staring into space or moaning senselessly in the background. Even my clothes weren't my own, I had to wear whatever I was given. Sometimes they weren't even washed properly.

But it wasn't a complete waste, not to me. Slowly things began to fit together - the therapist encouraged me to explore things, thoughts that I had shut down. She asked me one day, 'What is it that binds a family, what makes them cleave together?'

I thought it was a trick question. I couldn't answer properly. Love, duty, respect, need, expectation? Which came first? I saw it as an amalgamation of these things but how to juggle it so that all needs were met - was that possible, particularly when the goal posts seemed to be constantly changing? Then I got to thinking, what binds a couple together aside from the marriage vows? What does love really mean? How does it feel? What will you do for the sake of love? I thought of what I dreamt of as a child and what I wanted now and how I felt I had been let down, and how I had myself fallen short of my dreams and expectations. Who set me up with these expectations? Were these of my own making or had I absorbed them from someone, something else?

And my needs? My heart had been buried deep, ice-cold, white, numb, for an age. All I wanted was the touch of a hand, a gesture that reflected love and kindness, not judgement or pity but real, unconditional love. When had I ever experienced that? I held this image in my head. I'm skipping down the road, holding tightly onto my dad's hand. It's a big strong hand with a grip that held me safe, that said I was the most precious thing it had ever held. Dad and I were singing 'Rosy cheeks, rosy cheeks, rosy cheeks and dainty feet.' and he'd make a big ungainly jump on dainty feet making us both erupt into gales of laughter. We'd been up the lane nutting, looking for hazelnuts. Our pockets were bulging with them. He often took me foraging. Sometimes we walked up Cleeve Hill to sit by the washpool drinking hot sweet tea from his thermos. He'd tell me funny stories from his childhood, and I would sit captivated.

Then I thought of my mother, and I couldn't help all the talk that was going round and round in my head. It kept bringing me back to the same conclusion and the more I thought about it the angrier I got. Not a pathetic, little-girl anger where I'd cry into my pillow, but the kind that felt fierce and forceful, that made my hands tighten into fists and caused me to grind my teeth in my sleep. I longed to confront her, say out loud the things that were locked up in my head, bouncing around in there, desperate for a release. Why was I so afraid to challenge her? What hold did she have over me? Perhaps it was the fear of being wholly abandoned? I wasn't sure if I was strong enough for that or to take her on, but in my head the words clicked round and round. I was braver in my head than in real life.

I imagined saying, 'We will see this through. There will be casualties of that you can be sure. I will be that intact mirror in a riot. Think carefully now before you answer. What binds a couple together aside from the usual marriage vows? Do I have any semblance of that in my marriage? And yet you counselled me to stay, stay despite my abject unhappiness. Despite the fact that my children had an absentee father. So, what is it that ties me to this farce of a marriage? I'll tell you, shall I? I tied myself to your expectations, to your shame and guilt and then fed it with my own for good measure. I lost sight of my own needs - left them buried beneath a heap of shoulds, oughts and musts that were of someone else's making - Yours! Is that right? Is this what you really wanted for me?'

'Remember, you were the one that pointed the finger, accused me of loose morals, named me, your own daughter, as a trollop. What were the words that you used? Whore, guttersnipe. I took those words and wore them. You had no right to taint me so. I was so young and inexperienced. I still am. You shunned me when I needed you the most. Yes, I have regrets, but most of all I regret listening to you.'

It all made perfect sense to me, but the act of saying it all in reality frightened me, stifled my words and kept me still. Would I ever get away? Would the spectre of that god-awful trolley forever haunt me?

Finally, I got out, left that awful de-personalised place by the skin of my teeth and no more. I learned to keep my head down, not make a fuss, hide my tears. The thought of being kept in was enough. I had to play the game that was expected of me. Do what they wanted: the doctors, the psychiatrist, my parents, my husband, my child. Everything but what I wanted, what I needed. They piled their obligations and expectations on me in heaps until I felt buried under them. My emotional back creaking under the strain. I wanted to get back to normal, whatever that was. It seemed like such a distant memory.

I wanted Frankie to look at me as if I was her mother not a stranger to be frightened of. She stood behind my mother's skirts that time she came and peeked out. She wouldn't come anywhere near me. Not that I blame her. I could hardly say her name. I remember registering seeing her but for all that I may as well have been reading the back of a cornflakes packet. The foster carer told mum that Frankie had nightmares for days after the visit. She recommended that Frankie didn't come again as it was adversely affecting her. Surely it would affect her wellbeing not seeing her mother - did anyone query that? But I said nothing, just took it for what it was.

I also wanted Mum and Daddy to relax around me, not fuss or worry. Mum had aged, you could see it in her face, lines tracing round her eyes as if her salty tears had dried up all the flesh and left papery tired skin in its stead. Her hair had turned completely white since I had come here - referred to as a *shock* of white hair. I wondered what she had told her friends about me. Had she told them the truth, confided that she was at her wits' end or pretended that I'd gone away to stay with friends to avoid the disgrace?

I knew I had to change the way I did things or at least make it appear that way. I made my mind up to be careful of every move I made, not let any of the cracks show, not to my parents, my doctors, the psychiatrist. They had more power over me than I wanted or liked and that had to change.

To stay out and away from that bloody awful place I knew I'd have to batten my insecurities and fears down tight and make sure that those close around me did the same.

It was one great big act of appearing normal and I had to wear it like I wore my own skin.

Frankie cottoned on the quickest. She watched my every move, she could read me before I could read myself - she too learned to keep her head down, not make a fuss and never showed her tears.

Both my parents came to collect me. Mum fussed, making sure I had a blanket on my knees to keep me warm in the back of the car. She fed me barley sugars on the journey home, just like she did when I was a child. We went back to their house, arriving in time for tea – shepherd's pie followed by blackberry and apple crumble with custard. More favourites from my childhood. After that she drew me a long hot bath and allowed me to wallow in it until my fingers went all prune-like. She had warmed the bed with hot water bottles and put fresh, clean, cotton sheets down. She gave me my pills before kissing me on the forehead and closing the door. The room was dark, but the smells and sounds were familiar. That night I slept the best sleep I had had in a long time.

The following day was pretty much the same - all my physical needs were met but never once did ether of my parents ask how I was or about my experience. It was as if they were afraid to ask - that by acknowledging what happened meant that their daughter was flawed. And so, we continued in this way, bumping along, pretending that everything was alright. There was no question of looking at why it had happened and so, by avoiding, it just buried the problem deeper.

Days threaded in and out. Several weeks passed and life was one big monotonous routine. I watched the autumn leaves turn from gold to brown and gather in wind-blown heaps at the bottom of the garden at the dry-stone wall. Richard telephoned a couple of times, but our conversations were stilted. When he asked how I was I could almost hear him wincing on the other end of the line.

He referred to my illness as being 'a bit poorly' as though saying anything stronger out loud would somehow taint him or trigger me into a relapse. But what did he know? I was much stronger than he gave me credit. He had no real understanding of what I'd been through or what it took to keep my head above water, and I doubt he'd ever want to understand.

On the days I struggled and found things difficult, my mother would give me her steely look and admonish me. 'Now Diane, we're not going to have any of that nonsense today, are we?' She didn't even attempt to ask what it was that had upset me, just took me outside for some 'good old fresh-air walks' and made sure I ate properly. She was the gatekeeper and friends were kept at arms-reach. She monitored the phone calls, the length of the visits and probably our conversations. I know she primed my few visitors before seeing me.

I once overheard her saying to Val, 'You're not to discuss this or that and under no circumstances should you mention her illness.'

We were all expected to tip-toe round this 'thing' like it never happened.

But I was left feeling alone, isolated. I sensed that everyone was looking at me through a different lens as though they were waiting for me to break open again, start hopping round the room or howling at the moon. I hated it when on those rare occasions some of Mum's friends called by for a coffee and a chat. They would pop in on me in the sitting room and pointedly ask with forced smiling faces, 'How are you today Diane?'

I felt like an exhibit. What could I say? I had no opinions on anything apart from the weather. Not even that, really. Banal meaningless chit-chat. The pauses would get longer in our exchanges. Then they would turn and go back into the dining room and continue to gossip. I could hear their whispers, 'Oh, she's looking a bit peaky today.'

'Do you think she'll ever get fully better?'

'My friend, Dorothy, had a similar problem, has never been right since poor dear ... '

Frankie was brought to see me on occasion. She was pushed into the room the first time and gave me a frightened hug. I could see her looking, her eyes fastened on me - reading every nuance. She had this uncanny way about her that made me feel scrutinised.

She was very quiet and didn't say much apart from, 'Are you better now?'

I sent her away.

Frankie: August 1970

I only went to Sunday school because sometimes they provided jammy doughnuts. I got up really early to make my way through the Sunday-quiet streets. My stomach drew me there with the promise of diluted orange juice and sugar covered jammy doughnuts that oozed a blob of jam in the middle. I could even taste it before I got through the door, my mouth rinsed with saliva. This made God more palatable to me. I liked sitting at His table. Everyone was extra nice, and no one shouted.

Miss Avery, my Sunday school teacher, wasn't married probably because of her violet rinsed hair. She made a point of mothering me. Her neat, manicured hands cupping my face and telling me in her soft breathy voice that I was one of God's children.

'The Lord will always take care of you,' she would say.

All the sessions began and finished in song. I liked that bit best of all 'Yes, Jesus loves me. Yes, Jesus loves me. Yes, Jesus loves me …' I carried the songs absent-mindedly into my play - like mantras, protection spells.

God became a preoccupation, He fascinated me. Sometimes, on my way home from Sunday school I found myself looking for evidence of Him. Miss Avery's words rattling round my head.

'He is everywhere.'

I wondered whether He was there when I went to the loo and if He saw every single moment. It worried me just a little. I hoped He would forgive me for stealing chocolate bars with Marlon when I was at Nanny's and whether it would prevent me from getting to heaven when the time came.

I made a point of asking God every day for two things. One, to make my Mum happy - happy enough to love me - and two, to bring me a dog. It seemed that He hadn't heard me on both counts. Either that or I hadn't been good enough to warrant having the requests granted, but it didn't stop me trying. 'God loves a trier.'

Sometimes, when I felt a bit daring, I took the short cut home from Sunday school. I'd go through the private flats and climb over their wooden fence leading to my road.

Mrs Pearson caught me every time. Railed at me from her first-floor window with a skinny pointing finger and screechy voice, 'Get out of my garden. I'll tell your father!'

I ignored her. I didn't care for Mrs Pearson, she was mean and never gave any sweets or money at Christmas when Carol singing time came round. It was my biggest earner. Twice I'd been caught out, singing several songs to Mrs Pearson's face and all she said was, 'That's very sweet, thank you and Happy Christmas,' before closing the door.

Mrs Pearson was welcome to tell my Dad as I doubted that he would do anything about it.

It was during one of these encounters with Mrs Pearson that I met Patsy. Patsy lived in the flats. She was a whole year and a half older than me. Worldly-wise, almost. She had copper red hair and said 'bloody' a lot. Had it not been for the scabs on her knee and her flat chest, I would have thought her to be much older still. I was in the process of climbing the fence when she appeared.

'You know you're not allowed to be here unless you have permission, don't you?'

I shrugged.

'Why do you go that way anyway?'

'I live in that road,' I pointed beyond, 'so it's quicker.'

'My Mum says you'll get splinters in your bum if you climb the fence.' Her freckled face creased into a wide beam, 'Ha, made you look, made you stare, made you cut the barber's hair.'

I smiled back. I knew I was going to like Patsy and double bonus, she just lived up the road.

Returning home after my stay with Nanny had meant navigating a good many hurdles. A new school, a new domestic routine, missing Nanny and the other children, readjusting to being an only child and not having any friends or allies. Danny was gone. *'He went to heaven.'* It was said in way that made it feel like he was off staying with Grandma or away on a school trip. Whenever I asked questions about him, I was met with silence or blank stares and clamped mouths. Only Nanny seemed intent on telling me the truth.

Dad ruffled my hair and told me, 'You don't need to go bothering your head with that now Frankie,' but then added in lowered tones, 'And don't mention it to your Mother, it'll only upset her, and we don't want to go and do that now that do we?'

But I couldn't help it. Danny was a constant reference point in my thoughts, I kept returning back to it. Why had they removed all his things and every single one of his pictures? It was as if he had never been there. I worried that I'd forget what he looked like; even now his face was fading. Would it be the same if something happened to me? Would I be forgotten so quickly? And goodbyes, I never said goodbye or told him that I loved him, that I missed his place at the table, the hollow in his bed where he slept. Do you know things like this even when you're dead?

I had bitten my fingernails to the quick since coming back home. And sleep, I kept waking at strange hours. Sometimes I thought I heard Danny calling me, 'Frankie, Frankie, where are you? Frankie!'

I wished I was back at Nanny's where everything felt normal. My mind switched to the day Mum turned up at the door, unannounced. I'd become used to not seeing her. Yes, there had been a visit to that great big place with the large garden and lots of nurses and jangling keys. When I'd gone there and Mum was wearing odd shoes. Grandma told me to hush when I tried to point it out. I couldn't understand why Mum's hair was all messy or why she kept mumbling, nonsense. I wasn't even sure it was my Mum. She sort-of looked like her, but she wasn't right.

It frightened me. I decided that if I didn't see her, I didn't have to think of her and be reminded of how Mum just wasn't Mum anymore. So, seeing her at the door was a shock. I was pleased, but not enough to want to leave. Someone had come round to talk to me about it but I hadn't really taken it in. I hadn't understood that Mum was going to come and get me for good. Next thing I knew Nanny was on the front step waving me off, fishing out a fruit salad from her pinny for the journey.

Marlon lifted the front room window's net curtain behind his head and flattened his hand on the pane, I felt his eye's watching me as I climbed into the car. I couldn't bring myself to say the word goodbye or even lift my hand.

Mum, rattled her keys impatiently, 'Come on, hurry up, we haven't got all day.'

The next thing I knew I was being hurried into the car seat and moving away at speed, away from Nanny, her hugs, her laughter and the sense of safety. I kept my eyes fixed straight ahead.

Mum wasn't right. I could tell by the way she smoked her cigarettes and crushed them out in the ashtray. When she ate, she stood at the kitchen worktop stabbing at small mouthfuls of food with her fork, reminding me of black crows and their powerful beaks.

It felt like Mum would blow at any minute. Nothing had really changed. Yes, I knew she had been ill, but it wasn't clear why or how. She hadn't had an operation or broken a bone, there wasn't a getting better end date, just a poisoning presence that tainted the household. Fearful, I tiptoed round her. There were so many things that were taboo.

'Don't do that it'll upset your mother.'

Don't say this, don't say that. Half the time I didn't know what was expected of me. Slowly I became good at reading the signs - my Mum's tone or the way her shoulder's drooped, the number of cigarettes smoked, the way she tapped her fingernails, or the amount of crockery piled up in the kitchen sink. Some days Mum was still in bed when I got home from school. If the curtains were drawn I knew she was having a bad day. On such days, things were more precarious. I feared entering the house.

It was on a day when the curtains were closed that I hesitated at the back door. I watched as a colony of ants made their way, single file through a hole in the brickwork. I didn't try to prevent them, just hunkered down and witnessed their steady determined journey. It gave me time to slow my breathing down and think.

I couldn't face going into the house, so I turned round and headed back the way I came. As I passed the flats, I looked up, Patsy was at the window, waving. Wait, she signalled, then disappeared. I heard her feet clatter down the stairs until she appeared at the door, breathless. 'Where you off to then?'

'Nowhere.'

'You have to be going somewhere.'

'No, not really.'

'Fancy coming round the shops, I've got to pick some stuff up for Mum.'

'Yeah, alright then.'

The two of us set off, Patsy talking ten to the dozen. It was a throw away comment that made me stop. 'What do you mean your mum doesn't go out?'

'My mum just doesn't go out.'

'What do you mean she doesn't go out? Surely, she has to go out at some point. What about the school parent teacher meetings?'

'No. She doesn't do them. She's scared of leaving the house. It makes her ill.'

'Blimey, how long's she been like that then?'

'Forever. Well, at least couple of years. My mum's bloody mental.'

'Yeah, so's mine. Only she gets days where she can't get out of bed.' A smile flickered across my lips. I'd found someone who thought it normal to talk about what wasn't quite right.

The two of us had much in common; Patsy's mum was a single mum. Her dad lived in Kent and had remarried. Patsy's mum spent the bulk of her days confined to the flat, sitting in her tatty old armchair reading. Pills on the hour and opinions to be ignored. Patsy and her older sister ruled the sparsely furnished roost, bartering favours such as fetching the shopping, or taking the washing to the launderette for, what seemed like, outlandish demands to me. Their mother was imprisoned by her fears and her children. The requests ranged from staying up late and watching a particular tv channel to having a bag of chips and a bottle of Dandelion and Burdock on a Friday night.

Increasingly I spent more and more time with Patsy, we dressed, where possible, like twins, I learned to speak like Patsy, question the world in the way she did. She made my world seem bigger and far more accessible and laughed in the face of difficulties, positively showed it her bum.

Patsy encouraged me to try new things. Smoking for one, Patsy had apparently mastered the art and didn't cough or splutter. 'There's a knack to it. See.' She emitted a visible vortex of smoke blowing it in my direction. I was both impressed and determined to match Patsy's smoking ability, so I studied how my mum could make smoke funnel out of her nose, rather like a dragon, and resolved to try it out for myself. Besides, Patsy had double dared me.

Rising early the next Sunday morning I tiptoed downstairs to the kitchen while my parents slept on. My dad always kept his cigarettes on top of the fridge along with his silver Zippo lighter. With glee I realised I had all the smoking tools at my disposal: it was an opportunity too good to resist. Into the front-room I went, curtains drawn but letting in a crack of light. I knelt at the fireplace thinking that I would blow the dragon smoke up the flue. What I hadn't figured on was the effect the smoke would have on me.

Putting a Peter Stuyvesant, to my lips, I tapped its tip on the fireplace tile. It was a ritual my Dad did before his smoke. Then I flicked back the Zippo lighter lid - it felt so satisfying, that metallic snap, followed by the smell of lighter fuel, to me it was like a sweet perfume. Then, with the lighter aflame and the cigarette to my lips, I inhaled deeply...

One second, two seconds passed, and my exhale came in a sudden gasp as the bitter taste hit the back of my throat. I coughed and gagged violently. Smoke seemingly emitted from every orifice in my head. My lungs and throat on fire, breath failing, throat constricting, no air going in or out. Coughing I doubled over and experienced the strange sensation of my body taking over. Tears streaming, eyes bulging and retching.

With all the flailing and gasping for air, the tip of the cigarette fell off onto the new nylon carpet and began smouldering its way through. The hole burned bigger and brighter as the carpet fibres melted before me like some sort of weird sacrifice. Helpless, I gulped and gasped, spluttering and coughing so loudly that I woke the dragon.

I heard footsteps trailing across the bedroom floor above followed by the familiar creak on the stair and the sound of Mum descending, her knees making the tell-tale clicking noise as she got closer.

The carpet continued to glow like a small cigarette comet, smoke settled in ribbons about the room. The realisation of what was to come next made it so much worse.

Mum came in dressed in her pink slippers and nylon quilted Marks and Sparks dressing gown with her hair pinned up beneath its net. Her face said it all even before the verbal assault started.

Frankie: September 1970

We were sitting on the grass in the park after school. We were trading secrets: all the daft things we'd done and the different kinds of trouble we'd been in. We played Rock, Paper, Scissors to see who went first, Patsy won.

'The worst for me was when my sister annoyed me.'

'Doesn't she always annoy you?'

'Yes, she thinks she's always right - tries to boss me about like she's my other mum or something and mum doesn't even try to stop her. Anyway, it was my birthday and I wanted to spend my birthday money by going to the pictures. We got into this big fight about which film. She didn't want to see the film I wanted and said it was for babies. So, I picked up the nearest thing and threw it at her. It was a bottle of ink. She ducked and it smashed all over the front room wall. Blue ink on a white wall. Mum went mad. I thought she was going to kill me. So, my birthday money got spent on white paint to cover up the stain in the end. You can still see it now if you really look hard.'

My hand went to my mouth, I was shocked and rather gleeful.

Patsy could see that I was suitably impressed and flicked her hair back with renewed self-importance.

'My mum would have killed me if I'd done that.'

'So, come on then, what's the worst trouble you've got into?'

'Well, I'm not sure if this one counts because I don't think my mum ever found out.' I then told Patsy all about my short flight and the odious Esme.

Patsy was enthralled. 'I can't believe you did that! Did you really think that you were going to see angels and dead people up there?'

I looked at her quizzically. 'Well, maybe. But it didn't really bother me.' Then I tried to cover my tracks by adding. 'The air show was boring anyhow. One plane looked just like the other after a while. I thought I was going to a show where it would be more than just watching the planes take off and come back again.' Patsy sucked her teeth in a grown-up sort of way.

'But it did bother you didn't it.' She looked at me sideways.

I pulled at tufts of grass and watched the captured blades fall through my fingers, head down not looking up. Thoughts of Danny now circling in my head.

'It's okay Frankie, I get it.'

'No, you don't get it. You don't get it at all. No one gets it.' I got up, walking swiftly up the hill towards the edge of the park.

'Wait, Frankie!' Patsy sprinted after me. 'Frankie!'

'Go away. Just leave me alone. Leave me!' I hit out, swinging wildly into the air. Patsy hung back, confused. Then, thought better of it and, running, tackled me throwing her arms around me.

'Frankie, it's me, your bestest ever friend.' She held my arms fast. My struggle was weak, half-hearted. The anger subsided leaving me feeling embarrassed and exposed. With the warmth of Patsy's arms around me I allowed myself to give, let my guard down, just a little but doing so meant my throat tightened and tears welled up. I collapsed sobbing onto Patsy's shoulder.

'I know,' soothed Patsy. 'It's all bloody bollocks. Now say after me, it's all bloody bollocks.'

I snuffled.

'Hey, I hope you're not snottering on my shoulder, I've got to wear this for at least another week before it's washed. Bloody bollocks, come on!'

A weak smile appeared on my face.

'Come on, I'm waiting!'

'Bloody bollocks,' I proffered meekly.

'Eh, what was that?'

'Bloody bollocks,' I ventured, a bit bolder.

'Louder!'

'Bloody bollocks, BLOODY BOLLOCKS!' I screamed. The two of us shouting it from the top of our lungs until we collapsed in a heap laughing and breathless.

'Come on, we need cheering up. Let's go get some sweets.'

'But I don't have any money,' I protested.

'I know, nor do I, but that doesn't matter. Ve have vays and means.' Patsy pulled a pretend serious face, grabbed my hand and the two of us ran up the hill.

In Manton's all the penny and half-penny sweets were displayed in a finger-print-smeared glass cabinet with the chocolate bars in tiered accessible rows on top. I only got to choose from the penny or half-penny sweets when I went to fetch my Mum's cigarettes. That was all the change would buy. The tiered chocolates were something to dream and drool over

Patsy winked at me and asked the shop assistant to fetch down a large jar of sweets from the top shelf and, while her back was turned, quickly filled her pockets with chocolate bars gesturing to me to do the same.

Having climbed down from the steps after removing the jar the assistant asked, 'Do you want a quarter or half a pound's worth?'

At which point Patsy pulled a face and patted her pockets. 'Oh dear, I'm really sorry, but I seem to have forgotten to bring my money. I'll be back later.'

The two of us ran out of the shop and kept running until we reached the end of the road where we fell about screeching with laughter. We sat on the wall, pulling our ill-gotten gains from our pockets and stuffed our faces.

Frankie: May 1972

My school assemblies were held on Fridays. Only the Seniors got to sit on chairs at the back. The hall divided into girls on the right and boys on the left. I sat on the floor near the front with the rest of the first years.

I didn't notice all the looks and nudges going on behind my back. I thought the whispers and giggles were about something entirely different, certainly not aimed at me.

Then I caught a whisper from behind. 'Her Mum's a mental case.'

I snapped my head round. Two girls I didn't recognise looked straight at me, heads close together. How did they even know who I was?

'Is it true?'

'Is what true?'

'My mum said your mum got carted off to the loony bin ...' said one, '... by the straight-jacket brigade.'

They began to laugh.

'Yeah, the straight jacket brigade.'

'Cracked,' ventured the other girl, pointing to her head and twisting her finger.

'Was she making funny noises?'

'Frankie's Mum's lost it.'

'Aww diddums,' they chanted, cruel smirks plastered across their faces.

'Did she pee her pants?'

I tried to ignore them, but the constant whispers of 'nutter' or 'loony' were beginning to get to me. I sensed other eyes looking at me. Who else knows? I wished I could curl up and die.

When the bullies started prodding me in the back, goading me under their breath. 'Loony, loony, loony ...'

It was too much. We were at prayer, but I couldn't let this go.

Turning, I shouted, 'I'm going to kill you,' and jumped up to tower over them, smacking their two heads together.

All the kids nearby shuffled back to watch, shouting and jeering, egging us on. From the stage the headmaster called for order.

'Stop that at once!'

Teachers left their seats and waded into the fray, Oblivious I punched as though my life depended on it.

It took three teachers to pull me off, my blazer torn at the pocket, my hair dishevelled and my nose bloodied. I was still trading insults as I was carted out of the assembly hall with every eye upon me.

Mrs Malone, the deputy headmistress, viewed me with disgust. When she spoke, her lips turned white and small flecks of spittle appeared at the corners.

'I don't understand what came over you Frankie Miller. It's disgraceful behaving like that. What have you got to say for yourself? I remained tight-lipped.

'Come along, I'm waiting.' She looked at me over her glasses and fixed her sternest stare.

If I mentioned what the girls had said then I would have to talk about mum, more specifically what had happened to mum and how she went mad because of Danny, how could I explain that? I kept my head down, staring at one particular spot on the desk. 'Judy loves Dave forever' had been carved deep into the wood. I was tempted to trace it with my fingers to show that I wasn't listening, and I didn't care.

She stood over me. I could smell her perfume, sense her breathing. Her shoes were the flat and sensible kind, but there were scuffs at the toes. How did she scuff them? Had she tripped? I bet she didn't buy them from Timpsons or from the shoe shop at The Square.

'Miller, stand up.' I slowly got to my feet, my knees felt weak. I leaned against the desk and let out a sigh. She then issued a long lecture about appropriate behaviour and what was expected in the school. I stared out of the window my chin cocked defiantly.

Mrs Malone continued talking, I hardly listened it was all, disappointed, blah blah blah, do you behave like this at home, blah blah, blah. But when she insisted that I apologise to the girls I had *attacked,* I reacted.

'No! You can fuck off.'

She blinked at me from behind her owl-like frames.

'Miller, this behaviour and language will not be tolerated. You leave me no choice but to give you the cane. Come with me.' She made to grab my arm.

'Don't you bloody touch me.' I smacked her hand away and looked her in the face, defiant. Hands balled into fists. I was past the point of restraint and fled out of the door. She followed bellowing after me. I ran past the Janny's office, out of the back door and up the school field, crossing where Form Three were practising athletics. I ran past the rounders and cricket pitches and on to the end of the field and its five-foot chain fence.

Mrs Malone still trailing behind shouting, 'Come here this instant. Miller, if you don't come back, I'll have you suspended.'

Her threats made no impact. I was past caring. Sprinting towards the fence, I ran up the side of the concrete posts, vaulted over and disappeared into the park beyond.

I knew this park. Patsy and I visited it regularly. It was our place for building dens, hiding stolen sweets. We roamed the park's wild and secret places and made them our own. I loved the park, felt it to be mine. I liked nothing better than to sit very still and take in all the sounds; the drone of a lone bee, a chiff-chaff's twitter or a robin's cheery song. The sounds soothed, helped me find my happy place. I would have given anything to curl up in a feathered nest, close my eyes and make it all go away. I once decided that if things got too bad at home, the park would be the place to run away to. Was it time for that now? I needed to think, try and work out what just happened.

There was an old shelter in the forgotten part of the park where rhododendrons grew rampant with towers of green leaves and pink flowers. Bog grass pushed its way through the muddy patches amidst moss and dank puddles. The park keepers rarely appeared except to empty their grass cuttings on the fetid compost heaps.

I distracted myself looking for stag beetles. Me and Patsy had come across one once. It looked vicious with its horns, pincers and black armour. Patsy squealed when she first saw it. She leapt some four feet in the air like a giant human frog. Registering Patsy's fear, I screamed too. We must have shrieked for all of a minute until we realised how daft we looked. Then we fell about doubled up with laughter, tears streaming down our cheeks until Patsy sprang to her feet.

'Where is it? I'm going to stamp on it!'

'No Patsy! Don't. Leave it be!' I stood defiantly between the beetle and Patsy. I couldn't bear to see it harmed. We stared at each other with that I'm not backing down look in our eye, each wondering what was going to happen next.

'It'll probably bite us and then it'll be all your fault,' sulked Patsy kicking at a tuft of grass.

I let out a long breath. Then I squatted down to inspect the creature at close quarters, my heart still hammering in my chest. I feigned fascination in the beetle. Gently I prodded it with a twig and watched as it reared up on its hind legs ready to settle scores. Then, fascinated genuinely, I poked it some more for good measure.

I thought of that beetle now and it put me in mind of my own situation. 'Poor thing, I'm sorry we did that to you.'

Several hours passed before the daylight began to fade. I wondered whether to go home. Would it be safe? Perhaps the school hadn't been able to get hold of my mum before it closed for the day.

Maybe I should go home and try and put my point across before the school did? But how to tell mum that everyone thinks she's a looney? That would surely send her off the deep end. I just couldn't make my mind up.

Eventually hunger drew me out of the park. As I cut through the flats heading for the fence, Patsy appeared.

'You're in so much trouble. Your mum's been round looking for you.'

I felt sheepish. I went to speak but thought better of it.

'Frankie, what did you do?'

'Did you not see? Weren't you in assembly?'

'No, I didn't fancy school today.'

'Oh Patsy,' I hunched my shoulders as though trying to make myself small. 'Mum's going to kill me.' My voice trembled. 'Maddy Bloom and Grace Gifford started to have a go at me during school assembly. They said my Mum was a nutter ... in front of everyone...'

She stepped up to put an arm around me and smiling said, 'Well, she is a nutter.'

'But I don't want everyone knowing.'

'So ...?'

'So, I bashed them.'

'Eh?'

'Right in the middle of the whole school assembly. I kind of went berserk.'

'Bloody hell! This calls for a ciggy.' She disappeared into the dark of the bin cupboard, I could hear her rummaging about in the back.

'Keep the door open Frankie,' she hissed. 'I need to see what I'm doing.'

I carried on talking oblivious to the fact that Patsy - too busy searching for the half cigarette she had hidden at the back of the cupboard, wasn't listening.

'Aha, here it is.' She reappeared out of the dark, lit the stinking butt, took a drag and handed it to me. It was strong and burned the back of my throat. I thought of the hole in the nylon carpet, how I'd been grounded for a month and how I coughed til my eyes smarted and my lungs hurt.

'The teachers had to pull me off,' I continued. 'Look at the state of my blazer.' I showed her the torn pocket and missing buttons.

'Bloody hell. You did go mental,' she raised her eyebrows, looking suitably impressed.

'The deputy was going to cane me for not apologising ...'

'Did it hurt?'

'No, I told her to fuck off, then ran out of school before she could cane me.'

'No! Really?'

I pursed my lips and continued.

'She followed me, but she couldn't jump the fence.'

'The big fence? You mean the one at the end of the field?'

I nodded. 'Was my mum really angry then?'

A door on the top landing of the flats opened and a figure leaned out. 'Patsy, who are you talking to? If it's Frankie, tell her to go home this instant.'

Mum was waiting for me in the kitchen. Propped up against the worktop, she sat facing the backdoor with an ashtray full of spent cigarettes in front of her. I sloped in, head down, chin virtually touching my chest and waited. She lunged towards me.

'There you are you little shit!' and grabbing me by the collar she whacked me hard across the head.

'Where've you been? I've been worried sick.'

Reeling, I watched, as if in slow motion, as she arched her hand back to slap me a second time. I heard the resounding thwack first before registering the blow. Its bloom grew hotter as my face smarted. I didn't move; giving myself up to whatever was to come.

'I've had the school phoning me at work, saying that you've absconded, and you're suspended. What have you got to say for yourself young lady?'

I stood, my hands hanging limply, eyes downcast.

'Cat got your tongue?'

I shook my head, tasting blood inside my mouth and wincing as she seized my hair pulling it back hard to show my tipped back face. She ranted and raved until the spittle at the side of her mouth looked like foam. Her eyes wild as if something had pulled her eyelids up and back too far. Blows rained down until my knees weakened and finally gave way. All self-control lost, Mum hauled me back up ready to start again but stopped, mid-sentence, mid-motion, like a freight train slamming on the brakes. She moved in close and sniffed my hair. 'You've been smoking?'

I barely nodded and cringed, trying to pull away. I watched her stiffen. The words forming in her mouth as if in slow motion.

'You need to be taught a lesson.' She moved across the kitchen floor and lit the hob I heard the gas hiss before the fierce flames erupted.

'Come here. Give me your hand.'

'No,'

My heart hammered in my chest fear settled on my lips as they readied to stretch into a wail. My whole body was trembling.

'Give me your hand this instant.'

'No, mum, please!'

A struggle ensued. I was no match. My screams were full and shrill as she dragged me across the floor to the cooker prized my hand up and held it over the scorching flame.

My cries and mum's shouts mingled with the searing pain. Then I sensed a movement - something or someone at the back door.

'Diane. No. Stop.' Dad charged in and attempted to separate us but mum held fast, shrieking.

'She's an insolent little bitch and needs to be taught a lesson.'

'Stop. Diane. She's just a child. Diane, let go.' Exerting more force, he prized her hands off me and put his body between us.

'Frankie, are you alright? Let me see.'

White, fierce pain pulsed through me, I recoiled, unable to make a sound. He pulled me to the sink and ran cold water over my scorched hand. It hurt like a thousand red hot needles. 'Hold still Frankie.'

Mum was still raging only her attention had switched to dad, calling him all the names under the sun.

'Go upstairs and keep your door shut. It's over now,' dad ushered me out of the kitchen keeping a wary eye on mum.

From my room I listened to the muffled voices raised in anger. The fighting rumbled on for an age until finally I drifted off to a half-sleep, peppered with tears and pain.

Later that night I awoke to find Dad stooped over me. I tried to prop myself up as I whispered in the darkness. 'I'm glad you came home Dad.'

'Me too. Let me see your hand.' Blisters had formed, standing proud on my palm, the skin taut and red. 'Now, keep still. This is going to hurt a bit.' Gently he took my hand and applied castor oil to the wound, I wept softly at his touch.

'Frankie, what happened? I got a call at work from the school to say that you attacked some pupils and swore at a teacher before running away. Is this right?'

'Dad.' I sobbed, gulping down breaths. 'I'm sorry. I didn't mean it. It wasn't my fault.'

'Then tell me, what happened. It's okay. I'll not be cross.'

'Those girls I hit. They were mocking me, saying horrible things about mum. They said she's a nutter.'

'Frankie, haven't we talked about sticks and stones ...'

'Yes, but Dad. They started poking me and going on and on 'til my head was about bursting.'

'So, you were provoked.'

I nodded my face was streaked with tears. I cried about being made to stand out. I cried because my hand hurt. I cried because I felt ashamed. But mostly I cried because that's all I had left. Tears.

The next morning, I arrived downstairs to find pancakes on the table, radio one playing a jolly tune and the kitchen looking spic and span. Dad's eyes looked heavy and swollen, like he had hardly slept but he had a smile for me.

'How's the hand?'

'It still hurts,'

I lifted it to inspect the raised bubbles on my skin and wondered whether it would be a good idea to pop them.

'It's hard getting dressed with just one hand. I need help with my tie.'

'There's no point. You're not going to school today.'

'Oh,' I dragged my chair with my good hand up to the table. Tucking into my pancake I tentatively ventured, 'Then can we go and see Nanny?' Dad looked at me briefly before loading up his fork. 'We'll see.'

I watched dad's jaw, noting the muscles bulge at the side of his head every time he closed his mouth. When he was angry, the same muscles stood out. We sat and ate in silence. When he had finished mopping up his sugar and lemon pancake, he lifted his plate and rose from the table. Then paused, as though struck by an afterthought, 'Frankie, about yesterday evening... best you don't mention it to anyone, you understand.'

I bit my lip. My tight little 'I'm okay' smile faded, giving way to a quivering chin and misty eyes. I felt the blood pooling on my lip where I bit too hard. Dropping my fork, I stood up at the table. 'Why do I have to keep quiet?' My good hand was balled into a fist, but my voice came out like a gust of wind. 'Why do we have to act like everything is normal when it isn't?'

He reached out to stay my exit.

'Frankie!' he said softly. 'Don't take on so. You know your mother loves you. She didn't mean it. It's because she's been ill.'

'Why are you on her side?'

'Listen, you're too young to understand but your mum has had a rough time.'

I didn't hear. I didn't want to listen to any of it anymore. 'It's not fair. Can't I come and live with you?'

There was a long thin pause. I looked at him, desperate, trapped.

'Now Frankie, you know that isn't possible.'

'Then can I go back to Nanny?' I was half wailing half sobbing.

'No. Now be a good girl, just sit down and be quiet. This will all soon blow over I promise.'

I slumped on my chair. 'Now I know how Cinderella felt,' I muttered wiping my eyes with the back of my hand.

'That's enough of that! Now, I want you to write an apology to the teacher you were rude to. If you can do that, I might have a surprise for you.'

I knew it was pointless complaining. So, I took a leaf of Basildon Bond from the kitchen drawer and carefully wrote my letter.

Dear Mrs Malone,

I'm sorry for swearing and running away. You can cane me if you like but please wait until my hand is better.

Frankie Miller

Richard: May 1972

The phone rang in the hall. I wasn't in a great hurry to answer it. I hated phones at the best of times but answered it all the same.

'Hello,'

'Richard, Sophie said you were home. 'You alright?'

'Not really, it's a bloody car crash. Six days in and I'm still fire fighting.'

'Sounds serious, what's up?'

'Frankie got herself suspended from school and you can imagine how Diane took it. She totally over reacted.'

'What happened?'

'It's a mess. If I hadn't have got here when I did there's no telling…'

'Rich, No telling what?'

'When the school called, I knew it would cause a problem, so I dropped everything and came home. I got in to find Diane holding Frankie's hand over the gas hob.'

'Dear God!'

'Frankie's hand was blistered but it looks like its healing okay.'

'Rich, Do you think she's safe with Diane?'

'Frankie was shaken to start with but seems to have bounced back. She always does. Diane? I don't know, Simon. It all seems fine now.'

'Have you spoken with Diane about it, made her think about the consequences?'

'I may as well stick my head in a hornet's nest, you know what she's like. So no, I haven't but I have been considering all the other options.'

'Yes, well, it could have been a damned sight worse. However, ...'

'If she had any idea of what I've been thinking ... The result could be catastrophic for all of us. Yes, she has been quite volatile; that bloody temper of hers. I'm hoping it's a one-off, she's never over-reacted like this before. Frankie did provoke her, granted it was unintentional. It's still early days from, you know ...'

'The important thing here Richard is Frankie.'

'I don't think Diane meant to hurt her. It was more about teaching her a lesson. Whether Diane's stable, that's another thing. If I take it to the authorities you know what will happen, Frankie will go into Care and Diane will end up ... She'll end up back in that hell hole again'

'Have you considered moving back?'

'I've gone over and over in my mind but it's not an option. I'd end up out of work, no money for the bills or the mortgage - and me being here; it would end up in carnage. It's bad enough just for a weekend. I'll just have to keep a close eye on the situation. But for the now, I'm getting things sorted. The first priority is Frankie's school. Some kids were taunting her about Diane, and she attacked them.'

'Good for her.'

'This is serious Simon. It's been hard for her too.'

'Just think carefully about what you're doing. You know where I am if needs be.'

'Thanks Simon.'

'Anytime.'

.oOo.

The meeting with the headmaster went better than expected. I learned that up until her outburst Frankie had been a model pupil and that her actions were considered very much out of character. When asked if anything significant was going on at home I skimmed over the details:

'Yes, well. There had been some difficulties, but they've been resolved. Nothing to worry about.'

Seizing the opportunity, I turned the focus on the bullying, saying that this was the most likely reason why Frankie had overreacted. Catching the headmaster on the back foot I asked more pressing questions about why the bullies had not been reprimanded and why no one had picked up on this.

For the rest of the week, I occupied myself by attending to outstanding jobs in the house and having finished those, turned my attentions to the garden. It looked very much out of sorts. The grass needed cutting, the edges trimmed and the borders weeding but they were simple jobs and easily achieved. The only pleasing thing the garden had going for it was the cherry tree. It was in blossom and every now and then a glorious flurry of pink petals danced across the garden, brightening up the dark corners, reminding me of the cycle of life. As I worked, thoughts of how to tackle my family situation turned over in my mind. The image of my wife at the stove with Frankie made me drive the spade in deep. It broke at the hilt.

'Damn it.'

Panting, I picked up the broken pieces lying in the dirt. The spade had been in my keep for a long time. I'd kept it for sentimental reasons. It was my Grandpa Killick's. A reminder of how hands had long ago smoothed the rough wooden handle now ingrained and mingled with our sweat - but now the spade was well past its best and needed replaced.

Ah, the summers spent on Grandpa's allotment, chasing cabbage butterflies, eating peas out of the pod and raspberries off the cane. I liked nothing better than having a brew with Grandpa in his shed. Tea in a dented metal cup, one sugar and stirred with an old bent fork.

'The family silver' he would jest with a wink, smidgens of dirt smudged in his laughter lines.

Nothing else ever tasted so good. After tea I would read my comic while Grandpa studied the racing page and would fall asleep with the paper over his face. It was a happy silence built on contentment and affable comfort.

And afterwards, after the hours spent working the rich brown earth, teasing seedlings with fingernails black with toil, feeling the sun beating down on the back of our heads, the gardening tools were carefully cleaned and sharpened, especially the spade. Grandpa kept an old bucket in the corner of the shed. It was full of coarse sand and a drop of oil.

'You 'as to make right sure that you cleans the mud and grime off, son. Then work that spade in the bucket. Your spade will never know rust if you looks after it. You mind my words.'

I smiled at the memory and the sound of Grandpa's rich gravelly voice. I looked at the rusted spade with its woodworm at the handle. It was too far gone to repair now. Time to buy a new one. I took Frankie with me to Strait's Nursery rather than leave her in the house unattended. The last thing I wanted to do was impose her on the neighbours or give anyone any opportunity to ask questions.

The nursery was several miles out of town, out on the country roads. As we approached, we passed a sign written in bold handwriting.

'Free puppies. Enquire within.'

Frankie spotted it first. Straining in her seat to look back, she said, 'Dad, look, puppies. Can we have a puppy? Please. I'll look after it. I could train it to guard the house and keep us all safe too.'

'Hmm,' I lit up a cigarette, one hand on the driving wheel. The words 'keep us safe' struck a chord. 'I'll think about it.'

My mind sifting. A dog for Frankie, would it protect her? Would it fill the hole that Danny left? Do we need this right now, something else in the household to distract us? What about Diane? She loves dogs but would she, could she, love this one enough? Can we afford it? Who would care for it …?

'Please Dad. Please.' Frankie chirped on and on. She even came up with a couple of names. In her mind's eye the puppy was already installed in the house.

We went into the Nursery, but as I considered the various types of spades on display my mind was turning over whether to take on a puppy. *What would Diane think? Would she quash the idea and cause a scene? She hates surprises. But there again she might actually find the dog a comfort; she loves dogs. Would Frankie be able to cope with looking after a dog? The bulk of the caring would fall on her shoulders.* Making the decision was hard, but as I paid for my chosen spade at the checkout, I made up my mind. Having a dog was not a good idea.

Swinging out the car park and onto the road I clocked Frankie's innocent face brighten. I realised I hadn't seen her smile unguarded in an age. This smile showed her dimples. It banished that haunted look behind her eyes. As I drove past the 'Free puppies' sign, Frankie visibly shrank in her seat. I couldn't bear it and so made a U-turn in the road.

As we waited for someone to answer the door Frankie could hardly contain herself; she danced on the spot with excitement. From deep within came the sound of barking. A woman wearing a matching set of pearl earrings and necklace answered the door. She looked down at Frankie with a smile. 'Are you looking for a puppy?'

'Oh yes, please.' Frankie's eyes shone like they did when she won on the slot machine in the arcade at Weston Super Mare Pier a couple of summers ago.

'We've just come to look.' I hesitated, wondering if the puppies might be some enormous breed that we wouldn't be able to accommodate or afford.

'Come on in. Now, I've only got one left. He's the runt of the litter I'm afraid.' She led us along the hallway and into a bright warm kitchen. Over in the corner the mother and her pup lay in a large wicker basket. The room was suffused with the smell of puppy, all milk, pee and warm blanket. Wagging its tail ten to the dozen the puppy looked up and clumsily jumped out of the basket to land spread-eagled on the wooden floor. Frankie gasped out loud.

'Oh, he's beautiful. Look he's all fluffy.'

'What breed is it?'

'It's a mongrel, he's ten weeks old. Next door's dog got to ours. She's a Jack Russell and he's a Collie, they're both very biddable.'

Frankie was already sitting on the floor with the puppy in her lap. They looked like old friends reunited. He was jumping up, trying to lick her face which made her giggle. Two bundles of joy. Frankie stole a look up at me; her expression said it all.

'Oh, alright then,' I turned to the woman. 'Can we take him now?'

'Of course. He's been wormed already.'

We stayed for a little while so I could get some details. Frankie studied her new dog, from the colour of its wet nose, black, to the size and smell of its paws. She stroked the swell of his pink warm belly laughing aloud when his leg jerked at the tickle. But most of all she loved his fluffy mix of colours: black, brown, with a distinctive white flash on its chest and those three unforgettable white socks.

On the journey home Frankie sat cuddling the puppy.

'Dad, I'm going to call him Bonzo.'

'Why?'

'Coz he's just done a doo-dah in my lap!'

We looked at each other and smiled; it was an overt reminder of our last holiday, then we both spontaneously burst into song. 'In *the canyons of your mind … to the holes in your string vest.'*

Diane: May 1972

I clamped the phone to my ear, holding on to the mouthpiece. It was hard to keep the shock out of my voice. 'I beg your pardon?' The typists stopped and looked in my direction, I turned my back, and whispered, 'She's done what?' The voice on the other end explained that Frankie had attacked some pupils and fled from the school.

I had been playing things down, being calm and collected. Acting normal, being normal. But the call from the school threw me. It was the last thing I'd expected. I reached for my glass of water, trembling, hand on heart as I drank. I just couldn't think straight. My head went all jangly. All the office girls were looking at me. I could feel them watching my every move. It felt invasive and the more I was aware of this the more I fell apart. They began to close around me.

'Everything alright, Diane?'
'Do you need to leave early?'
'You're looking a bit peaky!'
'Shall we go and tell Bill?'

Panic rose, words cracked in my mouth making broken sounds, lost consonants and vowels jumbled and tumbling, my fluttering hands reached for my neck as my breath came in ragged and snatched. It took all I had not to scream and push them away. I made a sharp exit to the kitchen for a cigarette.

I knew that they knew that I *suffered from my nerves* but it didn't make me sub-human. Would I always be labelled this way even though I've been deemed better? They looked at me like I was some freak show, fuel for their gossip, sidelong looks and then exchanging glances. There were no allowances for being vulnerable or broken and I wouldn't, no couldn't, allow it for myself.

My glass had a fault, there was a line, a crack that ran the tighter I held it. Suddenly there was water and broken shards everywhere, blood, rich and red trickled down my wrist. I stood there feeling exposed and stupid. Shame washed over me all over again.

It was like when I went back to work. They were being so pleasant it was sickening. I knew they'd been told to be nice, but it was never anything more than that. None of them wanted to be around me. I never got invited out to lunch or birthday occasions. I saw them all one lunchtime piling out of the Chinese restaurant laughing, cards and balloons in tow.

I was the object of their tittle-tattle. My big scandal wasn't kept within the confines of the office, it was so new, so raw it was ripe for distribution. Lord knows who they shared it with. It added to my constant sense of humiliation. The woman at the grocer's whom I'd known for years, suddenly started reacting to me differently - like she felt obliged to talk to me but didn't really want to. Then one day she came out and said it.

'Are you better now?'

It didn't seem like a question though, more like she was mocking me. I gave her a withering look.

'What gave you the impression that I've been ill?'

She recoiled as though trying to gather in her words, feigning preoccupation with weighing the potatoes, the scales tipping back and forth as she dropped them in. 'Oh, I must have been mistaken. It was something one of your colleagues said.'

I drew myself up, 'For your information I'm perfectly fine. On second thoughts I'll not need the potatoes after all.' I turned and stalked out - inside I wanted to run, run as fast and as far away as possible. I was outraged, I felt as though I'd been defiled, judged, when there was nothing, absolutely nothing I could do about it.

Would I always be viewed like this? Then it struck me, what would be so wrong in saying, 'Yes, I've had a breakdown but I'm alright now?' What was it that everyone was so afraid of? I don't believe we can all be utterly perfect. I'd not gone back there since, even going so far as walking the twenty-minute detour, so I didn't have to pass the bloody shop.

So, when I got home to find that Frankie wasn't there it made me even more anxious. I imagined scenarios of calling the police, getting them to go and look for her; Social Work getting involved, the neighbours gossiping, their curtains twitching; all converged in my head; a hotchpotch of horrible images.

Would they see me as a bad mother because I'd had a nervous breakdown? Probably. Of course, I would be blamed, after all I was the one that had been broken, the one that had the cracks. The one people considered would never be normal like them, not after … but they never named it, not to my face at any rate.

I started to worry, all these thoughts, would they make me sick again? I didn't quite know what to do or who to turn to. I didn't want to bother Mum as she hadn't been well. The last thing I wanted was to bring more trouble to her door. Besides, she'd probably cast this up at me at some point. I needed to show I was capable of managing things for myself.

Richard - I'd telephoned him, but when was he ever any use?

Desperate, I went round to Gill's, knowing that Patsy and Frankie were like each other's shadows, joined at the hip. I'd never met Gill before, just exchanged notes to do with the girls.

'Please can you make sure Frankie gets home for 8pm' or 'Frankie has misplaced her jacket can you check to see if it's with you? Thank you.'

Neither Gill nor Patsy had seen Frankie. Gill was kind. She invited me into their sparse flat for a cup of tea. Noting I was on the brink of tears she gave me a warm hug.

'Don't fret Diane, Frankie will be back in her own good time. If she turns up here, I'll be sure and send her straight round to you.'

There was something about her that made me think that she understood. It wasn't just Frankie going missing - there was something more to it than that. I saw the Valium on the shelf where she kept the tea caddy. Had she been struggling like me? I wanted to ask but wasn't brave enough to broach the subject. Besides, Frankie was uppermost in my mind.

When Frankie finally came home, I was both relieved and angry. Angry at her for attacking someone, for swearing and running away and bloody furious that she had got herself suspended. What on earth was she thinking? And as if that wasn't enough, she'd taken off and failed to come home when she should. She pushed me to the edge, she knew my delicate state and still behaved so. As time passed my anxiety and anger increased. I trailed cigarette smoke around the house as I paced, tipping the blinds to look up and down the road. Nine o'clock was the deadline, if she didn't show by then I was calling the police. At five to nine she appeared through the back door bringing a flurry of cherry blossom in with her.

She sloped in - looking nervous and furtive, her head tilted to one side, the same slope of her shoulders, pursing her lips, fiddling with her fingers just like her father. It reminded of the way he sneaked about. She's her father's daughter alright, definitely a Miller. Nothing like my Danny.

I know I shouldn't have compared the two, but I just couldn't help myself. If it wasn't for her, I wouldn't be in the mess I was in. Married to someone I didn't love and tied to a drudgery of a life. So, I flipped. Next thing I knew I was striking out. The more I hit her the more she didn't say or do anything. She just looked at me through those cold almond eyes like I was pathetic - again, just like her father. This irked me so I rained more blows until she curled up into a ball.

Maybe I did go too far - but she needed to be taught a lesson. If I let it go at this stage where would she end up? 'Spare the rod and spoil the child.' She had been overly indulged of late. That little stint away with Vera Jackson, she came back with all kinds of silly ideas. Everyone tiptoeing around her because she'd lost a brother - but she never even mentioned him. Never asked what happened. All tight lipped and judging from behind those innocent little eyes.

And there we were, a week on and Richard had gone and bought her a puppy. Rewarding her for her bad behaviour - stupid man. Now I had something else to worry about. Puppies require a lot of time. Training, feeding, walking and then there's the vet's fees and I doubted he'd be about to put his hand in his pocket when it counted.

Bonzo. I ask you. Such an idiotic name for a dog. Mind you, looking at it, it does look like it's a Bonzo. It looked like it had been through a hedge backwards and if the paws were anything to go by it was probably going to end up the size of a retriever.

I reached down to pet him. My hand finding his head, smoothing the fur on his crown, feeling his silky ears. He sat perfectly still, lapping up all the attention. When I took my hand away, he looked up at me with his big doleful brown eyes and produced a couple of squeaky barks. He assumed the play position, front paws flat to the floor, back end up, tail wagging before scampering round in small circles.

I tried to ignore him, but my efforts were in vain. 'You're a beguiling little creature I'll give you that. But what to do with you during the day? Maybe I'll ask Bill if I can bring you into work.' Looking down again this time I saw Bonzo tugging at my shoelaces, tail wagging. I couldn't help but smile then I hauled him onto my lap.

'What are you after you cheeky thing?'

Bonzo cocked his head to one side then reared up onto his hind legs in an attempt to lick me, snuffling his little black nose into my neck and biting my earrings. I couldn't help myself and closed my arms around him. Despite my futile attempts to resist, I was falling in love.

Frankie: End of May 1972

I strolled through the school gates, head up and purposeful as if I didn't have a care in the world. I was good at giving off the wrong impression. In my coat pocket my fingers gripped onto my lucky stone following its smooth edges and curves. Several classmates eyed me from a distance, some nudged each other, whispering from behind their hands.

'Frankie's back!'

My head was a tumult of thoughts. I didn't want to go back to school. Didn't want to face the stares, the judgements or the inevitable telling off. But mostly I didn't want to leave Bonzo. Dad had made me solemnly promise to go back to school and not get into trouble; keeping Bonzo was part of the deal. Mum seemed less than pleased with his arrival so I was worried he wouldn't be there when I got home after school. I prayed that he wouldn't make a mess, but a day is a long time without going for a wee. I pondered whether to go home during the lunch hour to let him out - but that meant not staying in school all day which would have meant breaking my promise to dad

Making my way along the corridor to the headmaster's office, I knocked on the door and waited.

'Wait there,' boomed a voice from within. I tried not to slouch so I adjusted my socks, my tie, my newly repaired blazer jacket.

When the school bell rang, I jumped even though I should have expected it. Within a minute, scores of children filled the corridors, chattering, laughing, pushing shoving, eager to get to their registration rooms. After ten minutes the clamour had died to a hush, just the odd late child hurrying along the corridor.

I was left with nothing to do but study the school trophies locked away in a glass cabinet. I wondered who got the rotten job of having to clean them. It reminded me of Nanny - her monthly ritual of sitting at the Formica table in her kitchen, rubber gloved, polishing her dear departed husband's old dart's trophies with Brasso. I thought of the horrible smell the Brasso made, how it made my teeth go on edge, how the gloopy fluid took off the tarnish and made the cloth go black.

At the centre of the school trophy cabinet, in pride of place, stood an inordinately large silver cup. The engraving on it read, 'County Running Cup, awarded to ...' I pressed my face close up to the glass, squinting my eyes to try and read the name. No matter how hard I tried, angling my head this way and that, I couldn't quite make it out. I didn't notice Mrs Eames, the games teacher, sidle up beside me.

'It's Sarah Freeman,' she ventured, nodding at the cup.

'What?' I swung round to face her.

'The name on the County Cup is Sarah Freeman. She won it ten years ago. Went on to compete in the Commonwealth Games and came in third.'

'How did she get to the Commonwealth Games?'

'With a lot of hard work and dedicated training.'

I furrowed my brow considering what Mrs Eames was saying.

'You mean someone from *here* made it as a famous runner?'

'Something like that and I think you could do something similar if you put your mind to it, Frankie. Don't think it hasn't gone unnoticed.'

I couldn't help but let my mouth fall open as I looked up at Mrs Eames. I looked at the cup and then back at her. 'Really?'

'Why not? I saw you cover the field and clear the fence the other week. Pretty impressive.' Her wink was almost imperceptible, but her smile was open enough.

I looked down to hide my smile, my face pinking, 'Oh.'

Barely had the thought lodged there when the headmaster's door swung open and was framed by a tall figure. 'Miller, this way please.' He put his pocket watch back in his waistcoat pocket and turned on his heel and walked back into the room.

Mrs Eames patted me on my shoulder. 'His bark's worse than his bite. Come and see me some time, Frankie, if you'd like to talk more about running.'

I shuffled into the office my hands stuffed deep into my school blazer searching for my lucky stone.

'Take a seat.'

Obediently I sat on the chair positioned before the headmaster's desk. I felt dwarfed by its size. My chin barely reached its flat surface, I could just about see the headmaster staring down at me like one of those imposing statues in Montpellier Park. He sat back in his chair steepling his long tapering fingers.

'Frankie, we have decided to give you a second chance.'

I sat there wanting to fidget but said nothing.

'Your father has vouched for you and told us that you were provoked. But outbursts of temper and bad behaviour will not be tolerated in future. Do you understand?'

Trembling, I nodded

'In future you don't take the law into your own hands and any reprimands are left up to the teachers. Now, do you have anything to say for yourself?'

In a faltering voice I spoke, 'I'm very sorry Sir.'

'Good. Now don't let me see you in here again.'

I charged out of his office dodging a group of Fifth Years in my path. My footsteps thundered along the corridor and up one flight of stairs to Room 15, I burst through the door, breathless, to find the class already seated and settled. The teacher stopped talking. Heads turned in my direction.

'Sorry I'm late,' I mumbled, my cheeks flushing.

'Alright class, nothing to look at. Miller take a seat and be quick about it.'

I picked out an empty desk towards the back of the room and threw my bag down. Whispers flew. Julie and Karen sat glowering at me. *Just ignore them* I thought. I kept my head facing forwards. As I opened my workbook the blonde-haired girl sitting beside me gave a slight, almost imperceptible, nudge and passed a note. It read:

'*You dun great bashing Julie and Karen. Loads of us have wanted to do that.*' It was finished with a smiley face. When I looked sidelong at my blonde-haired companion, I caught the hint of a smile, then casting my eye around the class, I saw other girls smiling and inclining their heads.

I started to think that school wasn't going to be so bad after all, and suddenly I found I was able to inhale deep breaths.

I ran the whole way home after school. I didn't stop at the flats to see Patsy. My mind was fixed on one thing. Fumbling with the key in the lock I pushed open the door, heart pounding. The house was quiet.

'Bonzo! I'm home.' I rushed through into the living room where I'd left him that morning. He was not there. His bed was still in place, but his bowls were gone. Frantic, I ran into the hallway to look for his lead. Nothing, just an empty space.

I doubled over with my arms around myself I began to whimper, 'Please, no. Not Bonzo, not my dog.' I lay on the floor and cried until all my tears were spent, I vowed never to forgive my mother. Never!

The sound of mum's car pulling into the drive made me get to my feet. Taking the stairs two at a time I went to my room and slammed the door shut. As the key turned in the lock, I curled myself up tight.

'Frankie? Frankie, are you home?' I could hear her voice from the foot of the stairs. I didn't answer even when I heard the footsteps coming up the stairs and then my bedroom door was opened. I lay as still as possible.

Go away. Just go away. You can burn me, hit me, shout at me do what you like. I don't care anymore. I thought to myself but I knew better than to say it out loud.

Mum sat beside me on the bed. I could sense her looking at me.

'Frankie, is something wrong?' I closed my eyes tighter and held my breath.

'I've got someone here to see you. Look.' I sensed a slight movement, then felt a wet nose burying itself in my face.

I opened my eyes and sat up. 'Bonzo!' I folded him in my arms and felt the warmth of his little body. I whispered into the softness of his fur and kissed the top of his head.

Mum looked on smiling. She was quite calm. 'Did you think something had happened to him?'

Still cuddling Bonzo, I nodded my head and a single tear slipped down my face.

'Silly sausage, I brought him to work with me. He slept most of the day in my office drawer. Good as gold weren't you Bonzo?' Mum reached out to tickle him behind his ears. 'Now, he's going to need a little walk. Do you think you could see to that?'

I sprang up, Bonzo at my heels and raced downstairs to find his lead. I clipped it on and danced out of the front door.

Turning into the flats I lead Bonzo up to Patsy's front door and rang the bell. Patsy's feet thundered down the stairs, her wiry frame appeared in the door's glass panel. She opened the door sporting a new David Bowie haircut. 'Ta daaa.' She twirled for dramatic effect. 'What do you think?' Then the puppy caught her eye. 'Oh, he's adorable. Is he all yours?'

'Yes.'

'What's his name?'

'Bonzo.'

'Can I hold him?'

'Yeah sure, here.' I loaded Bonzo into Patsy's arms. 'I love your hair. Did you do it?'

Patsy was taken with Bonzo nipping her ears. 'No, it was my aunty. I could do you if you want?'

'Really? I'd love that. I didn't know you could cut hair.'

'I'm just learning.'

'Fancy coming for a walk?'

'I'd love to but we're just about to have tea. Tomorrow maybe.' She went to hand Bonzo back and stopped. 'What did you do to your hand?'

I stuffed it into my pocket. 'Oh that. Nothing much.'

'Frankie? Let me see! Frankie!'

I don't want to show her. I turned to leave. 'I have to go.'

'No Frankie, tell me,' she grabbed hold of my arm. I tried to resist but she held on.

'It was my mum.'

'Your mum!'

Patsy looked at me in disbelief. 'Your mum? Why would she do something like that?'

Even if I'd kicked her, she couldn't have looked more shocked. I shrugged.

'Liar. Mum's don't do that to their kids.'

For a millisecond I thought about protesting but I knew it wouldn't get me anywhere. *What's the point?* I thought. I shrugged, half smiling, and raised my chin up. 'Yeah, you're right. I was just kidding. I picked up the kettle when it was hot, didn't I, Bonzo?' I ruffled his ears with my good hand. 'Right, got to go.'

'God, you are such a weirdo sometimes'

'Tomorrow then.'

I took Bonzo down to the park. It was quiet. Everyone was probably having their tea. I led Bonzo down to my favourite spot, the big black pipe that stretches across from one side of the brook to the other. I took my shoes and socks off and let my bare feet feel the cool grass. I closed my eyes and listened to the brook's chuckle, to the wind moving through the trees, to the sound of Bonzo's steady panting. I felt stilled for a moment but in the back of my mind Patsy's words jarred at me, 'Mums don't do that to their kids.'

Some Mums do. Mine did, I thought conjuring up the image of my Mum. I went through the sequence of events frame by frame.

For the first time in a long time Mum was in a good mood. She hadn't called me 'sausage' since I was little. No, wait a minute, that's the name she kept for Danny. Was she pleased to see me? I'm not sure, her happiness is all for Bonzo. All she wanted was for me to take him out.

The only good thing was that Mum took Bonzo into work and came home in a good mood. That has to mean that she likes him; that he's going to stay? God, I'd love to ask ... but can't ... she's so quick to change her mind. I'll keep my head down like Dad says and not say anything, it's the best way.

Anything to keep Bonzo, even if it means he becomes Mum's dog. I can share. That's okay.

'You love everyone don't you Bonzo? No matter what!'

He thumped his tail on the ground.

Richard: June 1972

I was apprehensive when I pulled into the driveway that weekend, my legs felt wooden as I moved to get out of the car and hoovered with my keys in the front door lock. I didn't know what I'd find. Throughout the week I'd been wondering how things were going at home especially with the dog. I did try calling a couple of times but never got a reply; if I called her at the office to check in, she'd get mad with me. Getting the balance right between calling too early, (tea-time) or too late, (bedtime) was difficult to gauge. I thought it possible that every time I called they might have been out with the dog. It was hard to say. In the end I figured to just leave it be, I'd hear soon enough if something had gone wrong.

Standing on the doorstep I registered two things: the light of the television flickering in the front room and a vase of flowers in the windowsill. It looked like any household. As I went through the door, I heard a bark; a distinct, 'on alert' bark. The door to the living room opened and out rushed Bonzo, paws pattering across the lino tail wagging.

Frankie followed hot on his heels with a cheery, 'Hi Dad! Look what Bonzo can do.'

I struggled to get across the threshold with Frankie and a dancing dog blocking my way. In just a week Bonzo had grown upwards and outwards. He had more of a Collie look about his frame, but the shape of the head was unmistakably Jack Russell. A mix of His Masters Voice and Lassie, I chuckled at the thought and ruffled Bonzo's head.

'Yes, in a second, give me a chance to get settled in.' Deftly I high stepped over Bonzo, 'Tell you what, put the kettle on for me while I sort this lot out.'

I hung my coat in the hallway then scuttled up the stairs with my things. By the time I came back down the kettle was whistling on the stove and Frankie busy warming the teapot. Popping my head round the front room door I saw Diane curled up on the sofa, dozing. It was the most relaxed I'd seen her in a long while.

'Dad?'

'Yes, coming,' I went and sat on the only seat in the kitchen, it doubled up as a laundry basket for items that required hand washing and was situated at the side of the kitchen cabinet. Frankie handed me a hot mug.

'Ah, tea.' I threaded my fingers through the handle and took a long slurp.

'Thanks pet.' I slumped against the kitchen cabinet and gave my daughter my wearied attention.

'Now can I show you?' Frankie's face was lit up, she held her hands behind her back, pausing for effect.

'Go on then.'

She held her biscuit-filled hand high in the air and put Bonzo through his paces from sitting, to waiting and giving a paw. When he'd finished and having gobbled down the requisite rewards Bonzo dodged back into the living room to Diane.

'How's your week been?'

'S'alright.'

'And your Mum, has she been okay?'

'Yeah, good. We've been taking Bonzo out for walks and Mum's been taking him to work. He sleeps in her desk drawer at the moment, but Mum says he's going to be too big soon.'

I found it amusing. 'So, do you think Bonzo has Mum's approval then?'

Frankie gave an enthusiastic nod. 'Looks like it.'

There was something different about the house, something subtle that I couldn't quite put my finger on. Admittedly, it looked tidier: all the things in the kitchen put away, nothing sitting on the drainer and no rubbish spilling over the bin. Even the floor has been mopped. For a moment I wondered whether my mother-in-law has been for a visit but then I remembered she had had a hip operation only the other week.

It struck me that the house felt calmer - I didn't sense the usual tension; Frankie on edge, Diane hiding away upstairs listening to the radio. Can a dog be responsible for all this? Diane had been civil since I got in, that was a first, and Frankie was positively bubbly. Maybe there was hope for this family after all.

Throughout the evening I watched Bonzo and Diane interact. Bonzo stayed close, always facing her. He studied her every move as if she were a goddess. When she left the room, he followed close at heel. *He couldn't have been trained to do that already. It must be instinctive.* Occasionally, Diane's hand reached down to ruffle Bonzo's ears. And she always had a smile for him.

On Saturday morning, Frankie was up early making tea and toast and setting out the breakfast table. Diane and I came downstairs still in our night clothes. Sunlight shone warm into the room, from the table I could see the cherry tree, blossom gone now but a host of green leaves splayed out on the branches. This year, I thought, maybe this year it won't be blighted? We all sat round the table buttering toast, slurping tea, listening to the radio as if it was the most normal thing in the world. And yet, we had never breakfasted together as a family. Not even at Christmas. So, it seemed odd that it happened without any goading or prior discussion. Each of us sat with our reveries, wool-gathering as Grandpa would say.

I was mindful of the breakfasts in my household as a child. Dad at the head of the table carving the bread, Mum making a cooked breakfast and reminding everyone 'you must eat like a king at the start of the day...' while plates and hands darted across the table and everyone seemed to be talking at the same time.

I asked Diane what breakfasts were like in her childhood,

'Dick Barton on the wireless, buttering toast and smothering it with homemade jam from berries foraged from the hedgerows. Sometimes,' she said with a glint of mischief in her eye, 'there was bacon too.'

'Bacon? But what about rationing?'

'Daddy had a syndicate going, they all had shares in this pig.' She had our full attention, a pig! As she regaled this funny story about how her Dad nearly got caught with an illegal pig carcass in the car her face lit up. 'We were driving home late one night and were stopped by the Home Guard. Daddy would have been caught had I not been sitting on the pig with a large blanket over my knees.'

It felt like a breakthrough. Everything was civil, enjoyable even. With the tumbling of words and this new way of being, Frankie was keen to contribute. Rather shy at first, her words peppered with pauses, looking at each of our faces to see if were still engaged, she told us of the noisy breakfasts at Nanny's, rice crispies, orange juice and marmite on toast with a background of jabbering children and Nanny saying, 'put that down' or 'hurry up, we're going to be late.'

I looked at my family, sitting there, sharing, and it struck me how easy and natural it felt. How good it was and how it was what I had wanted all along.

Frankie's face was a picture, bright and open. She fidgeted in her chair as she tried to make further small talk. Being heard had given her renewed confidence. Her whole conversation was hinged on Bonzo.

'Bonzo wants us all to come for a walk down the park, don't you Bonzo.' And, as if fully understanding Frankie's every utterance Bonzo barked on cue. That made us all laugh.

A short time later our little family spilled out into the morning sun making its fledgling walk to the park. Diane and I walked awkwardly side by side while Frankie ran on ahead darting back and forth. It seemed like she needed to witness this spectacle from all angles, capture the image, keep it safe in her mind's eye.

Bonzo didn't need a lead. He walked to Diane's heel until we reached the park. Once there he busied himself with all there was to offer: all the other dogs, smells, new people, the brook and of course, romping with Frankie.

'The dog's really taken to you, hasn't he?' I ventured to Diane. 'Do you still think he was a bad idea?' There was a smile behind my voice.

'No. Not at all. I think he's the best decision you've ever made.' She continued to look forward, but the hint of a smile gave her away. I gave her a cheeky nudge.

'Well, I just might take that as a compliment.'

'Just you go ahead. I won't stop you.' She nudged me back.

There was a lightness in our play, a gentleness in our banter. It felt kind. For the first time in a long time, I dared to allow myself to relax, just a little, but enough to notice.

The weekend rolled by without incident. Bonzo's antics, unconditional love and steadfast loyalty provided a commonality, something to talk about - laugh about, communicate through.

I left for work later than usual that Sunday, stopping to kiss both my girls before closing the front door and stepping out into sunshine. I was smiling.

Diane: September 1972

Bonzo had grown on me, enough for me to want to keep him and ensure that he was appropriately trained so I enrolled in puppy training classes at the local school.

When I arrived, I found a motley assortment of some ten puppies and their owners gathered around the perimeter of the school hall. The dogs were making quite a din, barking and yelping. They lunged on their leads oblivious to their owners' orders. The janitor, clad in his brown lab-coat looked on from the side lines, sneering. In his nicotine-stained hand he held his shovel at half mast, all ready for use and eyed each of us pointedly. I prayed Bonzo wouldn't be the first to have need of it.

The trainer, a slim middle-aged woman dressed in outdoor gear entered the room with a flourish. The heels of her long boots struck the floor with some force for a woman of her size, she reminded me of sergeant about to drill his battalion. All she needed was a riding crop and the outfit was complete. In a shrill voice she bid us line up in front of her. We shambled about and made a rather pathetic line. Unimpressed she put the plastic whistle that hung from her neck to her mouth and blew enthusiastically.

This made the dogs yelp and bark with the owners struggling to maintain any sort of control. It took a good ten minutes and a couple of 'accidents' before any sort of order was achieved.

She was fascinating to watch. I decided that if I could translate her into a dog breed, she'd be a Yorkshire Terrier. This amused me and made my observations more entertaining as I watched her standing in the centre of the hall shrieking orders. 'Now remember, the problem is not the dog but the owner.'

It was obvious that she had fashioned herself on popular television personality, Barbara Woodhouse. The tweed skirt and sensible long boots were a give-away. The commands, although precise and sometimes having the desired effect with the dogs, bordered on the comical to everyone else, including the janitor who frequently resorted to openly snorting with his hand smothering his mouth. Most of the time us dog owners teetered on the brink of collapse, made worse by the janitor egging us on.

By week two I was beginning to wonder what the point of the course was as training didn't seem to figure high on the agenda. It was proving to be a great source of amusement though and for that I stayed.

Occasionally a dog ran amok and had a set-to with another dog, or an accident would happen: Cue for the janitor who would run on from the side lines like a Wimbledon ball boy, stopping all proceedings until the accident was appropriately shovelled, disinfected, mopped and the janitor had ceased muttering beneath his breath. On one such occasion I thought No *wonder he looks like he's been sucking lemons.*

The idea had hardly entered my head when the tall willowy woman with butter blonde hair behind me said in a loud American drawl, 'Oh my gawd, he looks like he's been chasing parked cars!' I looked round and caught her eye and we both stifled a laugh.

'What is so funny?' snapped the trainer. 'Would you like to share it with everyone else?' The American bent double, slapping her lean thighs, tears rolling down her cheeks. She shook her head, unable to speak, inciting me to more convulsions. In the background the janitor deftly shovelled another large steaming turd off the floor and glared at the culprit and its owner.

The rest of the class, as though buoyed up by our amusement appeared to suddenly get the in-joke and began to laugh, quietly at first but then worked up to full throated guffaws. The trainer was on the brink of melt-down, her face and throat bright red, stiffly called for a short break to which a large body of the class shuffled outside for a cigarette, myself included.

The tall American stood before me, my partner in crime.

'My name's Carla and this,' she pointed, 'is my dog Woody.' I was struck by Carla's engaging smile, perfect white teeth and incredibly long nails. Carla followed my gaze. 'Oh, they're not real. They're false.' She tapped them on the top of her cigarette packet. 'I chew the hell out of mine. Drives my hubby mad. Want one?' Casually she offered me a cigarette.

I groped about in my pocket for some matches, but Carla quickly produced a slim gold lighter with the words *You light up my life* engraved on its side. It didn't take long for me to realise that I liked this curious woman who made me laugh. Her dog was something of an oddball too. Small with bandy legs, woolly hair and it had Marty Feldman eyes that gave it an odd expression rather as if it had caught sight of itself in the mirror and had had a shock.

Soon we began meeting up of an evening to take our dogs for a walk. Carla didn't live that far from me and having only recently moved there, she was keen to know all the hot spots and make new friends.

She had a head for mischief. Her irreverence was infectious and matched well with her New York drawl. 'You just gotta have fun where you can get it,' was her catch phrase. I thought I would die laughing when Carla took me into her confidence and admitted that she had written a cheque out to Mr Morgan the milkman entitled 'For sexual favours,' just for the hell of it. I laughed even harder as Carla regaled Mr Morgan's reaction complete with exaggerated facial expressions. 'He did a double take like this, then stammered a response. Course, I kept a very straight face ...' Carla's take on life was as refreshing as it was ridiculous.

We had a number of things in common. Both of us trained as secretaries, albeit in different continents. We were born in the same year with birthdays in the same month. Both of us married with a child.

We looked forward to our walks. We didn't talk deeply, but we laughed a lot. I enjoyed her company. Soon, I thought, I'd have a new best friend.

'Hi, Di. It's Carla. I'm taking Woody out shortly, wanna come?'

My fingers wrapped round the telephone cord as I cradled the phone against my neck. 'Sure, I'll see you there.'

I put the phone down and called up the stairs. 'Frankie, I'm taking Bonzo out for a walk. Won't be long.' As soon as I'd reached for the lead hanging on the coat rack Bonzo began to dance, spinning about with excitement, his paws skittering on the floor. 'Keep still, silly boy so I can put your lead on. Now sit. Sit!'

Bonzo tried to do as he was told but just couldn't contain his delight, half sitting, his bottom hovering a few inches above the floor, with his big brown eyes fixed on me.

'Alright, that's good enough.' I clipped the lead onto his collar and we stepped out of the front door walking at a swift pace towards the park.

Carla greeted us with a warm smile. She looked as though she has just stepped out from a fashion shoot in her gingham peddle-pushers and cropped top. Her style was easy, effortless and very American.

'Hey Di, how was your day?'

She bent down to greet Bonzo, offering him a treat. 'Hey Buddy.'

I tried to do the same to Woody but quickly recoiled.

'Eeew, has he been in the brook? He's all wet and he stinks.'

'Yeah, I know, he's a very naughty boy - aren't you Woody?'

She gave him a look that spoke of love and mild annoyance, he responded with an exuberant wag. 'My hubby will have a fit. I'll have to get him cleaned up before we go home. You don't have a garden hose by any chance ...?' She looked at me, the late evening sun reflecting in her big blue eyes. How could I refuse?

'Of course. Just come to mine and we'll wash him in the back garden. I'm sure Frankie would be happy to oblige.'

'Are you sure?'

'Yes, absolutely. Come on let's walk before we lose the light.'

As we set out from the bridge, spots of rain begin to fall. With measured steps we made our way along the banks of the brook, its bright water babbling over pebbles and stones, as if laughing at its own jokes. Further up, its passage slowed, pouring into a deep leafy pool hidden beneath a glade of trees. It was a place where scores of midges gathered, circling in small bundles of black. The rainfall increased. We were getting saturated, so took shelter under the canopy of the trees and stood a while listening to the patter of the rain.

I was the first to break the silence, peering up into the tangle of leaves and branches.

'It doesn't look like the rain's going to let up.'

Carla shivered, goosebumps standing proud on her pale skin.

'You're going to catch your death without a coat. Shall we make a run for it? I'll lend you some of my clothes when we get back - a mac at the very least.'

'You mean a raincoat? Thanks, that's really thoughtful.'

She beamed her huge smile, like the one she flashed at me the first time we met.

Carla's hair was wet through. It lay flattened against her head in a 1920's flapper girl style. She looked so fresh and yet somehow vulnerable.

'I love running in the rain. Don't you?' Carla stepped out from beneath the canopy, arms flung wide as she twirled round and round laughing, Woody joined in the fun, scampering at her heels, barking.

'Come on Diane, join in. It's wonderful. Come on!' she stuck her tongue out tasting the raindrops, her white shirt now thoroughly wet so that her flesh showed through.

But I remained beneath the canopy wishing I could experience the joy Carla so easily accessed. I was envious, wondering how it was that Carla was so carefree, at one with herself. Then it occurred to me that I'd never really tried running in the rain. The last time was probably when I was at school. A games session; being made to run round the hockey field while the teacher watched from the staff room, a dark silhouette standing at the window, cup and saucer in hand.

It was getting a stitch that stood out so vividly in my memory: having to slow up to catch my breath and holding my side because of the pain. I thought I was going to die, that perhaps the running had brought on appendicitis. I didn't want to die in my Airtex shirt.

The dark silhouette was unsympathetic. She hammered on the staff room window, gesticulating to keep going. Later, when the appropriate number of circuits had been completed, she chastised me in front of the class with the remnants of her milky coffee still riding on her whiskered upper lip. I was furious. How dare she scold me in front of everyone?

'Did you see the state of her?' I later said to my friends. 'All that mess on her upper lip, those ugly whiskers. What a mess! It's unforgivable and embarrassing. This is an elite private school for young ladies and attention to self-care and presentation is paramount. *She* should be setting us an example, conducting herself with utmost decorum and look at her. She's sloppy and she looks like a man - do you think she might be a lesbian? And anyway, my stitch couldn't be helped.'

After that, I wouldn't give the woman the time of day. It was a grudge I wasn't prepared to let go. Even when the teacher retired, I refused to sign the leaving card. 'I'm not writing good wishes when I don't mean them … you can't make me either.' Despite the class prefect's pleadings, I didn't budge, claiming the teacher was entitled to my disdain and nothing more. I never liked running after that.

'Hello Diane! Are you in there?'

I came to with a start. 'Sorry, I was well away there, off in my own little world.'

'Yeah, the Valium has a tendency to make you do that.'

I gave Carla a double take. 'What?'

Carla had caught me unprepared. Was *it that obvious?* My mouth opened ready to say something, but Carla spoke before me.

'You'll catch flies like that,' she cackled. 'It's okay, I get the same thing.' She was smiling but her eyes said otherwise, they had a glassy look about them that belied a sadness.

'Come on Diane, run!'

I paused and looked at her anew, 'No, wait! Please.'

I needed time to order my thoughts. Never, in a thousand years would I have thought Carla to be someone who was struggling. She seemed so sunny and carefree. A front perhaps? We all had fronts, didn't we? And yet what I liked about Carla the most was her realness, or what I thought was real. That and her 'not giving a damn' attitude. She was intriguing and inspiring, something I wanted more of and to be more like.

So, was Carla's joie de vivre down to the cultural difference, being American? They were known for their brashness, weren't they? Carla had a strong sense of self-awareness and a mercurial ability to assess a situation accurately. But in spite of all that, there she was, emotionally exposing herself.

I was confused, unsure what to make of her. It wasn't something I'd really experienced before. Val, my old best friend was very different to Carla, she was kind and thoughtful, certainly, but not warm like Carla. Val had certain boundaries that you just didn't cross, and being vulnerable was one of them. She baulked at any displays of emotion or anything that contravened her idea of what equated to 'appropriate social etiquette.'

I'd never opened up to anyone before, I hadn't dared. It felt alien. My parents didn't; none of my friends did. To behave in that way was perceived as being rather ... vulgar, weak even. Add 'she's a bit sensitive' into the mix and people crossed the street when they saw you. Either that or patronised with pitying looks and pithy comments. *People like me are a stain on society, something they don't like to acknowledge in case it infects them too. It's akin to saying I've got gonorrhoea. Don't speak to her in case you catch it. Come away. Run.*

As though sensing what I was thinking Carla turned back. She ducked under the canopy and stood next to me. The features on her face changed from fun to serious, as though her face changed from bright to dark. She tilted her head to one side and said, in almost a whisper,

'Diane, I don't know what I'm doing with my life right now.'

Her confession confused me, as though she had slapped me across the cheek and caught me unawares. Her eyes searched mine pleading for help, for someone to throw her a lifeline. I knew she was telling the truth for it was a look I had seen in myself.

'I married a man whom I thought I was in love with, but now I realise I'm not. He's a nice enough but he's too reserved, too uptight.' She started to tear up, distracting herself by looking for her hankie. 'Too bloody British for me. I feel such a heel.' She wiped her nose and dabbed her eyes. 'I have to admit, I fell in love with the potential. I just got carried away with his charm, his British panache. He had me the moment he opened his mouth. That accent with its rounded marbly vowels, it made him sound like royalty. Back home we all love the Royals, my mom especially. He was so different to all the other guys, so polished, witty and charming. All the girls wanted a piece of him, so I wanted him too. Do you get that?'

I nodded.

'He was the prize, the one who I thought would whisk me off to his big countryside pile with whiskeys by the fire, a butler, a housekeeper and all the British society friends with their horses and dogs. Oh boy, how wrong was I. I sold myself out on my own stupid fantasies. England seemed so exotic until I moved here. But now the rose-tinted glasses are off and all I'm faced with is damned tradition and etiquette that makes no sense to me.' Her face crumpled, tears, streaked black mascara lines down her face.

'Now I'm stuck here. No family, no allies. A child that screams all the time and a mother-in-law who looks down her nose at me. *We English don't do it like that, we do it like this.* She's always putting me down for one thing or another. If it's not my parenting skills, it's the way I cook or clean the house, even down to the way I iron her son's shirts. There's hardly a day when she isn't at the house, getting in the way, interfering. Sometimes I think she's competing for my husband's attention. I made a shepherd's pudding the other day...'

I smiled affectionately 'Pie, dear pie.'

'Oh, whatever, and then she appeared, about an hour or so later in her kitten heels wafting that revolting Tweed perfume with her very own frozen shepherd's pudding-pie.

She pulled an over-exaggerated face, '*No, my son will prefer mine I'm sure. He will only eat it if it's made from lamb's mince and you've used beef.*' She held her hand up with the little finger extended and swivelled her hips to emphasise her mother-in-law's demeanour.

I laughed out loud. 'She's a trout!'

'A what?'

'A trout. An obnoxious, interfering old bat; probably wears a twinset and pearls too. Am I right?' Carla's eyes widened as her face creased with a smile.

We both squealed with laughter. Carla pulled a long face and making a moue spoke through her teeth in a faux Groucho Marx voice:

'A man was watching a fisherman at work. The fisherman caught a giant trout but threw it back into the river. Next the fisherman hooked a huge pike and threw it back. Finally, the fisherman caught a little bass. He smiled and put the little bass in his bag. *Hey*' yelled a guy who was watching. *Why did you throw back a giant trout and a huge pike and then keep a little bass? ... Small frying pan,* yelled the fisherman.'

Carla gave me an impish look and made her eyebrows dance.

I laughed so hard I had to hold on to my sides. 'Stop now, or else I'll have an accident!'

'Childbirth eh!' Carla looked knowingly, 'Catches me out every time.'

I was now bent double, my face a mix of mirth and impending disaster and somehow, I managed to splutter. 'Okay, okay, enough, you win.'

Carla dropped her mad expression, tilted her head and looked sidelong at me all conspiratorial. 'So, come on. What's your story?'

I felt a rush of anxiety. I wasn't ready to share. It was too early, may be never. Much as I liked Carla, I worried she might judge or worse ignore me, label me as mad and dangerous, so I evaded the question. It was safer that way.

'Oh, my goodness, look at the time.' I showed Carla my watch. 'We'd best get back. Frankie will be wondering where I've got to. Come on.' I set off, leaving Carla standing.

'Hey, wait up. I'm coming.' she called after me.

We clambered and slid up the steep hill as fast as we could. Our breaths came short and fast as we neared the top. My feet were sodden from the wet grass. My shoes squelched and sucked as if I had some terrible bowel problem which in turn made us laugh.

At my house we made quick work of changing out of our wet clothes and getting warm drinks inside us. Frankie was tasked with hosing down and drying the dogs. There was a point where it was difficult to distinguish who was hosing who. She squealed with mirth, the dogs barked, and water went everywhere. Overly excited the dogs raced up and down the garden and round the cherry tree with Frankie hot on their heels, her cheeks rosy with exertion and her face lit up with a wide grin. The kitchen was awash with dirty wet paw marks and a pile of damp towels, but the house pulsed with laughter and warmth.

Carla and I sat in the front room, our heads wrapped in towels, we looked like a scene out of a Turkish bath. Carla nursed a hot teacup in her hands while I hunkered down to make a fire. She watched as I crumpled up bits of old newspaper, added kindling, coal and the gas poker for the final stroke. It hissed and burst into blue flame when I lit it. With a fire tamer's panache, I thrust the poker through the gravelly coals into the fire's heart, before long there was heat and a red-hot glow. We chatted as I worked, easy talk that wasn't forced or trite, for the first time in a long time I felt myself unwind.

Carla cast her eyes around the room taking in its sparseness. One well-worn two-seater couch, its piping frayed in places. A battered wingback chair which, despite its sagging seat, looked like the most comfortable stick of furniture. At the hearth, a colourful rag rug and in the farthest corner of the room on the floor was a Dansette record player. Two 45's sat in their sleeves. Curious, Carla went over to see what the records were. I watched her crouch down and examine them. She nodded her approval.

'Oh, I love this one. *The Locomotion* and oh yes, *The Night has a Thousand Eyes.* Good choices. Do you have any more?'

'No, not yet.'

Her eyes cast round again. I saw the quizzical look on her face and the flicker of a frown. She's noticed it, I thought, the lack of anything personal in the room. No children's toys, no books, no family pictures. She probably thought it rather odd but then perhaps she might have thought that finances were tight so didn't press any further. There was an oblique silence.

'Diane, I hope you don't mind me saying, but where is your other half? Come to think of it, I don't recall you mentioning having an other half. I don't see any pictures anywhere.' I stiffened and sat up a little straighter as though preparing myself for a reprimand.

'Oh, I do have both, pictures and an other,' I hesitated, 'half. His name's Richard. He works away during the week and comes back at the weekend.'

'Oh Lord! Are you okay with that? I mean, who puts the trash out and does all the hard chores?' We both laughed, polite hollow laughs that held no joy or humour.

'Actually, it rather suits me,' I said, trying to make light of it.

'So, what does he do to keep him away? Is he a long-distance driver or something?'

'No.' I paused, collecting my thoughts. 'He works for a garage as a mechanic. Not a regular mechanic, it's a bit more specialised than that.'

'Oh. Please tell me you don't have to deal with his overalls. I bet it's a nightmare getting the oil and grease out.'

'I don't do his washing. He does his own.' I raised my chin haughtily and lit a cigarette. As I exhaled a long stream of smoke I smirked, cockily pleased with myself.

Carla's eyes opened wide as she clasped her hands together in glee. 'No way, really? How did you manage that? I have to wash and press every day. It's such a pain.'

'Well, I suppose I'm a bit like you. I'm not in love, I just ended up in this marriage.' I cleared my throat and lowered my voice checking around me before I spoke.

'We had to get married.'

Carla let out a long sigh and touched my hand. 'Oh, I see,' she said. 'That must have been so difficult for you.' Her words were like a balm to me. Like Mrs Webb, she seemed to understand. Her approach was uncomplicated, without judgement or implying that I had transgressed what was socially acceptable. I wanted to hug her in that moment.

'Difficult, you don't know the half of it. I had so many dreams... but marriage and babies put paid to that.' I leaned forward and roughly towelled my hair.

'Babies? I thought you had just the one.'

I sat up, composing myself to say it. 'I do now. My little boy died.'

'Oh Diane, I'm so sorry,' she reached out and touched my hand again.

'Me too! It was the worst thing I've ever been through.' I hesitated. as if checking myself; stoppering my words. I turned my face towards the fire watching as it crackled and blazed and coals shifted and slipped in the grate.

Frankie burst into the front room giggling. Both dogs were dressed up, Woody in a scarf and Bonzo in one of Danny's shirts. 'Look, don't they look funny!' she giggled. Her face was bright and happy. The excited dogs raced about the room. They yelped and tugged at the clothes. But the amusement Frankie anticipated backfired badly. When I caught sight of Danny's shirt, the one that got missed in all the packing away of his things, I snapped.

Grabbing hold of Frankie, I swung her round by the arm to face me. Raising my hand high I slapped her hard across the face. Her expression changed in an instant, her face screwed up as the tears fell but it didn't deter me. And just like that the atmosphere was ruined. Even the dogs sensed something was awry and sloped away to a corner cowering, ears flattened, tails between their legs.

'You little bitch.' I growled, 'How dare you disrespect Danny's memory. You, vile, hateful child.' Frankie cringed, holding her free hand up to prevent further strikes. Her face had started to smart showing a red hand mark on her pale white cheek. 'I'm sorry Mum, I'm sorry... I didn't mean it.' Her voice was small and quavering.

Carla leapt to her feet and tried to intervene. 'Diane, stop! She didn't mean it.' I ignored her as I marshalled Frankie out of the room by the scruff of her neck.

'Get up those stairs and out of my sight. I don't want to see or hear you. Do I make myself clear?' My throat was tight, constricting my voice but it still had a menace about it. Gripping Frankie's shoulder, I yanked her closer and hissed. 'You will never match up to Danny, never.' I pushed her away roughly before turning and slamming the front room door shut.

Carla's hands were shaking so much she could barely light her cigarette. 'Was that really necessary? She's a child for God's sake!' I wasn't listening, the anger was still pulsing in my ears. She tried grabbing my arm but the look on my face made her think better.

'I think it's time for me to leave.'

Folding my arms, I looked away. 'Yes, I think that's best. You know where the door is.'

With an exaggerated sigh Carla took the scarf from Woody's neck and folded it with care, then clipped the lead on Woody and left, closing the front door quietly behind her.

I didn't show up at the next dog training class.

I missed the following class too.

Diane: Late September 1972

The phone was ringing in the hall.

'Get the phone Frankie. Frankie!' I heard her feet run across her bedroom floor upstairs and then bound down the stairs.

'Cheltenham 53078, Frankie speaking.' There was a silence as she listened to the voice on the other end. She responded in her brightest polite voice. 'Yes, I'm fine. Yes, thank you.' She put the phone down on its side and called, 'Mum, it's for you.'

'Who is it?'

I suspected it was Carla, but was determined not to show I was pleased. Frankie popped her head round the door and smiled. 'It's Carla for you Mum,' I put my magazine down with a sigh and traipsed out to the hall.

'Hello…' I said flatly, a tone that doesn't invite further conversation, the kind that says I'm not interested, go away. But Carla persisted. 'Hi Di, I'm phoning to see how you are.'

'Fine, thanks.'

'I, errr, I'm sorry how we left things last time. I didn't mean to interfere. Listen, tell me to go away if you want, but I like you. I know I don't know you very well but I thought we were friends, good friends. I want to support you Di. It seems to me from where I'm standing you could do with it. What do you say Di?'

I twisted the phone line round my fingers as I tried to process. It wasn't anything like I was expecting.

'Diane?'

My breath came short and ragged as if snagged at the back of my throat. The wall of anger I harboured receded allowing a different sensation to seep through in subtle slow drops, like treacle from a spoon.

'Diane, are you okay?'

I cried softly.

'It's okay honey, just let it out. I'm here for you.' Her words made me cry harder.

My words interspersed with tears came out clipped and small. 'I don't know how to connect anymore.'

'Talk to me honey. Would you like me to come round?'

'No. No, it's okay.'

'You don't sound okay to me. Put the kettle on. I'll be with you in ten minutes.'

I examined myself in the front room mirror. My eye was drawn to the twitching muscle at my jaw. My mouth was clamped tightly shut, like a carp. An unhappy carp. My heart thumped rhythmically like it was punching the inside of my ribcage. *'Keep away, keep away, keep away.'*

I wrestled with the rising sense of losing control. Forcing myself to stand closer to the mirror. I hissed, *'What is it you're afraid of?'* My breath fogged the glass as my eyes tried to read those looking back at me.

A voice, my voice, came from deep within, it was breathy and unsteady.

'I'm scared. Scared of being let down. I hate being lonely. It terrifies me. I feel abandoned and nobody understands.' I wiped the condensation from the mirror.

'I want, no need to feel close to someone but it has to be on my terms. Is that too much to ask?' I shook my head then held my own gaze.

And what were my terms? Where has that girl with all the dreams gone? The thoughts wearied me, like wrestling with my hands tied. I slumped on the settee, as though the weight of them had pressed me deep into the fabric and held me there... I tried to steady my breath and focus.

Bonzo settled at my feet, his head rested in my lap willing me to notice him. I stroked the top of his head and fondled his silky ears. When I lifted my hand away he sought it again, nudging with his nose, licking with his soft pink tongue, *I'm here,* his actions said, *I'm right here.* He calmed me. He looked at me like I was his world, the one he would do anything for and in that brief moment I felt safe.

When the doorbell rang, I jumped to my feet. Bonzo bounded to the window and barked. Frankie thundered down the stairs and answered the front door before me.

'Hello pumpkin.' came Carla's voice, a smile in its melody. Through the part-open door, I watched her stoop to hug Frankie's little frame. A flicker of a frown crossed Carla's face; the child was stick thin. Frankie's response was stiff and guarded and yet she leant in.

Carla hunkered down and stroked a piece of hair out of Frankie's face. 'You okay?' she whispered.

Frankie said nothing, just nodded her head and glanced back at the door where I was standing.

'I have to go to bed now. Nighty-night Aunty Carla.'

'Nighty-night, Frankie.' Carla called after her as she scampered up the stairs.

Then Carla looked up and caught me peeking. I felt a bit awkward as though I was caught in the act of doing something I shouldn't.

She swept in and enveloped me in an exuberant embrace. I responded woodenly, 'You Brits,' she chided warmly and continued to hold on, holding me tight. Then something changed and I felt myself give. My shoulders dropped, melting almost, until my head rested heavily in the crook of her neck. The two of us stood a long while in the middle of the room as I gave in to my tears. A mere whimper at first but expanding into a full body-shaking sob. And once the floodgates had opened, I spilled my heartache and hurt out onto Carla's shoulder.

There was a noise on the stair. Frankie. I wondered what she made of the muffled sobbing and whispered *sshh?* She'd probably crept down several steps to watch from the top of the stairs. Did what she see and hear frighten her? Was she thinking *she was all right five minutes ago, what's caused this?* I could guarantee though, that she would not say a word about this to anyone.

I looked up through the open door and spotted a pair of eyes taking the scene in. Carla saw it too. She manoeuvred me slightly so that Frankie could see her mouthing the words, 'She's okay.'

I sensed Carla signalling to Frankie to go back to bed but Frankie did not move. Carla called, firm but polite. 'Can you give us some privacy honey?'

I turned my head in Frankie's direction again, but she was gone, disappeared into the darkness at the top of the stairs.

Richard: Monday, late September 1972

It had been a rough start to the week. I'd seen all the activity in the office. All the coming and going, the phone calls, and Geoff's strained face. Things in the workshop were no better either. Some of the equipment had disappeared with no explanation. The bookings diary was empty too.

Come Wednesday, Geoff beckoned me into the office and shut the door. He looked grey and awkward, his fingers fidgeting with a paperclip.

'Take a seat, Richard.'

'I'm okay as I am, thanks.' I thrust my hands deep into my outfit pockets bracing myself for what was to come.

'There's no other way to say this … we've gone under. We've run out of options and the bank has called time on us. I'm really sorry Richard, I'm going to have to let you go.'

I left the office in a daze. I don't recall getting into the car. Somehow, I made it back to my digs, packed the few things I had there and got back in the car. Throughout the long journey to Cheltenham, I tried to sequence what to do and what to say. Diane wasn't going to like it. She might even throw me out. Then what? What if she found someone else? My mind played through the scenarios of never seeing Frankie grow up, not having access to her or worse, seeing her being brought up by someone else. These thoughts remained with me throughout the journey.

It was evening when I pulled into the drive and applied the handbrake. I could see two figures in the front room, small black outlines through the blinds. My heart sank.

That's all I needed, my mother-in-law witnessing my failure. No doubt she'd have something to say about it and rile Diane up further.

As I put the key in the lock and pushed the door open, I heard animated voices coming from inside. Laughter even. I dropped my bag at the foot of the stairs and went into the front room.

Diane was sitting next to a stranger, the two of them giggling. Her face changed the moment she saw me, like the tripping of a switch. An awkward silence followed, irritated she flicked her cigarette into the fire and looked away. It was her way of saying *Go away, you are not welcome here.* I stood, hovering in the doorway, half in half out, feeling embarrassed in my own home. Then her guest put her glass down and standing, held out her hand.

'Damn it, someone's got to make the first move. Hello, I'm Carla, Diane's friend from puppy training school. I take it you're either her husband or a very bold burglar!' I was a bit taken aback. *Friend! Diane doesn't have friends, not ones that call round. Most of the people she knows are essentially just associates and nothing more.*

'Yes, hello, I'm Richard. I apologise if I'm intruding.'

Diane glared at me. 'What are you doing home?' Her voice had an edge to it.

Carla picked up her handbag. 'That's my cue to leave. Di, do you mind if I use your phone to call my husband? Where's the phone?'

'No Carla, you don't need to do that, Richard will give you a lift home. Won't you Richard?'. Diane looked at me pointedly and inclined her head.

Carla was quick to respond. 'Ah, no. I don't think so. That's very kind but like you said, your husband works away, he's probably tired. Where did you say your phone is?' Diane waved a hand in the direction of the hall.

'It's out there. Are you sure you don't need a lift?' Again, Diane glared, as if to say, *Do something.*

'It wouldn't be any trouble,' I sighed, still taking off my jacket.

'Thanks, but no thanks.' Carla brushed passed me out into the hall. I heard her lift the receiver and start dialling.

Diane fixed her narrowed eyes on me, 'What are you doing home?'

I tried to respond but she cut me off.

'Shut the door. I don't want our guest to hear us.' Obediently I pushed the door to then squatted down to greet Bonzo, his tail whirled like a helicopter, but Diane grabbed his collar, holding him back. 'Well?'

'Now is not a good time. I'll explain later. After your guest has gone.'

Carla breezed back into the room. 'He's on his way, should be here in five minutes.' She sat beside Diane, took out her compact and applied some lipstick.

'I'll go and make a cup of tea. Do you want one Diane?' I waited for an answer but nothing came.

With the kettle on I searched my pockets for my cigarettes and lighter.

'Damn it!' I realised I'd left them in the car. I was on the point of picking up my keys from the top of the fridge when Frankie bounced into the kitchen.

'Hi Dad, what are you doing home?' I gave her a tentative hug then holding her at arm's length looked at her directly. 'And what have you been up to young lady?'

'Oh, this!' she fluttered her eyelids. They were covered in a gaudy coloured turquoise and looked as though she had applied it with her toes. 'There's a Halloween disco at school next week. Do you like it?' she smiled, 'I've been practicing.'

I appraised her a little more. She struck a pose - on Diana Dors it would have been suitable but on my daughter it was hideous. 'It's not a great look and I'm sure Mum won't like it. Has she seen it?'

Frankie shook her head.

'Where did you get the make-up?'

'Patsy from the flats, she lent it to me. She wears make-up all the time now. Even to school - although they always make her wash it off.'

'Go and take it off now before your Mum sees it. Go on.'

'But Dad!'

'Go on.' Taking her by the shoulders, I turned her round and gave her a gentle push into the hall. I watched as she took the stairs two at a time and disappeared behind the bathroom door.

'Now, where was I? Ah, keys.' I picked them up and headed out of the front door.

A Vauxhall Viva pulled up outside the house as I was leaning across the dashboard to retrieve the cigarettes. A man stepped out of the car. My heart gave a jolt.

'What the bloody hell...?' Pulling myself up to full height and squaring my shoulders I faced him.

'You've got a nerve...'

'Richard!' Tom looked just as stunned as I was.

'I've just come to collect my wife, Moni.'

'Who? Do you mean Carla?'

'Well yes. I call her Moni, but she goes by the name Carla.'

Tom stayed close to the car his hand rested on the open door. He was at pains to make it look like a casual pose, like he was in control, unfazed, but the pinched expression on his face said otherwise. To me, it looked like he was considering his options for a quick getaway.

He cleared his throat then adjusted his tie and glanced at his watch before casting his gaze towards the house. A moment later the front door swung open, I saw his sharp intake of breath. Carla and Diane emerged saying their goodbyes on the doorstep. Their silhouettes standing out against the hall light.

On seeing her husband Carla's face lit up. She half skipped to him and kissed him on the cheek.

'Aw, sorry honey,' she giggled, making a thing of trying to smudge off the lipstick mark she made then turned to make the introductions. A huge smile stretched across her face.

'Di, I'd like you to meet my husband, Tom. Tom, this is Di, my puppy-training friend that I've been telling you about.'

Diane froze. Her face drained of colour. She put out a hand to steady herself, catching the door frame.

'Diane, are you okay?' Carla moved to hold her up.

'Yes, I think I stood up too quickly. Thank you.' She brushed Carla away trying to compose herself, her voice barely a whisper. I watched her look from Tom to me. Her mouth set in a thin smile.

Tom looked tense his eyes could barely meet Diane's.

'Come on Moni,' he jangled his car keys. 'Mother's at home, she's made supper and she's waiting.'

Both Diane and I looked like we'd been slapped hard in the face, which Carla misread. She was still all smiles, keen for us all to get on.

'Oh, I didn't tell you? Monica's my Sunday name. Tom insists on using it but I prefer Carla,' she giggled nervously. Diane barely registered what Carla had said, her facial expression remained unaltered. Her attention was elsewhere. Tom fidgeted with his pinkie ring, thumb pushing at the gold, turning it over and over.

Diane was struggling, the shock was written all over her face. Her chest heaving in an out as she fought to breathe.

Diane: Same day

I felt a fluttering stirring in my chest, like the tiny heartbeat of an emerging panic. I battled to put those thoughts behind me.

Focus. FOCUS.

I was finding it hard to think. His voice. His voice! Hearing *his* voice again, it was something I'd dreamed of … but not like that. *Oh my God, not like that.*

'Nice to meet you Diane.' His eyes lingered on me but he acted like he'd never met me before, like I was nothing, as if I had never meant anything to him. 'Richard.' He turned to walk away, Carla on his arm, then he looked pointedly back at Richard.

'Oh, do give my regards to your sisters, especially Sophie won't you.' He sneered like he had the upper hand. Why was he behaving like that?

Richard's response was swift, his movement athletic. The punch landed squarely on Tom's face.

'You cocky bastard!'

The blow caught him off guard, blood gushed scarlet from his nose. Carla screamed and Woody barked. She leapt between the two men, pushing them apart. Tom made a show of trying to retaliate but I could see he was relying on Carla to hold him back, all swearing and bravado. And Richard, goading him, trading insults from the driveway. I'd never seen him so angry.

'Stay well away from my sister. Stay away from all of us. Go on. Clear off before I give you a really good hiding.'

When they left Carla was driving. I'll never forget her expression, her face, black as thunder as she wound down the car window and rounded on Richard.

'Goddam it, what was that all about?'

'You'd better ask him.' Richard pointed an accusatory finger in Tom's direction. I looked askance between Carla, Richard and Tom.

'Go home Carla and take him with you before someone gets hurt.' Then I turned and went into the house praying that my knees would carry me.

My head was full of noise.

Did Richard know about Tom and I? Did he know about Danny? Was that why he reacted like he did? I couldn't think what to do. How Richard was going to react I wasn't sure.

My hands shook so hard I had difficulty lighting my cigarette. Was I about to be thrown out of my own home? Perhaps I deserved it for all the lies I'd told. But then hadn't I been the one who had taken all the backlash? Wasn't I the one who had done most of the donkeywork in this marriage?

Deny it. He has no proof. All the evidence was gone. Tom didn't know anyway.

And Carla? My new best friend, how do I tell her? Would she understand?

And Tom…?

My breathing changed, lost its rhythm. It came in snatches, thready and short. And then I heard that distant flapping noise - those birds, those black birds of my nightmares back again. I clenched my fists ready to beat them off.

Richard: Same day

I watched the car disappear up the road, its taillights disappearing as it turned the corner. Finally, I exhaled. My hand was throbbing. I checked my knuckle and found a small cut. I admit I felt smug. I'd been itching for an excuse to do that for a long time. One for Diane, one for Sophie and one for my bike all those years ago.

The neighbours were watching me. I could see their outlines at the windows, the faces between the half- closed curtains. I wanted to shout, 'Show's over now.' but what was the point. I headed back inside.

The instant I stepped through the door Diane slapped me hard across the face. The blow cut my lip.

'You bastard. Why do you have to ruin everything for me?' Her mouth folded bitterly around the words.

'Diane.' I tried to remonstrate, wiping blood from my mouth. 'Diane!' But she was no longer listening, her lips curled into a snarl, summoning venom.

'I hate you. I hate everything about you. I wish…' She raised her hand again and instinct made me grab it. I gripped it tight and tried to reason with her, get her to listen. She was hell bent on attack vicious as a cornered vixen.

'Let go of me, you bastard.' She struggled to break free. 'You're always there, spoiling things for me. It's always you.' She started to cry her face twisted as though collapsing in on itself. She always looked ugly when she got that upset. 'And now you've destroyed things for me and Carla. She's the one good friend I've had in a long time. You! You've ruined it! And for what?'

I was still holding onto her wrists as she wrestled to break away. Her efforts were useless, she may as well have been a puff of air trying to push me over. Her skin lay soft over her slim wrists. How could something so delicate be so wild?

I tightened my grip and drew her closer. 'Diane, listen to me. Listen to me!' We were straining to the point of breaking.

'Why should I?' You never listen to me. You're always hell bent on bringing me down. It always boils down to you. You're nothing but a selfish bastard. You ruined my life and then you walked away and left me to pick up the pieces and you continue to walk away.'

The next-door-neighbours banged on the wall, Bonzo started barking, Diane shouting.

'How can you say this?' It feels like my voice is wailing into the abyss. It took all I could muster not to over-react. Oh, she would have just loved that, martyrdom on a plate. I imagined her trotting off to tell her mother, any excuse to blacken my name further. I pushed her away as though she was something distasteful, her wrists white where I had gripped her so tight.

'Is that what you've been saying about me, that I walked away? Take a good look at yourself. I did try to come back. I did try to be with you, be a family, create something solid. But ooh no, nothing was ever good enough for you. It's always been my fault because it suited you to be that way, blame me for not being the person you want me to be rather than seeing me for who and what I am. You've pushed me and my family away at every opportunity. You have never tried to work at this, work as a team like a normal family. You're the one that's wrong, not me.'

The words spilled out of me and even as I was saying them, those hurtful, truthful words I knew they would sting. But it stopped her in her tracks. She stood there looking at me, registering what was said, the moment seemed to expand for an age. Then I saw the hurt in her face, like a wounded animal and I felt pity. She was incapable of seeing her own faults. She had always been like that, a bloody princess, and I always relented.

The banging stopped.

'Diane, I'm sorry you feel the way you do. Let's be honest, its never really worked when I'm about has it?' She relaxed, she dropped her hands by her side and closed her mouth into a sharp line, the fire receded in her eyes. She turned her head and strands of hair fell over her face. Gently I moved forward and tucked them back behind her ear. She pulled her head back, like a skittish horse, but didn't move away, not completely. Her body shuddered as she sighed. A coal slipped in the grate something had shifted for us but we were both at a loss to know what to say next.

She spoke, her voice quiet and steady.

'But why did you react like that? And what has your sister got to do with it?'

I hesitated, knowing that the news I was about to deliver would devastate her. But she needed the truth. She deserved that. I hoped it would help her see what a feckless bastard Tom really was. Perhaps it would break the spell. And maybe, in time, she would learn to understand and appreciate what I did. She lifted her head to look me full in the face, the first time in a long time. Now I had her attention.

'He got Sophie pregnant.'

Her face reflected the changing emotions. Disbelief, shock, rejection. I could see she couldn't take it in.

'No. He wouldn't. 'You're making it up. 'It's not true. Not Tom.'

Then something else - like a shadow crossing her face. Betrayal.

Her jaws worked but no sound came out. And then I hated myself for doing this to her but as they say, the truth hurts.

Diane: Same day

'He got Sophie pregnant.'

It was like a bomb had gone off, sparks of words, concepts, trains of thoughts clattering through my head. I could barely take it in. My mouth gaped for a second then began working without sound. It was as though my thinking was a scratched record, jumping over the unpleasant bit.

'Liar, that's not true. It's not true.'

My voice rose - more to convince myself than anything else. I wrung my hands, pressing them together, squeezing as though the pressure will bring about some sort of release. Stop me putting my hands about my head and covering my ears. Richard continued speaking. I didn't want to hear it but it filtered through anyway.

'She had a termination, not long after he left for the States.'

'No, he wouldn't. He couldn't.' My legs buckled beneath me.

I lay on the floor, facedown, eyes closed waiting for my head to stop crowding, my hands fidgeting involuntarily.

Richard loomed over me holding out his hand. It appeared to be larger than hands should be. I saw oil ingrained into its rough creases. It was outstretched, coming towards me.

'Come on, get up. Let's take this into the front room.'

I swatted his hand away. 'Don't touch me! Leave me alone.' I struggled to my feet. The word termination repeating over and over in my head.

Frankie's small voice called out from the darkness at the top of the stairs. 'Mum, are you okay?'

I heard myself say 'Go back to bed this instant!' but it didn't sound like my voice. It was as if I was disconnected from myself. A roaring noise filled my ears, like a thousand drummers drumming simultaneously. Rising and swelling, occupying every thinking space in my head. I put my hands over my ears, but it persisted.

'No. No. No. Nooooo. Stop it!'

'Diane? What do you need?' Richard's voice, sounding concerned. *Is he concerned? Can I trust him?*

'Diane, let me help you.'

He shouted through the noise. Hunkered down, big knees, shoes. His voice up close, buzzing, distorted.

'Breathe. Come on, deep breaths.'

I saw his face loom in large, it blurred and spread, merged with the wallpaper. Something was squeezing my hand, but I was pushing it away. I could see, or was I imagining scores of birds flapping and scuffling around me. Crowding and squawking. I blinked and it was gone, like Alice, down the rabbit hole. Free falling …

'You'll frighten Frankie if you carry on like that.' His voice, distant, what was it saying? I lashed out, flailing my free arm weakly, still doubled over.

'Frankie … ?'

Frankie, I don't care about Frankie, can't care about Frankie.

His voice was indistinct, words coalesced into a far-away sound, like shouting under water.

I surfaced, as though coming up for air aware and wailing, emptying my lungs, pushing out the sound. It came from a place deep within me, a strange resonant noise that boomed and pressed like savage crushing waves.

Richard: Same day

I was standing there, helpless - useless. Unable to calm her. The more I tried the more I saw her retreating from me. And that sound, that animal sound, so raw. God, what had I done? I remembered the last time Diane was lost, her mind closed in on itself as her body trembled involuntarily and spittle flecked her chin. She was so medicated that I hardly recognised her.

I only went to see her the once. It wasn't what I expected - although I didn't really know what to prepare for. I'd stopped at a florist on the way, bought flowers, peonies, her favourite; had them all wrapped up in nice paper with a big bow. But seeing her there, through the reinforced window, her hair half matted and unwashed, dressed in ill-fitting hospital clothes, rocking back and forth, was a shock. I broke out in a cold sweat. I dropped the flowers, crushed them under foot turned and almost ran. For weeks following, the smell of disinfectant or urine made my stomach lurch. Her vacant eyes, like hollows, haunted me. I couldn't get the image out of my head. The prospect of another re-run was one of my biggest fears. My wife lost to me. Tangible evidence of my failure as a husband and father, fodder for the gossips to throw me and my family to the wolves. How to deal with it was beyond me then and now ...

And then there was the guilt, the guilt I'd heaped upon myself and added an unhealthy dose of shame for good measure. It was a twisted shame, hewn from generations of fear and misunderstanding, from what we tell ourselves is wrong and not right. Pointing our sticky fingers anywhere but close to home. *His wife's got that nerve problem; they had to lock her away she was that unstable.* I'd seen the pitying looks, heard the platitudes, even dealt with the stupid awkward questions. But in reality, I had no answers, not ones that convinced me or fully protected Frankie. It was wearing. So bloody wearing.

With a firm hand I led Diane into the front room and sat her on the sofa. She continued whimpering. It was a quiet sound that came with each out-breath, making her face screw up and mouth gape. Dribbles of snot and spittle escaped to the corners of her lips and nose.

Suddenly I snapped, compassion gave way to irritation. I told myself she was just being over dramatic, we had all pandered to it. Being upset was one thing but wallowing in self-absorption was too much. 'Diane, stop it! Stop it!' I slapped her lightly on the face. 'Pull yourself together!' My hands were about her shoulders. 'That's enough now.'

Bonzo got up from where he had been lying at the side of the couch to stand between us weary-eyed. When I leaned in closer to Diane's face, Bonzo curled his lip back and emitted a deep low growl. His hackles were up. Startled, I stood back as if taking stock of myself. As I left the room, I saw that Diane had her arms wrapped round the dog, as he tried to wriggle free to lick her face.

In the kitchen I lit a cigarette, snapping the zippo lid shut and threw it onto the counter. I needed to calm down, my heart was pounding like fists against my ribcage. *If she ends up sectioned, we'll all be back to square one.* Was the spectre of her illness back again? A wave of frustration gripped me. I don't have time for this and don't want to hang around and play nursemaid to all this over-dramatic nonsense. I threw the ashtray across the kitchen. It crashed and scattered but that didn't placate me. I wanted to destroy more.

If she finds out there's no money coming in... she's clearly not fit to work in her current state. Christ, do I call her parents? Her mother will have a field day. Course, all the blame would be heaped on me but then she'd start on Diane and only make her worse. I should have listened to my father. 'She's not right son.'

I gritted my teeth as I tried to think through my options, I gritted so hard my jaw ached. There was so little room for manoeuvre. Diane had agreed when I said, 'It never really works when I'm about.' Perhaps that was the answer?

Frankie: Monday night and into Tuesday

That night, when the house was quiet with Mum in a deep Mogodon-induced sleep and Dad snoring in the spare room, I slipped downstairs making sure not to step on the creaky step. I tiptoed into the kitchen making my way to where Bonzo lay and snuggled up next to him, half curling my body around his. He licked my face and hands, a swap for belly rubs and ear strokes. I did this quite often. He made me feel safe, loved me without question.

Those were my happiest moments. When all the house was still. Only its ticks and creaks - the hum of the fridge, the slow drip of the tap, the steady tick of the kitchen clock and the rise and fall of Bonzo's warm body as he took his big easy breaths. Those sounds reassured me, they *sshhhed* my busy head, blotting out the shouting and crying and staved off my nightmares. I had lots of nightmares. But most of all I felt safe with Bonzo.

I'd heard my parents earlier, the shouting, the argument between them. I heard Mum's broken sobs and Dad trying to reason with her. I knew then, without doubt, that Mum was bad again.

Would this mean I could go back to Nanny? A part of me would have loved that but the other part wanted to stay home. Be with Bonzo, keep going to school and having Patsy nearby.

As the hours ticked by I kept thinking up my worst fears, feeding them snippets of worry and scary things. I got into such a state that I clung to Bonzo and sobbed. My tears fell on his coat as I made a pact that the two of us would never be parted, no matter what. Curling closer around him, I whispered stories into his silken ears, and told him of the adventures we were yet to have, the places we were yet to go and the people we would meet on the way. And all the stories included finding a special little boy called Danny whose face I could barely recall and a family that took happy holidays together with their dog. I told these stories until sleep took over and the morning light pooled into the kitchen.

It rained the next morning, not the sprinkling the lawn type of rain but a real downpour, streaking windows and gushing down the gully type. I guess the sound of it battering against the windows woke Mum.

She was lying in bed. I noticed her blank swollen eyes staring at the ceiling. When she rolled over she got a bit of a surprise to find me standing there with a cup of hot tea.

'I thought you might like a cup of tea, Mum.'

She snapped, 'How long have you been there? What time is it?' Hearing her voice, Bonzo jumped up and put his front paws on the bed and stuffed his wet nose in her face.

'Oh Bonzo!' Mum protested half-heartedly which only got him more excited. He plastered her with loads of licks and little *mmmnnnaa mmmmnna* cries. 'No, that's enough now,' she said, but was only half trying to push him off so he'd wriggle back again. Her voice was a give-away; you could tell it was a smiling voice which Bonzo knew better than anyone. So, he kept on licking and creating a draught with his tail.

I managed to rescue the cup just seconds before Bonzo's tail swept it off its perch. I clocked Mum's feeble smile and watched her reach for her pills on the bedside table. She took two from the Valium bottle and motioned to me to hand her the tea. She threw her head back as she swallowed and washed them down.

'You'll be late for school. Go on, off you go.' She waved me on dismissively and turned her attention to Bonzo. I stomped out of the room, my throat tight where anger and tears snagged. Not that I ever held it against Bonzo, there was no getting away from it, he was adorable. Sometimes I wished I was a dog.

From the landing I saw that Dad's bedroom door was ajar, so I pushed it open a little further. The room was empty. It still smelled of him, a mix of motor oil, sweat and Old Spice. His little blue suitcase had gone. A drawer left open was empty bar one stray cufflink. I looked about the small room and noted that even the picture of me was no longer there. My heart sank. For a moment I wondered whether I should tell Mum but then thought better of it. It would only send her into a spin, and I knew who she would take it out on. I let out a big sigh, then fastened up my shoes and took off for school running all the way.

Richard: Later that night

I lay in the single bed in Danny's old bedroom considering my options. Simon suggested I sleep on what to do next, but I couldn't dismiss the recurring thought; that this was the only sensible and practical way to go about it.

Leaving would be a hard decision, but one made out of necessity. I turned it over and over in my mind and couldn't see how my being there helped the situation. None of us was happy and Diane would probably get more support with me being out of the picture. Besides, if I was truly honest with myself, I found the whole situation too much of a struggle. She pushed me, really pushed me. She had that uncanny knack of knowing my tipping point and, boy. had I come close. There were times where I didn't even trust myself. It would be so easy to lose it and really hit out. I knew I could do some damage without any effort. Snap her like a twig and what good would that do? Where would it stop? She would use it as emotional leverage, she was good at that, suffocating me with guilt, tears and tantrums. And Frankie? It would break the spell. In her eyes her Daddy was not a bully or a wife beater. If I went down that path her fear and disappointment would consume me and that's one thing I couldn't handle. And yet, somewhere in my mind, I thought she would eventually come to understand why I left.

I knew then that my next move would be seen as selfish, but if I didn't do it... What I really needed was peace and quiet. I worked better being by myself. And there it was - the bare ugly truth unmasked. Despite loving my family, I didn't love it enough.

I was just not cut out for it. This was not how I'd imagined family life to be. A loveless marriage that left me feeling drained, inadequate and guilty.

Bleary-eyed I got out of bed and dressed in the semi-dark. The house was quiet. I looked at my watch. Its luminous hands said eleven ten. It was late but not too late for my purposes. I didn't dare switch on the bedroom light; it was too bright and might wake someone. Instead, I relied on the streetlamp that beamed through the crack in the curtains. Its orangey glow gave me just enough light to see what I was doing. Carefully I slid open the drawers and threw the few items I possessed into my suitcase. Just as I was about to exit the door I looked up to the shelf where I had the picture of Frankie. She was standing awkwardly, head tilted to the side, hands clasped in front of her daring to be happy in a shy sort of way. I'd taken it the week she was suspended from school, just before we had gone to fetch Bonzo. I picked up the frame, savouring the memory, then carefully tucked the picture into my inside jacket pocket. On the landing I found myself hesitating outside Frankie's door. The pangs of guilt were almost overwhelming, but I knew that if I stopped and popped my head in to say goodbye, I wouldn't be able to leave.

Bonzo waited patiently at the bottom of the stairs, tail wagging. I reached out and ruffled his head. 'Take good care of them, boy.' Then I opened the door and left.

As I pulled away from the neighbourhood, I wasn't entirely sure where I was going but I steered the car along the familiar roads towards town. It was as though I was on automatic, driving out of habit, because, before I knew it, I had driven to my old family home.

Stopping outside, I felt my heart sink: it was a cloying, sickening feeling. Looking up I saw that different curtains hung at the windows, closed against the night sky. Closing me out. The brass plate at the front door saying 'Miller' had been removed and in its stead was a gaudy replacement that read 'Arnold Residence.'

Just past the gate to the side of the front path was our family cherry tree. Once resplendent with blossom and admired by many but now, it too showed signs of disease. Seeing it in that state was like being punched in the gut.

It was a sudden physical realisation. Mentally I knew that my parents were no longer there, but sitting there outside my old home, all the feelings of love, safety and security flooded back. I felt bereft. I would have given anything to sit at the big kitchen table nursing a strong cup of tea while Mum busied herself at the stove. She would pass across tid-bits: 'Here, try this,' she would proffer a scone or a spoon laden with something tasty. Then, hands pressed into her tabard pockets she would closely watching my reaction. 'Do you think it needs a bit more salt then?' She often held animated conversations with her back to me, busy with whatever was bubbling in the pots. But she always knew when something was up, said it came from her 'mother's milk.' Without fail she dragged whatever problem that bothered me out into the open. She made it feel like a joint endeavour. Together we'd scrutinise it and winkle out a solution with pointed questions. encouragement, reassurance and all topped off with a warm embrace. She was completely at my disposal, just like she was for all of the family.

And Dad, I couldn't think of Mum without thinking of Dad. I could be stilled by his calming presence. There he'd be, sitting in 'his' chair in the corner of the kitchen, engrossed in The Times, muttering disgruntlements at the articles behind the pages. Identifying Dad's moods was like reading semaphore. It was all in the way he held the paper. High signalled that he didn't want to be bothered, half-mast meant he was listening in to what was going on, lowered meant that more than likely he was snoozing or very close to it. If only I had heeded his warnings. 'Be careful with that one son - she's not right.' But pride and immaturity rode rough-shod over common sense. Even when Diane was sectioned I kept quiet, played it down. I told no one the real truth. Couldn't bear to hear the *I told you so's*. Defiantly I toughed it out, manned-up by keeping quiet. Pride, shame and ignorance won the day.

Looking back now, I was naive to think that I could protect Diane and also protect my parents at the same time - I thought that if I kept them in the dark the shame wouldn't touch them.

But when I was finding it all too overwhelming - my life disintegrating before my very eyes, I worked up the courage to confide in Mum, my champion, my unswerving guide, but she suddenly took ill and died. I was left with an unfathomable confusion and fought to repress my grief. 'Keep it together son,' Dad chided, slapping my back a little too heartily. 'We don't want to be letting the side down now do we?' And so, I forced it down - like swallowing the cod liver oil Mum had pressed upon me as a child; its vile aftertaste lingering - until finally I became numb. It was part and parcel of what it was to be a man. 'The done thing.' This, I realised, was the heart of the problem. Diane and I had existed at opposite ends of the emotional scale and ne'er the twain should meet.

Suddenly, as if a wave had washed over me, I gave myself up to the grief I hadn't allowed myself when my parents passed. One after the other they went, in quick succession. I felt tired and hollow - like all I wanted in that moment was to swallow the soup of my mother's love and hear the comforting rustle of Dad's newspaper. But they were gone, resting in a cold cemetery not three miles away.

It was late. I looked at my broad hands on the steering wheel. I wanted to punch something, smash it to smithereens and keep punching until there was nothing left, until I was completely spent. But I knew that it would not curb the tide of pure anger and futility I felt. It was a familiar cycle, feeling it rise, like bile from my belly, then forcing it back down. I'd been doing it for so long it had become second nature until now, when I finally realised that I'd had enough, a belly full. The cycle's velocity had increased from slow turns to such a giddy whirl that I knew I had to get off.

I found myself at The Club, a late-night drinking hole that smelled of desperation and loneliness. It was situated in the lower end of the High Street, a less than salubrious area. Bar flies gathered in shady corners, drinking, shoulders hunched, eyes at half-mast. I drank shot after shot, slamming each glass down on the counter with a finality akin to the spaghetti western cowboys I'd watched as a boy. Then I called Simon from the payphone

'C'mon Simon, let's go have some fun.' But my voice didn't sound like it wanted to have fun, there was nothing jovial in its tone. It sounded like it needed a friend.

I felt relieved when Simon came. His smooth voice: 'Steady Richard. I think you've had enough for now. Shall we get you home?' He took me by the elbow and steered me, pin-balling, to the exit. Outside in the fresh air, away from the dull music and fetid smoke, I launched into a tirade.

'Home?' I looked at Simon through squint eyes, swaying on my feet, 'What home? That bloody woman never made me feel welcome. In my own bloody house, I tell you.'

'I know Richard,' Simon soothed. 'It's a damned shame. Come on.' He held out his hand. 'Now come on Richard, give me your car keys.'

He loaded me into the passenger seat of my car, strapped me in and got behind the wheel. He'd just inserted the key in the ignition when I began to offload. I looked straight ahead as I spoke, my glassy eyes not focused on anything in particular. My words, in that padded silence of the car, were laced with a whisky-truth. Simon had never witnessed me so wretched, not even when Danny died. But there was something else, a change, an opening up of what was once a very tightly shut door.

'I knew the boy wasn't mine... but I never said anything. Never, not one teeny tiny word.' I shook my head and half wagged a finger in an exaggerated attempt to emphasise the point. 'I didn't mention it - not to her, not to anyone. No one knew.' I paused as I hung my head summoning up the words. 'When I realised, he wasn't mine I felt ashamed and humiliated. Was she laughing at me? Stupid Richard being a soft touch, grafting all his days to bring up someone else's child. I was angry. Really bloody angry. But strangely, not with her, I didn't even give her a hard time.' I turned my head to look at Simon. 'I forgave her, Simon.'

As our eyes momentarily locked, I saw a look of complete incredulity. 'You might find that hard to understand Simon. Even I don't fully understand it. Perhaps it makes me appear weak. Maybe I am weak? It's hard to explain.' I hung my head.

'I loved Danny as my own. I gave them everything I could and yet still she treated me like the bad guy.' I thumped the passenger door and shook my dizzy head. 'Why? Why?'

Simon remained quiet and still while I fought to regain composure. My forehead creased as my eyes began to pool.

'I've had enough, Simon, beyond enough.'

I fumbled in my pockets for my cigarettes, needing a distraction. When I fished them out my drunken fingers couldn't extract one from the packet. Simon obliged and, lighting it for me, encouraged me to continue.

'And now her nerves are frayed... I feel I'm watching her about to tip over the edge all over again. For crying out loud, I don't know how to help her or what to do.' My voice cracked with desperation. 'I'm not even sure she wants my help. Everything I try just makes her worse. Do you know Simon, there was a point when I thought we were turning a corner? And then, tonight, Tom showed up again.'

'Tom!' Simon was taken aback. 'I thought you'd seen him off.'

I felt a little more sober at the mention of Tom.

'So did I. Turns out he got married and came back here. His wife got really friendly with Diane. Neither of them was aware of the connection... He turned up at my place to pick his wife up. When I saw him, it took everything I had not to...' I clenched my fists until the knuckles showed white. 'Then he went and said something smart. Full of himself he was, goading me, taunting me.'

My face twisted as I recalled the moment. 'I snapped and ended up smacking him one. Look.' I showed Simon the cut on my knuckle. 'I got him right where I wanted to, it was so...'

'Richard, you really need to decide what to do, one way or another. You can't go on like this.'

'I know. The only thing I can come up with is to re-enlist. It would give both of us space. I can't divorce her. For a start I can't afford it and, given her mental state, I'd probably end up with Frankie.'

'Couldn't you...?'

'I'd have no home to provide her with. Given what she's been up to lately I think she'd need more care than I can give. She'd probably end up back in the system.'

'What about your family, your sisters?'

'That's just it, they don't really know Frankie. Diane wouldn't let her near any of them, you know what she's been like.'

'What about the in-laws?'

'If they take her, I'd probably end up never seeing her again, but I doubt they'd be considered, not with Madge's health being as it is. They wouldn't have her last time, anyway. If I re-enlist, and get stationed nearby, it covers most of what I need.'

'But that's just it, Richard, there's no guarantee where you'd get stationed. You can't demand it either.'

'But I can't think of anything else.'

'Richard, I've got plenty of contacts. Do you want me to put some feelers out? I could sort you out with accommodation until you're up on your feet. Leave it with me.'

Diane ... Tuesday, the next day

I called in sick, claimed I had a headache. From the hall window I could see that Richard's car had gone. I didn't really think much of it, he was always coming and going.

Then I went back to bed. When I closed my eyes, my body began to tremble and the more I became aware of it the more erratic my breathing became. Deep inside I felt myself constrict and twist as though from a distance a million doors were slamming shut until, finally I exploded with one great scream. The cry came for what seemed like an age. Waves of rage, fear, hurt and pain coalesced into one. My mouth gathered around it as my body went rigid, my hands spasming as they gripped onto the bedding.

When the scream ebbed, I drew breath and realised there was still a fire within me. The will to fight showed itself through my fists and gritted teeth as I pummelled the pillows until one burst. Feathers filled the room, caught in my hair, my mouth, floating and drifting over everything. I howled and punched until I had nothing left to give. Then the tears and shaking took over.

This can't be happening. Please God not again. My mind flicked from one confused fragmented memory to another. A soul-less hospital ward, hypodermic needles, being strapped down, *'Here bite on this.'* Tom's tender words, Richard's voice 'He got Sophie pregnant,' Carla's mischievous grin. 'The Valium does that honey.' Danny, his laughter, memories of him running barefoot in the back garden clutching Duffy, and then his cold white face beneath the hospital strip lights. Still. My mother's face: 'Pull yourself together … the shame you have brought upon this family.' Frankie: holding out a cup of tea, her little face so open and trusting.

Why could I not love Frankie? Why do I always push her away? Perhaps it's the way she looks at me, like she could really see me. Does she judge me? How ridiculous, how could a twelve-year-old child judge? Yet even now, Frankie makes me feel inadequate.

I wrestled these thoughts until they distilled into worrying about what lay ahead. It seemed like one great big empty road of nothing. Just a routine of work, childcare, housekeeping, a loveless marriage and an endless draining of energy. Each in their own way were tying me down with their shoulds, oughts, and musts. A collection of expectations and shame. They all collided together into one big black, unscalable wall and an unending sense of exhaustion. Merely thinking about it leached my energy. The phone rang a couple of times, but I ignored it. Just the thought of picking it up overwhelmed me. My head was too full, too tight to let the real world enter.

I had a vague recollection of the sound of the letter box flapping but turned over and went back to sleep. Frankie brought the note up when she got home after school. It read:

Dear Diane,

I stopped by to say goodbye. I believe I owe you that. Tom told me everything but I'm not mad at you, please believe me. We were both victims of circumstance and immaturity.

I know that in another life we would have been the best of friends. I'm leaving Tom and going back to Connecticut. It's just not working for me here.

Diane, have a nice life and be happy.

Your friend, Carla.

I pulled up the covers, turned over and shut my eyes.

Frankie ... Tuesday/Wednesday

I couldn't concentrate in class. I sat at the back in the seat nearest the window watching the wind in the trees and a magpie collecting twigs and bits of paper to build its nest. The teacher's voice faded into the background like the radio does when it's there and you're not really listening. I felt kind of weird and hollow like all the colours in my world had been watered down until they'd fused into bland. I didn't have words to explain it, where to begin? After school I went to see Patsy. She was warm in a sarcastic Patsy sort of way. She answered the door sporting her new David Bowie haircut, her eyebrows standing out pink and proud where she had recently plucked them, 'Just like David Bowie's.'

'So, you still playing happy families or has the shit hit the fan?'

I shrugged, Patsy had seen through it all. She'd grown up weary. Being a child of a single parent family had seen to that. I first saw it when she'd got a parcel from her dad for her birthday. Some jewellery and a dress she was never going to wear. Her fingers traced the earrings then she threw them across the room screaming. I couldn't understand why she was so upset, going on about them being presents to make her dad feel better, that he didn't even know her. It took a while for me to figure it all out, but I get it now.

We charged up the wooden stairs sounding like stampeding elephants and into the kitchen. Patsy's mum was sitting where she usually sat in her tatty armchair reading a book and smoking a cigarette. She looked up briefly, 'Frankie, you alright?'

I nodded but didn't look at her directly.

'How's your Mum, she okay?'

I grimaced and went into the kitchen, Patsy had gone back to eating her tea - fish fingers, chips and peas. Dousing her fish fingers in tomato sauce and talking between mouthfuls, barely stopping to taste her food.

From the other room Patsy's Mum nagged, 'Patsy, eat your greens. It'll make your tits grow.'

We giggled, it was something that we shared in common - flat chests. It had become something of a joke in Patsy's household. Three months before we had hatched a cunning plan because both our Mums had point blank refused to buy us trainer bras. It just wasn't fair.

We had planned our bold adventure at the kitchen table. We forged sick notes for school and spent days practicing how to steal, using information gleaned from Patsy's recollection of Oliver Twist. The target: trainer bras from the Ladybird shop in town. We stashed non-school clothes in the bin cupboard and changed in the subway, stuffing out school skirts and jumpers into our bags before running through the estate's back alleys to catch a bus into town.

Things went wrong when we were confronted by the shop assistant, a middle-aged woman with a strip of lurid red lipstick plastered on her lips. She looked like someone had gashed open her face and her uneven bottom teeth made me think of sharks. She watched us closely and threw us out of the shop because we weren't buying anything. As we left, we walked smack bang into Patsy's auntie who clipped us round the ears and frog-marched us back to school via the number 37 bus. She nagged us all the way there, even made us change back into our school uniform on the bus. I don't know what excuse she gave to the school secretary, but no questions were asked and our Mums were none the wiser. .We loved her for that. Oh and the sweeties of course.

'How many bloody peas do I have to eat before they start to grow then, Ma?' I marvel. How I would give my eye teeth to be able to be as free as Patsy. She could swear, even use the word bloody, and there was no kick back. Her Mum might have given her a sharp rebuke or stern look, but that was as far as it went. Patsy was lucky. Even though her family were poor, they were tight knit. Patsy belonged she knew her family accepted her without question no matter what she did. I felt a tinge of envy every time I witnessed it. Most especially when Patsy left the house:

'Love you, Ma!'

'Love you too, Mini Moo!'

There were no words for me; I left my house to silence. There were no words to pad the hurt spaces, to bind me to something hard and concrete or to bolster how I felt about myself. I had no sense of belonging. If my Mum didn't love me, then who could? When I left Patsy's, I was twenty minutes late home.

Mum was waiting for me in the kitchen. The moment I stepped through the door when I was met with a hard, stinging slap.

'Where've you been you little bitch?' She towered over me, menacing like an angry dog. 'Answer me, where've you been?' I cowered in the corner, feeling the door handle in my back, wondering whether to make a run for it.

'Patsy's. I was at Patsy's, Mum.' My voice was small, small for my size and age.

'Liar. I bet you were hanging round with those boys at The Square, weren't you?'

'No Mum, I swear.'

'Swear? You sound just like a bloody Miller.' She spat the words out, like they were something to be reviled, something repulsive, ugly. 'Look at you,' she looked me up and down as if I was something horrid she'd picked up on her shoe. 'Do you know how disappointed I am with you? And there I was, thinking you could do better, better than the Millers. But no, you're lazy, thoughtless and stupid just like them. Richard's sister was a trollop, flaunting herself round town. Common as muck, and here you are following in her footsteps.' Confused, I felt frightened and angry all at the same time. What did she mean *just like them?* I had never met any of them, not that I could remember any way. I knew I had aunties and grandparents, well, did have grandparents, they had died a while back. I would have loved to have been given the opportunity to meet them, make up my own mind about them but ...

I didn't quite know what to make of it. Dad never talked of them - probably because Mum kicked up such a fuss if he did. They were the enemy as far as Mum was concerned and to even think about them was like taking sides.

But I did fleetingly recall one Christmas, Dad giving me and Danny presents saying they were from my grandparents. 'My Mummy and Daddy,' he said pointedly. Mum was upstairs at the time. Danny and I opened them in front of the fire where Dad disposed of the wrapping paper. Mine was a Post Office set complete with pretty pink writing paper, envelopes, stamps and a Letraset. I was so happy I started writing an immediate thank you note to these kind people who didn't even know me but sent great presents. I couldn't recall what Danny had got but I did remember the blissful peace as we were lost in our play worlds. And then it all changed when Mum appeared. I remember the shrieking and the presents being ripped out of our hands 'Take them back. Take them back,' Mum kept shouting. I can still see our outstretched hands and hear tearful pleas. The sting of the slaps on the back of my legs and Dad leaving the house at high speed, leaving me and Danny too terrified to do or say anything. I'd almost forgotten the memory but thinking of it now made me narrow my eyes and look defiantly at my mother.

'How dare you!' Mum grabbed my wrist in a vice-like grip, her long red fingernails digging into my flesh. 'Take that look off your face this instant, before I knock it off. Do you hear me?' She tightened her grasp and brought her face close to mine. 'Do I make myself clear?'

Through gritted teeth I whispered. 'Yes.'

Diane ... Tuesday, late morning

The banging was insistent, a rhythmical thumping on the front door made worse by Bonzo's frantic barks. For a moment I thought it might be Richard, perhaps he had changed his mind and come back, he took all his stuff last night. But why bang on the door when he has a key? I turned over and tried to ignore it but it didn't stop. I tried pulling the covers over my ears, but that didn't work either. Finally, I dragged myself out of bed, pulled back the curtain, opened the window and leaned out.

'What? What do you ... ?' My stomach lurched.

Tom was standing on the doorstep. He looked up. 'Diane, please, we need to talk.'

I looked at him with all the contempt I could muster. *He got Sophie pregnant. He got Sophie pregnant.* My mouth dried, my fingers felt brittle against the sill. I willed myself to imprint the image of the Tom I saw below me, saying to myself, *Remember this moment, remember what an insipid bastard this man really is.*

He looked unkempt. I could tell he hadn't shaved; the twelve o'clock shadow was just forming. His shirt was wrinkled, and his shoes scuffed. He looked dowdy and pathetic. *My, how the mighty have fallen.* I'd never noticed his rounded shoulders before. Daddy had always said men with rounded shoulders weren't to be trusted. *They keep secrets, that's what makes their shoulders hunched.* Tom's insincerity and shallowness marked him for the man he was. Looking down I could also see a thinning of his hair at the crown, a small patch, the size of a child's fist. I imagined it wouldn't be long until complete baldness was upon him. It was not a good look; it aged him. Besides, he didn't have the right shaped head, all bone and shine. At least Richard had a full head of hair.

It seemed like an age before I spoke, the moment stretched on and on, wrapping itself around my heart, girding it. 'Wait there.' It was more of a command than a request. I threw on a top and a pair of slacks over my nightie and ran to the bathroom to splash my face. Then I loaded my toothbrush with toothpaste and shoved it round my mouth. As I looked at myself in the mirror, I rehearsed the words that I was going to say, tasted their potency in my mouth, on my lips and fed them the fire they needed.

At the door I stood, arms folded, sneering. The imaginary wall couldn't have been higher if I had tried.

'So, what have you got to say for yourself?' He seemed to have shrunk from how I remembered him. It was as if I was seeing him for who he was for the first time. Even his voice seemed nasal and grating.

'Diane. God you're even more beautiful than when…'

'Oh, please! Don't patronise me - it serves no one.' I thought of Carla and I felt instantly sorry for her.

'I don't know where to begin,' he looked weasel-like; conceited and untrustworthy. He shifted his weight and put his hands in his pockets and fidgeted with the loose change. I could tell he was frantically searching for something to say, something that would hook me, draw me in.

'Firstly, I should say I'm so sorry.'

'For what, the other night? For not turning up all those years ago. For shagging Richard's sister? For betraying your wife by even being here. And why do you need to apologise? Why now? Is it to assuage your guilt or to see if you're in with a chance?'

'Diane, I've … can I come in rather than say this on the doorstep?' He looked around as though afraid of being seen. But I didn't care, I wanted it to be out in the open, this humiliation to be public. I wanted to see this snake squirm.

'No! Say what you have to say and leave.'

'You're not making this easy for me, are you?' He tilted his head to one side trying to play coy, but this just fuelled my resolve further.

'No, and why should I?'

'Diane, I still love you. I've always loved you.'

'Huh! But not enough to stick around - and what about your wife. Carla? Doesn't she figure in this somewhere? You have a child too, remember?

'They've gone.'

'Gone?' I feigned surprise just to see how far he would take it.

'I never should have married her.'

'Where's she gone?'

'Back home and good riddance. Diane, listen to me. It's always been you.' He stepped closer, his face inches away from mine. I smelt the stench of stale alcohol on his breath. I saw him in the years to come, vulgar and bloated sitting in squalor in his string vest, his bald head shining beneath a strip light. Still thinking he had all the charm and smarmy moves, still thinking he was *it*. I didn't move a muscle.

'So, you think you can just pick up where you left off, do you?' I fixed him with a hard-bitten glare.

'You have no clue about what I went through after you left - and don't flatter yourself thinking it was all because of you either, because it wasn't.'

'Then tell me Diane, I'll help you.'

I couldn't bear the idea of Tom knowing all my business - getting to judge and reject me. Because that's what he would do if he knew. It's what everyone did. There was still a part of me that didn't want to admit to my *nerves*. The shame and stigma continued to haunt me, made me feel inadequate, made me work hard to appear normal to the outside world... whatever that meant. I shut people out, kept the *real* Diane out of reach. It was safer that way. Carla had been an exception with her I had felt I could be myself ... and look where that had got me.

He put his foot on the doorstep as if he were about to just step through, the stitching was coming away at the toe, soon the leather would lift, and the shoe ruined. He wasn't listening to what I was saying, I could tell by the way his body was set, stooped forward a little, his neck muscles taut, a hand curled around the door frame, his iris' pinpointed. He was thinking that he could win me over, get what suited him and his ego. It was written all over his face and that incensed me more.

I felt a presence. Bonzo pushed his way forward between Tom and I, he stood stock still, hackles raised baring his teeth. I didn't check him, in-fact I enjoyed the moment. Tom hesitating, unsure what to do, the wind knocked out of his cocky sails.

'Tom, I'm saying this just the once, so listen up. Piss. Off! Now leave me alone and don't ever bother me again.' I pushed him hard, he reeled backwards and lost his footing. I left him sprawled across the shrubbery covered in dirt, called Bonzo in and slammed the door shut.

Only Bonzo saw my angry tears. I was livid with myself for being so gullible and naive, angry with him for being such a rat, and angry for the pain I'd endured over the years and for what? Him? *Oh, what a bloody fool I'd been. Why did I not see it? How was I to pick up the pieces and move on?* Grappling with the banister rail I climbed back up the stairs in a slow laboured fashion. In my bedroom I made straight for my pills - slugging back two Valium with the dregs of the tea Frankie had brought me that morning, then I forced myself with shaking hands to get ready for work. I'd changed my mind and decided to go in after all.

Frankie - Thursday

Sleep evaded me that night. I tried counting the cars passing on the main road, then counting sheep. I tried to remember Danny but couldn't conjure up his face - not all the features at any rate. I could recall his brown eyes and how, when the light shone in a particular way, they looked conker brown. I remembered the shape of his chin, the way it trembled when he cried. The tear-shaped mole at the side of his eyebrow. Was it left, or right? These things were now fragments becoming more and more difficult to piece together. But his shirt, the one I put on Bonzo, that held a strong memory. Not the type recalled by smell, but a hardly noticeable stain just below the collar. A small blob of what was once tomato sauce. I remembered him vigorously shaking the bottle then taking off the lid and holding it up above his head at eye level to see if anything would come out. Nothing happened at first but then a huge blob tumbled out and caught him on the chin and neck and ultimately his shirt. We both creased in a fit of giggles. Then I reached out my index finger wiping up the blob from his chin before smartly popping it into my mouth and smacking my lips for show. This made us laugh even harder - his mouth open with half chewed food, shoulders squeezed up, slit-eyed-laughter. Oh, how I missed him.

Early the next morning I was up and out running across the park with Bonzo. A mist lay in knee-high layers above the grass giving it a magical feel. As I ran the mist swirled, billowing around us, I pressed on faster just to prolong the other-worldly effect.

Running helped to clear my head, shake out the jangles. I never felt happier than when running with Bonzo at my side.

We were back home by 8 o'clock, time enough for me to have a piece of toast before heading off to school. This time I left without waking Mum or taking her a cup of tea. *She can make her own for all I care,* I thought, and that was just it. I was beginning not to care.

At registration I was told to go and see Mrs Eames the games teacher at break time. I wracked my brains, had I done something wrong or forgotten to do something? When the bell went, I made my way to the staff room, threading through the bunches of kids streaming through the corridors. I knocked, a timid knock, on the staffroom door. It swung open and I was told to, 'Wait here,' while Mrs Eames was summoned. Peering inside, I saw sheets of smoke settling in the room. It made me think of billowing net curtains drying in the back garden. I heard the murmur of teachers chatting and laughing, and I could pick out some of their voices. The husky Welsh tones of Mr Edwards the English teacher, who frightened me with his big hands and booming voice - 'I will send you home crying' - and the shrill pitch of Mrs Atkinson the needlework teacher, she was rather overweight and had such eye-watering body odour in the summer months that I had to hold my breath. I found it spellbinding to catch a glimpse of the teachers all loosened up.

I watched as Mrs Eames weaved her way through the groups of teachers, stopping here and there to respond to colleagues' questions. It was like watching a series of false starts and to my twelve year old head, took ages.

Always cheerful, Mrs Eames greeted me with a warm smile. Short, barely three inches taller than me, yet compact, she stood out in her black track suit with white piping down the sides of the trousers and a silver whistle on a rope around her neck.

'Ah, Frankie, thank you so much for coming. Now, I wonder would you like to help me out? One of the school's runners has managed to twist her ankle just before a race meet and we are in dire need of another one.' Her look was direct; she smiled as if to invite me to respond. It took a moment for me to process the information. My mouth fell open.

'But Miss, I've never competed in a race. I wouldn't know how to do it and besides, I don't have the right kit.'

'I'm sure all these problems can be surmounted Frankie. Would you consider running in the 800 metres next week?'

I stood a moment, trying to think it through.

'Why me, Miss?'

'Frankie, I've watched you run up the main road every morning for the past three weeks. Did you know you that from the subway to the school is just over 800 metres and from what I have seen you are able to cover it in very good time. You are a natural.'

'Oh, I didn't know you were watching me, Miss.' I could feel myself going a bit red, I was a bit embarrassed but secretly pleased.

'Now, the meet is on Thursday. It would mean taking you out of your normal classes for the last two sessions and you would probably get home for about 5pm. Would that be alright?'

I chewed the side of my mouth, trying not to frown. 'Thursday night? I'm not sure, Miss.'

'I'll give you a note for your parents. The school bus will take you there and bring you home. Or better still, I'll come and speak to your parents, given it's such a last-minute arrangement.'

'No. No, Miss.' I felt a rising panic. 'You don't need to do that.' I already knew how Mum would react. She would be all smiles and politeness to the teacher's face but as soon as the door was shut and the teacher safely out of earshot it would be a different matter altogether. I decided that I'd figure a way, somehow.

'So, Frankie, are you on board with this?' Mrs Eames inclined her head and raised her eyebrows.

I half-smiled, still preoccupied, 'Okay, I suppose.'

I climbed on the school bus going to the race venue. In my carrier bag I had the new items of sports kit Mrs Eames had given me. A white Airtex T-shirt, black shorts an armband and a new pair of black plimsoles. I got so much pleasure from their fresh-from-the-factory smell that I kept opening the bag every so often to get another whiff. There was something about having a new item, all for me. It meant the world. I could physically touch those plimsols and remind myself that I had some worth, but even better than that, someone cared.

I didn't tell Mum about the race. I'd thought about it. I thought about nothing else. But after looking at it from every angle, I knew Mum would have put a stop to it and that would have been harder to swallow. For once I wanted something all to myself - so even the prospect of getting caught and the fall out that followed would be worth it. I had to have a moment to shine - just this once at least. I hoped beyond hope that fate would smile on me. *Maybe Patsy'd let me hide the kit behind the bins.* But one thing I was sure about - nothing would get in the way of me running.

On the day before the race, I went out on the school playing field to take my place on the track with other runners - we were practising our starts. Walking onto the track was scary. I could sense all the other kids looking at me. It made me want to run off. All those kids, who had the right kit with name tags that their mothers had sewed in for them. They all appeared so much more able and sure of themselves. I kept my head down, half waiting for the snide comments to start. I felt so self-conscious, running in my vest and home-made shorts. Ones that I'd cut down from an old pair of slacks and sewn up with the wrong colour cotton because that's all there was.

I took my place on the starting line, head down, crouched low, ready to spring at the sound of the 'Go'. I practised in my bare feet - I didn't possess a decent pair of plimsoles. Not that I really minded. The grass felt good, I enjoyed the feeling of dirt between my toes. Yes, the bare feet attracted a bit of attention, but I did my best to blot it out, I used it to make myself more determined. Every time I heard 'Go', I felt as if my life had been suddenly kick-started.

Taking off quickly. I sprinted, pretending my shadow was Bonzo as it matched me. I ran as though my very existence depended on it, keeping within the lines, bending on the curve, feeling the wind in my hair, arms pumping, legs stretching, heart beating as though it was trying to break out of my chest. It was total bliss. I forgot about everyone else. In my head I felt braver with the thrill of it all.

I enjoyed competitive running more than I'd imagined I would. It was quite a revelation. Now I'd found something I was good at. It made a huge difference. To think I nearly didn't go. I had moments when I worried whether I would be accepted because of my outfit. Then I'd worry about whether I would be able to keep up and if not, would I end up making a show of myself straggling along behind everyone. This stupid skinny girl running bare foot in her home-made shorts and Keynote-kiddie vest. But what I thought would happen and what happened was quite the opposite.

Keeping up with the experienced runners was easy. I not only kept up, but at times out-ran them. After a while, when I began to not worry, I could tell they were charmed, and they even said nice things to me like 'that was ace.' It felt so good it made me want to cry. Mrs Eames was encouraging, and it felt good, really good.

Finally, I had found a part of myself that made me feel connected, powerful even and I knew I didn't want to let it go. But a niggle began to rear its ugly head. What would happen when the runner with the sprained ankle came back? Would I have to leave?

At the race ground, loads of school buses lined up as the kids piled off. Teachers with clip boards shouted them into the grounds. They walked in single file and then spilled in higgledy-piggledy groups along the benches in the wooden stands. The noise of their voices sounded like a flock of twittering birds. You could hardly hear the teachers voices above the din of kids' chatter.

Out front the competitors started to warm up, running on the spot, bending, stretching, jumping up and down. The track, all newly painted, stretched out into the distance. A tannoy squeaked into life as the town mayor gave a long speech that echoed across the field. He welcomed everyone to the event and finished with the lines, *'It's not about the winning, it's the participating and teamwork that counts. Do your best and good luck to you all.'*

The first heats took place, starting with the younger runners and the one hundred metres sprint. The crowd roared from the stands. From where I sat on the wooden bench, I could feel the bouncing bodies and stamping feet. The noise and atmosphere infectious, the stands positively vibrated with excitement. I found myself getting caught up in the euphoria, jumping and shouting wildly along with the rest of competitors. The heats whittled down the winners until the deciding races for each category and age group took place. It came to my turn to run the 800 metres, I felt light-headed. I took off my shoes to put on my new plimsolls but found that my feet had swollen, and they no longer fitted. I knew I wouldn't be able to run in them, even if I took my socks off. There was no time to try and explain to Mrs Eames, hardly any time to think, so I did the only thing left to me, I took off the plimsolls and the socks and went to the start line in my bare feet.

Crouching down, my mind closed off the outside world. All the noise, movement, smells around me blotted out, even down to the fidgeting girl hunkered down further up the track. My mind had telescoped down. I sensed the sun on my back, the light breeze across my forearms, the strands of grass and hard dirt beneath my feet. From the corner of my eye, I watched the track judge shifting position making ready.

His words rang out, 'Take your marks ... '

A single empty crisp packet drifted across the track, its foil glancing off the ground reflecting flashes of light then lifted with the breeze as though yanked by invisible string.

'Get set.'

I was primed, all geared up, every muscle, every sinew flexed. Energy coursing through me, so much so I could hear my blood pulsing in my ears. I was ready, more than ready.

The gun fired, CRACK!

I had a strong start. I bolted out arms pumping, one of three out in front, pushing hard till my lungs felt like they were on fire. My breath fast and laboured, for an odd second or two all I heard was my feet hammering the ground one after the other in quick succession.

My heart pounded more from fear than over-exertion. But I knew that sensation, something I had learned outside of running, something much closer to home. As I ran, I mentally battled with myself, fighting for control, pushing myself to stretch my stride, focus, blot everything else out with a fierce determination.

Another runner came up fast on my near side. Just a glimpse of a body moving in was all I needed to spur me on. Then, for a split second my mind let in the sound of cheering. Above the roar and din I picked out a name.

FRANKIE, FRANKIE, FRANKIE.

It carried on the wind across the track, spurring me on, as though, somehow, I was riding the crest of an enormous crashing wave of noise. Miraculously I found the strength, the capacity, to push myself, my legs powering ahead, my arms pumping, tilting towards the finishing line, my chin jutted out for that extra inch. All around the stadium, the crowd was on its feet, roaring and cheering. I hit the tape with my chest. A bulb flashed, I'd won my heat.

It felt fantastic, like I was walking on air. All those faces beaming at me. *Me.* They were reaching out, touching my head, my shoulders, patting me on the back, shaking my hands. Through the noise I heard congratulatory voices saying my name. Having surrounded me, my team-mates lifted me up and threw me in the air. I felt such joy to have been claimed to belong. My confidence couldn't have been any higher if it tried.

When the final heat was called for my category, I took my place in my lane. I was so much smaller in comparison to the rest of the runners, all at least a head above me. Their bodies had filled out, showing womanly curves and shapely legs in their sports kits. Not that I took any notice - I was light as bird bones. I had that advantage. In my mind I was the equivalent of a peregrine falcon with an airspeed exceeding two hundred miles per hour.

The gun went off and we launched ourselves off the starting line. My every movement was precision timed. Gradually I threaded my way through the huddle of runners. It felt natural to me, knowing when to push myself out and up front. I ran against another runner whose form was strong, but I was holding my own; we matched each other stride for stride. As we took the final bend we jostled for position, our legs tangled and suddenly I tumbled, ending up sprawled on all fours at the side of the track. I stayed there, watching the runners' feet rumble past. I couldn't help but collapse down on myself and bury my face in the grass and cry. My knees smarted like I had carpet burns but that wasn't the cause of my tears. My disappointment burned.

Mrs Eames was the first to get to me. Kneeling beside me, her voice was soft with concern.

'Frankie, are you hurt?'

I shook my head, unable to speak for fear my sobs might overwhelm me. I felt an arm around me. 'Come on. Can you get up?' I felt myself being lifted up but didn't dare raise my head. I was consumed with shame and disappointment.

'For your first event, Frankie you were magnificent. We all saw it. Well done indeed. You should be proud of yourself.'

'But I let you all down. I didn't win.'

'Nonsense. You let no one down. You ran with all your heart and that's what counts Frankie. You have the makings of a great runner. Now stand tall and show everyone you are alright and take the applause you are due.'

Slowly I stood to my full height and wiped my face with the back of my hand. When I looked around everyone was standing facing me whistling and applauding. I responded with a weak wave and a smile before Mrs Eames took me off to have Germolene and plasters applied to my scraped knees.

Mrs Eames dropped me off at home after the event. She let the mini-bus engine idle while she reiterated how pleased she was with my efforts. 'Would you like me to come in and tell your mother?'

'No.' My response was almost too emphatic.

It was gone five o'clock when I let myself in. I was anxious that Mum might be home at any minute but when I saw the note on the table it gave me a huge sense of relief. Mum was going to be late home. She was staying on to make up time from when she had been off.

I fed Bonzo, peeled the potatoes and then took him for a quick walk. As I walked, I filled my lungs with air and my face lit up with a beaming smile. I had participated in the races, won my heat and there were no repercussions.

However, the next day, at 6.30pm I heard mum's key in the door. She slammed it shut. I instantly felt my breath go shallow. Bonzo leapt up and stood waiting at the front room door, tail wagging. I sat on the edge of my seat, knee jumping. Something wasn't right. Mum moved into the kitchen, filled the kettle and put it on the lit hob. I heard her light a cigarette then call, in her *I'm annoyed voice*, 'Frankie, come here this instant.'

I began to tremble. I went through to the kitchen. Mum had a face like thunder, she was brandishing the local Friday newspaper. Its headline read 'Barefoot winner' and beneath was a picture of me bowing into the tape as I crossed the line.

She grabbed me by the hair and slammed me against the door. 'How dare you. You little bitch, you did this deliberately to show me up didn't you?'

'No, Mum,' I recoiled, my hands on her arms trying to gently ease them off.

'Don't you 'No Mum' me. You little vixen, now everyone will think that I'm a bad mother. Bare feet! Whatever possessed you?'

'Mum, I promise faithfully, I didn't even think that ...'

'That's your problem, you never think. You just go ahead and do what you please never thinking of the consequences. Isn't that right?' I felt her grip tighten, straining my head backwards. I know the fear showed in my eyes, I felt it racking my body.

'Well ...?'

'Yes, Mum.'

'On Monday you are to go to school and tell that bloody teacher that you are not allowed to make a public display of yourself. Do I make myself clear?'

'But, Mum, please,' I pleaded but knew that it was futile.

'I'll hear nothing more about it. You will learn your lesson about being thoughtless the hard way. Do I make myself clear?'

'Yes.'

'Yes who?'

Through gritted teeth I said the words, 'Yes. Mum.'

'Now get upstairs, straight to bed. I don't want to see or hear a peep out of you. You're nothing but an ungrateful child. Valerie's children would never behave in such a way - bringing shame and embarrassment to their family. They're perfectly polite and well mannered, they know where their priorities lie. But you, you bring nothing but shame to my door and now everyone will be talking. Talking about me and you. You have caused this. Do you know how hard it is for me?'

In my bedroom I lay on my bed. Tears pooled at the side of my face as I thought of the potential things running could give me. All the joy that now had to stop - it was so unfair. Mum was unfair. I wished I could talk to someone, try and explain what was going on but I didn't quite know how or where to begin. Who would understand me anyway and besides, I was just a child. No one would believe me and even Patsy would probably laugh.

As I lay there, I thought of all the reasons why living one more day was just too much effort. Trusting my parents was not an option. They were too wrapped up in themselves. Not that I saw it as a fault, it was what it was.

I thought of all the times I had been hit or shouted at, of all the unkind things said and done. I thought of Dad. Yes, he did care, but not enough to stay around, not enough to intervene when Mum went off on one and, oh yes, he had witnessed enough of them but said nothing. He would retreat into the front room to watch telly with the volume turned up to drown out the shouting. Surely this was not the norm - or was it?

I felt sure that Mum didn't care - so many examples came to mind, and as for Grandma, she never really listened. She would just squeeze my cheeks and tell me to be patient and to help around the house.

'Your mother's got her nerves problem Frankie so you have to make exceptions.'

And even when Grandma had listened and quizzed mum, her explanation made it all sound convincing and my description a complete over exaggeration or figment of my imagination: 'big fibs.' It happened so often that I learned to shut up and shut down.

Nanny listened, she would sit and give her undivided attention, hands patiently folded in her lap, eye's warm and all on you. When I thought of her, my smile was wider than a mile and even after all these years I still missed her. I felt sure she would have been on my side but at the end of the day she would have told me to go back home, that her hands were tied because of the authorities. I would have given anything to go back there, for the routine, for knowing what was going to happen, for feeling safe, for the love that Nanny showered on everyone, and for the sweeties.

Bonzo was the only thing that gave me an excuse to stay. But I figured that he would be looked after even if I wasn't around so there was no need to fret about him.

I couldn't bear to carry on like this. There was no working with or against it anymore. The rules were always changing, and I couldn't keep up. I didn't have any money to run away with and besides I had nowhere to go. I had only one option available. *If the opportunity presents itself, I'll do it tomorrow* I thought.

On Sunday Mum left the house late to go shopping and see Grandma and Grandad. She left strict instructions for me to clean up the kitchen and my room. I saw to the chores as best I could. I hoovered, dusted, polished. Washed up all the dishes in the sink. Emptied the bins and washed the kitchen floor. After all that, I took Bonzo out to the park. We ran along the length of the brook that threaded directly through the centre of the park. We skirted the hawthorn and ash trees, climbed over the fallen tree that was the meeting place for the local kids at night. On the return leg it started pelting it down.

Alone in my room, I had too much time to think. I crept into Mum's bedroom, lifted the Mogadon bottle from the bedside table and emptied its contents - four tablets. In the bathroom I washed them down with water from the tap and went back to my bedroom. Hastily I wrote down a few words for Patsy thanking her for her friendship and telling her that she could keep my platform shoes that were hidden in the bin cupboard. Tears blotted the paper as I wrote - telling how I couldn't cope anymore. How everyone would be better off with me out of the way - that no one would really miss me except perhaps Patsy and Bonzo. With the note finished I lay on my bed, draping myself dramatically with my candlewick bedspread like a version of The Lady of Shallot. Finally sleep took over and the late afternoon hours crept into the darkness.

It was 8am when I woke on the Monday, all groggy and dry mouthed. I opened my eyes and looked around me. Everything seemed grey. All my favourite little possessions had no meaning: stupid gonks, books, pictures - what was the point? I was still in the clothes I had been wearing the day before. Evidently Mum hadn't looked in on me. She didn't notice that I hadn't come out of my room. I felt unimportant and, even worse, a failure. I couldn't even get taking my own life right. I cried for a good while, until my Mum's voice, coming from the landing pulled me up short.

'Frankie, Bonzo needs a walk before you go to school. Hurry up.'

Bonzo, that's right. Bonzo needs me. I dragged on my school clothes and hurried downstairs. I fed him, pulled on my jacket and the two of us set off up the road to the park.

I arrived early at school and made a point of going to speak to Mrs Eames before registration. I'd called her out of the noisy staffroom with its rumble of voices, rattle of teacups and plumes of cigarette smoke. We stood just outside the staffroom door when I woodenly delivered my mother's decision.

'But, Frankie, I don't understand. Why ever not?'

'She just said no, Miss.'

'And what do you want, Frankie?'

I looked away, barely daring to breathe. 'It doesn't matter what I want, Miss.'

'Frankie?' Mrs Eames tried to catch my eye as I turned my head. She reached out and gently took my chin between her thumb and forefinger, making me look up. 'I'm going to call your Mum and see if I can get her to change her mind. Okay?'

'Thanks Miss.' My eyes were beginning to water. 'But I don't think it will do any good.'

The bell rang and the corridor swarmed with hundreds of bodies.

Diane - Monday

I'd been nursing a cup of tea in the kitchen while trying to decide whether I had the energy to go to work. I had been watching my cigarette burn down in the ashtray when the phone rang. I was loath to answer - I was loath to do anything. It all seemed like too much effort. The phone rang long enough to draw me out of my lethargy. Clearing my throat, I picked it up and answered in my bright telephone voice.

'Hello? Cheltenham 53078'

'Mrs Miller? It's Mrs Eames here from the school. Is this a convenient time?'

'Not really ...'

'Your daughter tells me that you have told her that she is not allowed to participate in competitive running. Is that correct?

'Well, yes, that's about the long and the short of it. She disobeyed me and she knows that to do so has consequences. This is the only way to teach her a lesson.'

'Mrs Miller, I appreciate that a parent needs to reprimand a child when appropriate, but this does appear to be a little excessive. Frankie has ...'

'Excuse me? Who are you to presume to tell me what I should and shouldn't do with my child? Frankie has been incredibly difficult since being suspended and I have to take a strong stance with her.'

'Mrs Miller, I understand your concern, but your daughter has a remarkable talent. With the right support and encouragement, she could go far. I believe it could also present a solution to the difficulties you have been experiencing with her, something to engage and motivate her.'

'I'm afraid I've made my decision and I'm not about to change it. Now, if you'll excuse me, I have to get to work.' I dropped the phone in its cradle as if it were burning my fingers. Under my breath I muttered 'Who the bloody hell does she think she is, telling me how to bring up my daughter? I'm her mother so I do with her as I please.'

I crushed the butt of my cigarette out in the ashtray, picked up my keys and left.

Frankie - Monday

Mrs Eames's facial expression spoke volumes. She said she would call Mum during the break and for me to wait in the classroom for her. When she came in, I clocked her guarded smile, the type that looked forced, that said, 'Everything's okay,' when clearly it isn't. I'd seen enough smiles like that to know what they meant.

Before Mrs Eames was able to speak, I butted in. 'It's okay Miss, I knew it was going to be a 'no', but thanks for trying.'

'Frankie, I'm really sorry that it's gone this way.'

'Me too, I really liked running.' I turned and started to head out of the classroom before my disappointment showed. Mrs Eames called after me,

'It doesn't mean you can't run, though.'

I stopped and looked back over my shoulder. 'Yes, it does.'

'Your mother said not in competitive events. She didn't say anything about giving up running completely.'

I felt hopeful. 'Oh?'

'You could run in school time - and train too.'

'What's the point of that if I can't compete?'

'You will be competing against other pupils within the school. And you'll be preparing for competitions, building up your stamina and form. It's the training that makes all the difference.'

'So, I can run but not in competitions like the other day. Miss, would I still be able to run when I leave school?'

'Well yes, I suppose, but you would have to join the Harriers. Look,' and then she produced a small leaflet on a running club detailing its events and club news.

Diane: Three years on, 1975

'Take the pills.' That's what the doctor told me.

I sat in that surgery waiting room shaking from head to foot, my hands virtually bouncing I was trembling so hard. I pressed them together and pushed them between my knees, so it didn't show. But I could tell that the woman next to me had noticed. Out of the corner of my eye, I could see her looking at me. She was openly gawping, staring at me with her beady eyes from behind those hideous tortoiseshell frames. She shopped at Cavendish House, had the bag at her feet, a blatant advertisement of her place in society; entitled.

She made me feel awkward, ashamed. In my head I was screaming at her. 'Go away. Leave me alone. Stop judging me!' But of course, I said nothing. These days I could hardly get a word out without stuttering and if I stuttered then I started to blush. There were so many situations then that I had to avoid incase … incase …

Inside I was screaming. *Please God, help me.* But He wasn't there. There was no-one there for me.

So, my turn came round. The doctor stood at the threshold of his door calling my name. I stood, then fumbled about for my bag and coat, all eyes were on me. I could see I had his attention. He waited, but there was something about his stance that implied impatience - was it the tilt of his head or the way his mouth was slightly downturned? That and the look on his face that said it all, that 'Oh no, not her again' look. I followed him into his surgery and sat on the appointed seat. When he asked, 'What is wrong with you?' all I could do was cry. Tears spilled down my face, I sobbed and snottered and that was before I'd managed to even say a word. What's wrong? I didn't know what's wrong, all I knew was that I wasn't right. I didn't feel right. I was constantly tired, everything overwhelmed me. I cried at everything. I couldn't sleep and yet I was so tired.

I was so incredibly lonely. It seemed that everyone had left me, or those that should be there avoided me. I felt outside from everyone. I was afraid of everything; things that had happened, things that might happen and people, where did I start? I felt old, really old and I wasn't even thirty-five. 'You've made your bed...' is what my mother tells me. But I didn't want this and yet I don't know how to change it or if I could. I'm stuck, in limbo.

Richard was only half out of the picture. He wouldn't divorce me and dropped in and out of our lives as and when it pleased him. And Frankie, there's just nothing there, no bond, or deep love. I don't and never have understood it. I hate myself for that, but I didn't attach like I did with Danny. I was the one left with her, not Richard and there was always something, to remind me that I was tethered because of her.

'Take the pills Diane,' the GP said, more emphatically, breaking through the chatter inside my head, and pushed the prescription toward me. My mind threw out the image of the child-catcher in Chitty Bang Bang, and somehow, I connected the pills and his words and felt cornered, imprisoned and worse. To him I was just a set of symptoms to throw pills at. I'd been labelled and that label had stuck, there was no coming back or out of it. I tried to form words... I tried to say that I thought that the pills were part of the problem - a big part. But all I could do was make stuttering noises. Frustrated, I reached out a shaking hand and put the prescription in my bag.

The first thing I did when I got home was take the pills.

It took the journey back for me to consider whether to or not. But I was worn down, it seemed like the most sensible and easy option. The dosage had doubled. As I swallowed them, I hoped that maybe this would numb me completely, blot everything out so I didn't have to feel anymore.

Bonzo was at my side the moment I sat down. His wet nose found my hand, nudging, insistent. I'm here, that's what he was trying to tell me, *I'm really here!* He rested his head on my knee. His eyes held me as though they were pouring love into me. How could I resist? Putting my arms around him I held him close, burying my face in his coat. When I finally pulled my head up, he licked my face, his tongue tracing my salty tears with such tenderness, such care.

Then he stopped, stock still, sitting up in his alert stance. His ears pricked forward, indicating that he had heard something?

'Frankie. Is that you?' There was no reply. Bonzo turned himself fully round, putting himself between me and whatever was that disturbed him. I loved that he had made me his number one priority, on guard, ready to protect. I heard another movement, a rustling sound from the kitchen. 'Frankie, is that you?' I called again.

Excited, Bonzo began padding his front paws on the spot, wagging his tail ever so slightly, anticipating, Frankie's appearance. She poked her head around the door, stooping to greet the dog first. He lay on his back, pink tummy exposed as she tickled his sweet spot. She kept her eyes fixed on him as she spoke.

'Alright?'

'Where've you been?'

She looked up briefly. 'Nowhere, just coming home,' but she had that guilty look about her. She clamped her mouth shut tight when she was hiding something, and it made the sinews in her neck stand out. 'What have you been up to today, Mum?'

I was caught off guard, my words come out slow and slurred, like I was drunk and had no control. Frankie looked at me strangely, a frown settled on her forehead.

'Mum, are you okay?'

Her question made me feel defensive; it raised a doubt. *Did she think I'm acting oddly? Am I acting oddly?'*

'Do you want me to take Bonzo out and fetch some chips from the chippy?'

I nodded my head and gestured towards my handbag. When she leaned down to take my purse, I noticed that Frankie was beginning to blossom. Her breasts had begun to bud, she was a late developer, but better late than never. I saw the curve showing through her school shirt. She was still as thin as a rake, but I was like that as a child. She was turning into a young woman - not far off sixteen. Almost the same age I was when my life fell apart and I got pregnant with her.

I felt a tinge of sadness, but it was fleeting in comparison to the pang of jealousy I felt. It was bitter and sharp, tangible almost, cutting much deeper than the sadness. There, I admitted it. I envied her youth, the opportunities that she might have. The future she had stretching out before her. Would she realise her dreams or make the same mistakes that I had? God forbid she becomes a mother at the same age I was. Would she be able to cope? It was hard to tell, Frankie always kept her cards close to her chest.

Frankie

Saturday morning. I'd already been up and out running across the park with Bonzo. At 7am there was hardly anyone about. It was as if we had the park to ourselves. Nothing but the whispering trees, the babble of the brook, the wind in the grass. I loved that time of day best of all. Summer was coming, I could smell it on the air, tell by the way the trees looked green and fulsome. Beyond, from the top of the brow of the hill, I could see a milk float busy wending its way around the housing scheme, rattling its bottles as it went. An occasional paperboy whizzed past on his bike hell bent on delivering the contents of his bag as quickly as possible, probably because it was going to rain.

I ran with Bonzo at my heels, and he kept up with me stride for stride. His pink tongue lolling out of his mouth as he ran, as though he was smiling. Having Bonzo with me buoyed me, filled me with an intense love where everything else in comparison felt empty.

Lately the emptiness felt more tangible. It twisted and churned in my stomach, it sat on the edge of my thoughts. I sensed it as a gradual closing in and around me and I, in response withdrew as if a part of me was slowly fading away before my very eyes. What to make of it and how to respond left me with a sinking feeling of hopelessness that defied description. *It's not like I've got a broken leg or an open wound,* I thought. *It's just a sensation. Like anticipating something horrible is about to happen any moment.*

I worried that I'd inherited something from Mum that would cause me to be as unhappy as her, but Patsy set me right.

'Don't be so daft. You're only feeling like that because you're a teenager. It'll be your periods messing with your head.'

I hadn't thought about that, but she probably had a point. She usually did.

I missed my Dad. I missed his gentle words, even his chastisements, for they were never harsh. They weren't said in a barbed way that made me feel bad about myself. Mum constantly put him down, reminded me how he didn't care, how he had forgotten my birthdays, parents' evenings and wasn't even there when I took my first steps. I struggled with the doubt, the steady drip of vitriol. It didn't match my own picture of my Dad. Mum even planted a seed that he had another family, one that he loved more than me and that hurt like hell. But did I blame him for leaving us? Not really. In a way I understood. Mum had made it impossible for him and continued to do so, but he never said a bad word against her. He was living in Tewkesbury now, staying in a pokey bedsit and working in a garage. We met every few weeks, did fun stuff but I didn't tell him much about what was going on at home, only what Bonzo was doing.

As I got older, I hadn't really thought much about Danny. He was there, but in the deep recesses of my mind. Until the day Mum had asked me to fetch something down from the loft. I'd never been up there before. Dad had said in his sternest voice that I wasn't to go there, that it wasn't safe.

I climbed the ladder with trembling hands and lifting the hatch, entered into its dark dusty space, head half in, the rest of my body standing on the top of the ladder. It took a while to find the light switch. I reached out with the flat of my palm against the splintered bare boards feeling for the switch while trying not to think of the big spiders that probably lurked there. Having negotiated the light, I hauled myself into the space. It was stacked with boxes, books, unused items such as stair gates, a piano stool, an old-fashioned lamp stand and plenty of bric-a-brac. Mum wanted me to look for an old photograph album of hers, containing a picture of a recently passed great aunt.

As I stood there my eyes found something familiar, something that dislodged a memory: it was a gun, fashioned out of Meccano, sitting on top of a large cardboard box. The moment I saw it a flood of reminiscences came to mind. I lifted the gun and opened the box. On top were pictures, framed pictures of Danny, followed by layers of his toys and at the very bottom some of his clothes. I cradled the gun, thinking of his sticky little fingers screwing the parts together, his tongue twisting in concentration. Rooting through the box I grabbed a photo. How young he looked now, his big brown eyes staring back at me, the corners of his lips still stained with whatever sweetie he had been eating.

I stopped, squatted down and stared. Danny, suspended in time, captured in a photo. I remembered the day it was taken. We had been to a party. Danny cried every time the parcel didn't land on his lap, howling louder and louder as it disappeared further down the line. But his face spilled over with joy when the music stopped, and he won the prize. It was only a white chocolate Mouse, but from his reaction it was as if he had won a whole sweet shop.

'Have you found it yet?' Mum's agitated voice called up from the bottom of the ladder.

'No, still looking.' I stayed a moment longer before lifting the picture of Danny to my lips and gently kissing it. 'Love you,' I whispered before carefully tucking the picture under my arm and willing myself not to get upset. Then I rummaged around the boxes and corners of the loft until I finally found what I was looking for.

'Found it!'

But there was no reply. Mum had already gone down the stairs leaving a trail of cigarette smoke and ash in her wake.

The following Monday morning I skipped school. I turned up for the day's registration then neatly jumped the fence adjacent to the local park. The domestic science teacher didn't bother checking the register.

Patsy was waiting for me in the park's gazebo. It was a small wooden structure that provided shelter from the rain and a great place to have a crafty cigarette. Patsy had brought a small bag of clothes for me to change into, a Harrington jacket and a maxi skirt plus a new pair of wedges that we took it in turns to wear.

Deftly pulling up the maxi skirt I asked, 'So, what's the plan, where are we off to?'

'We're going into town. There's someone I want you to meet.' Patsy flashed a mischievous smile.

'Who?' I was hopping on one foot trying to pull off my socks.

'It's a surprise.'

'Is it someone I know?' I was busily stuffing the clothes into a carrier bag, wondering whether to bring it along with us or leave it hidden behind the gazebo.

'Like I said, it's a surprise. You'll see. Now come on or we'll miss the bus.'

We ran along the side of the fence furthest away from the school and across the road to the bus stop. We sat on the front seat of the top deck smoking cigarettes, pleased with ourselves. Then the atmosphere changed between us when Patsy said 'My Dad's coming to visit. He's coming all the way from Scotland.'

'Holy shit. Scotland, is that where he lives now?'

'Yeah, he moved there a while back.'

'When did you last see him?'

'I think I must have been about eight, I can't really remember. My Mum's totally wigging out over it.'

'What's she worried about, that you'll run off with him back up to Scotland?'

'No. She thinks he's going to die or something.'

'That would make her happy, wouldn't it?'

'You'd think. But he left her for someone else and I don't think she ever got over him really.'

'Oh, so what're you going to do?'

'I'll meet him and get him to buy me some new clothes and pay for driving lessons. Maybe even ask him to buy me a car!'

'Yeah, like that's really going to happen.'

'We can all dream, can't we?' Patsy shrugged, indifferent.

I leaned over to fiddle with the strap on my shoe. 'I think my Mum's getting worse. Sometimes it's as though something has taken her over.'

'You know what they say,' Patsy pulled a gruesome face and spoke in a strange strangulated voice. 'It's an excellent day for an exorcism.'

'No,' I punched her softly on the arm. 'Not like that! She acted really weird like she had been slowed down somehow; she's been like it for months.'

'Oh.' Patsy took a long drag on her cigarette and looked pensive. 'Have you asked her if she's okay?'

I rolled my eyes. 'If I ask if she's okay she'll claim she is even when she isn't. I'm not sure what to make of it. Does your Mum do that?'

'No, mine's exactly the opposite. She never bloody shuts up about how she's feeling. It's always: Patsy I've got a headache, Patsy turn that music off, Patsy get me a cup of tea, Patsy if you do that, I'll have to take another Valium. I'm sick of it. Have you told your gran?'

'If I mention it to Gran I'll get into trouble. Mum went mad the last time I did, said I was exaggerating. She tried to make out I was lying and really went to town on me when we got home. It's like she doesn't want help. And she definitely doesn't want anyone to know.'

'You can't blame her, really.'

'How do you make that out?' I turned to look Patsy full in the face, but Patsy was busy trying to apply her makeup, mouth open, eye squinting as she looked in her compact mirror.

'Well, from what my Mum told me, your Mum had it really bad. She got sectioned, didn't she?' Patsy snapped her compact shut as if to emphasise the point.

'Oh, I kind of forgot about that. I suppose you're right. But that was years ago, eight at least. That could be why she is the way she is. But how did your Mum know about that? Did my Mum tell her?'

'No, it's like everyone knows. You know what it's like round here.'

Stunned, I turned my head to look out of the window. I found myself struggling to keep my breathing even, as a prickle of hot tears welled up in the corner of my eyes. And in that moment, a little piece of my life's jigsaw fell into place.

Still looking out of the window I spoke quietly, 'It's always up to me to try and smooth things out. Some days I don't know who I'm dealing with. I have to say and do the things that she wants to hear and that changes depending on her mood.'

'Thank God my Mum's not that bad.'

'I can't tell her I'm late home because I was mucking about with the running group or hanging out with you. She just wouldn't believe me. Even if I tell her the truth, she'll claim I'm doing something else. Mostly she accuses me of doing *it*. I wouldn't mind, but I've never had a boyfriend.'

Patsy cackled. 'Well, you'll just have to change that then won't you.' Her remark fell on deaf ears; I was still figuring things out loud. 'It always comes back to that, back to how disgraceful and shameful I am. She's always on about *What would your grandparents or the neighbours think and blah blah blah, and how bad it makes her look*. So, I end up having to lie and then I have to lie, on top of the lie to try and cover my tracks. I hate it. I can't keep up with myself.'

Patsy lit another cigarette and forcefully blew out smoke as she spoke. 'Sounds shit. My old dear couldn't give a toss what I do. So long as I'm home safe and don't get myself knocked up, she's happy.'

'Yeah, you're lucky. I'm the one that ruined my old dear's life. I mustn't forget that.'

'No. Your Mum wouldn't say that would she?'

'Yeah.' I nodded my head emphatically. 'She reminds me nearly every day.'

'So just tell her.'

'Tell her what?'

'Tell her *she* was the one that got herself bloody well knocked up. Not you.'

Patsy's voice was defiant as she wagged her finger in an over-dramatic fashion. The two of us collapsed into a fit of giggles, rolling round on the top of the bus, holding our sides we were laughing so hard.

Patsy bumped shoulders with me. 'Here,' she proffered her cigarette, 'have a drag on this. It's not going to be like this forever. You'll be able to leave home soon, then you can do what you like.'

'Yeah, no more slavery Frankie put the bins are out. Frankie walk the dog. Frankie, take the washing to the launderette, light the fire. Do this, do that! All so Gran can think everything's fine and dandy. Not that she ever visits us now.'

'Aww diddums, poor Cinderella!' Patsy pulled her face into an exaggerated frown. We both cracked up laughing again.

'All I want is to be a normal kid, mess about with my friends, go to discos and have a boyfriend.'

'You wish.'

Patsy jumped up out of her seat. 'Come on, here's our stop.'

We rang the bell and thundered down the stairs.

We walked quickly through town heading towards the Lower High Street. As we turned down a small side street I stopped in my tracks when someone called out my name.

'Is that you Frankie? Frankie Miller?'

I turned round and there before me was the figure of an elderly woman wearing a dark gabardine mac loaded down with shopping bags. Her hair, now silver grey was fashioned into a neat perm. She seemed smaller than I remembered her but perhaps that was due to her stoop. But her face, although wrinkled with years, was still as kind as it had ever been.

'Nanny?' my voice choked. 'Nanny, is that really you?'

Patsy, impatient, stood a few yards ahead. 'Come on Frankie, we've got to go.' I ignored her and walked slowly towards Nanny who engulfed me in an enormous hug. 'It's so good to see you, Nanny.' This time I towered over her, my skinny arms barely reaching all the way round. I nestled my face into Nanny's shoulder taking in the faint whiff of lavender and wind-fresh laundry. The smell reminded me of comfort and love, of mince and taters, of afternoons playing beneath the kitchen windows in the sunshine but most of all it reminded me of unconditional love.

Tears of happiness spilled from my eyes. I was bowled over with joy; how often had I dreamt of Nanny? Yet at the same time I was shocked to see how much she had aged and shrunk. I had almost forgotten her rich Cornish accent. Honey in contrast to the Gloucestershire accent.

'Aright, me luvver? I 'ave often thought o' you. Look at you,' she looked me up and down. 'You're a young woman now. Now, 'ow's your mother, dear?'

'Frankieee,' Patsy's face looked like thunder. 'I'll see you at Benny's Cafe then.' She marched off as best she could in her high heels.

'Oh Nanny, I've really missed you. I was so happy staying with you, those were my happiest days ever. Mum's … she's doing as best as she can.'

Nanny looked at me closer and clasped my hand, 'Is that for 'er or for you.'

I half smiled, tight mouthed.

'You wuz never one to speak up, even when you wuz a child,' She patted my hand and touched my cheek. 'And your Dad, 'ow is he doing?'

'He left, Nanny. He left a long while ago.'

'So, it's just been the two of you? I am sorry, my luvver. That must 'ave been 'ard. Oh, look at the time, I'd best be off or else I'll miss me bus. You know where I am, please come and see me.'

'I will Nanny, but I can't remember the address …'

Nanny placed her shopping bags down, then opened her large handbag and took out a pen and a piece of paper. Carefully she penned her address.

'Now keep it safe, and don't forget.' she said as she folded it into my hand. Then with a smile she picked up her bags and slowly made her way up the road. I watched until she disappeared round the corner before I went off to find Patsy.

Frankie: Four months later

It was a double celebration party, a final gathering for us school kids at the end of school and a birthday. The school holidays had been and gone and we had all started to separate and make our own way, finding work or starting college. I hadn't found either, but I did make it to the party. It was hosted by Sam, who lived in a big house on the outskirts of town. Getting there was quite straight forward: one bus into town and another onwards. The main event was held in a barn where we all danced to Motown and disco tunes and drank vodka disguised with soft drink. There was also a lot of snogging in corners going on. Sam's parents stayed subtly out of sight and didn't seem to cotton on to the snogging or the vodka. At the end of the night some of the party kids stayed on. The boys kipped down in the barn and the girls stayed in the main house at Sam's mum's insistence. I left at about ten to take the bus back into town but realised that I must have missed it when it didn't show after waiting some twenty minutes. So, I did what I thought was a sensible thing and went back to the house. I tried to call Mum, but she didn't answer. She never answered the phone after 9.30pm.

I was tired when I got home early the next morning. I had hardly slept all night worrying about how she was going to react. She was sitting in the kitchen, facing the back door, waiting. The ashtray was full of spent cigarettes. 'Where have you been you little guttersnipe?'

'Mum, I told you. I was going to the end of school party at Sam Jordan's.' I already knew that trying to explain was futile. I could tell that Mum had made up her mind about what had gone on.

'Liar. I know exactly what you've been up to. Staying out all night and coming home acting like butter wouldn't melt, you little trollop.'

'But Mum. I couldn't get a bus home. Believe me.'

'You couldn't get a bus! Do you think I was born yesterday?'

'You can phone Mr and Mrs Jordan if you don't believe me.'

'I have no intention of calling them. I've already made up my mind. Behave like a whore under my roof and you will be asked to leave.'

'But Mum …'

'And staying out all night leaves me no option but conclude that you have been behaving inappropriately. I want you out.'

'Mum, no.'

'I want you to leave. Now.'

At first, I was panic stricken. My feet seemed welded to the ground. I felt my throat constrict, and my mouth go dry. Where was I to go?

'Get out,' she screamed as she hurled a cup at me from across the room.

I ducked and ran from the kitchen upstairs to my room. I grabbed a small carrier bag and randomly filled it with a few things, then emptied my piggy bank of its loose change. Lastly, I retrieved Danny's picture from beneath my pillow and put it in my pocket. My heart was still pounding, but my thinking was crystal clear. This was my opportunity, the huge get-out clause I needed to leave. It was a gift. But where was I to go and how was I to cope?

There were no more tears. Just a calm sense of clarity. Leaving now was a much better option than staying. I knew, had known for a long time that I didn't want a carbon copy of Mum's life. A life un-lived, mired in bitterness and resentments. Then it occurred to me that she wasn't far off my age when she had me. That was a mistake I was determined not to make for myself.

Now I had the chance to seize life by the horns and I was going to take it with both hands. I regretted leaving Bonzo, but I knew that he would fare ok. At least Mum loved him.

I picked up my bag with its meagre contents. Took one last look around the room, its faded wallpaper and threadbare carpet, the salmon pink candlewick bedspread on my bed. On the windowsill was my lucky stone. As I lifted it to put it in my pocket, I looked out the window to the old cherry tree at the bottom of the garden. How sad, I thought, it had never found a way to grow properly. I left without a backward glance.

Diane

I heard the click of the snub as she closed the door behind her. I watched through the blinds as she trailed past the front room window, kept her head facing forward, carrier bag in her hand. She didn't look back. That's pride for you, but you know what they say, pride comes before a fall. I felt smug snuggling down into the cushions on the sofa, anticipating my favourite programme on the telly.

Bonzo had jumped on to the back of the sofa trying to look out, ears cocked forward, tail half-mast. He stayed there for half an hour, waiting to see if she would return. I saw the heart of his hope fade. His ears flattened and he hung his head. Sighing he jumped down to curl up at my side.

I was convinced she would be back, confident in the knowledge that she had no money, nowhere to go. Richard perhaps? He might put her up for a night or two, but eventually, it would prove too inconvenient and he would talk her into coming back. There would be delicate phone calls where I would have the upper hand.

I would make her grovel, cry even, 'I'm sorry Mum, I didn't mean it. You were right.' Then she would appreciate what she has here. Then she would listen, do as she's told.

Nine-thirty, I can't help but clock watch. Why is there nothing interesting on the telly? I flick back and forth through the channels. There had been no phone call. I was expecting Richard to call to say she was with him and she was staying overnight. Nothing, it was disappointing. Perhaps they were doing it deliberately, to make me worry. I wouldn't put it past them. It was always the same, leaving me out, not telling me anything. They've always had their secrets. Spiteful, nasty creatures. Whispering and giggling behind my back. Disrespectful.

I lit a cigarette, inhaled deeply, all the while my head turning like it was on a loop, winding it tighter and tighter until it physically hurt. Throbbing at the temples, radiating across the top. I was getting more annoyed. She was doing this intentionally, just to provoke me, make me ill. I knew it. She knows not to countermand me she knows how ill I get with my nerves. How dare she. The little cow!

Ten-thirty, the newscaster was finishing up the news on the telly. I switched it off leaving the room in semi darkness, just a feeble lamp in the corner. I heaved myself out of the sofa then plumped the cushions, punching them resoundingly, muttering, *'I don't care. I'm glad she's gone, ungrateful wretch.'* I'd practically convinced myself that it was a good thing, less responsibility, less worry. Then I thought ... I bet I was right, I bet she had a boyfriend all along. Now it all made sense.

Well, she can bloody-well go to hell if she thinks she can turn up here with her illegitimate child, because that's how she'll end up. A single mother living off the State, trailing the streets with her pram and snotty nosed brat expecting hand-outs. I'll not be her bloody nursery. My parents didn't do it for me, and I'll not do it for her.

I heard a shuffling noise in the back garden. *Ha, that'll be her* I thought as I unlocked the back door and peered out. But instead, an outline of a fox slipped by, the white of its tail disappearing towards the cherry tree at the bottom of the garden.

I flushed with anger. Every time I looked at that tree it made me seethe. That bloody tree! One day ... one day, I'll have it ripped out, roots and all, and finally rid myself of Richard, Frankie and the bloody lot of them.

It's their fault my life was ruined, their fault I'm stuck. All the hard work, all the pain and effort and look at me now. Yes, I may not be that old but I just don't have it in me to start over and who's to say the same wouldn't happen all over again?

I thought of Frankie and felt a pang of disappointment.

She'll be back, she needs me. Every girl needs her mother ...

The Author - L Taylor

The House Beside The Cherry Tree is Lea Taylor's debut novel. Miraculously crafted in between life as a busy working Mum, pet to two boisterous rescue dogs and wife to her scientist husband. Lea lives in Scotland and works as a professional storyteller, writer, performer and trainer. She has a number of publications to her name: *Midlothian Folk Tales*; *Animals Beasties and Monsters of Scotland* and is a contributor to *An Anthology of Scottish Folk Lore* - with The History Press.

Lea is a member of The Scottish Federation of Writers and The Society of Authors. *The House Beside The Cherry Tree* is a fictionalised account of a family dealing with mental health issues and considers it from different perspectives. It also explores a fractured relationship between a mother and her child, a bond that should be one of unconditional love. How the relationships unfold lie at the heart of the novel and touches on subjects that are both sensitive and taboo.

Lea can be found on Twitter:
Lea Taylor - Author @leataylor5783

The story continues with
Frankie's own journey of discovery, in

BLOSSOM IN THE WIND

Out soon!

Printed in Great Britain
by Amazon